Creatures of Dust

Scott Hunter was born in Romford, Essex in 1956 and educated at Douai School in Woolhampton, Berkshire. His writing career was kick-started after he won first prize in the Sunday Express short story competition in 1996. His fantasy novel for children, *The Ley Lines of Lushbury*, was long-listed for the Times/Chicken House Children's Fiction competition in 2010 and his archaeological thriller, *The Trespass*, is a Kindle top twenty bestseller. He continues to work as a semi-professional drummer with *The Book of Genesis* (UK) and Italian prog rockers *Analogy*, and lives in Berkshire with his wife and two youngest children.

www.scott-hunter.net

Creatures of Dust

Scott Hunter

Creatures of Dust

A Myrtle Villa Book

Originally published in Great Britain by Myrtle Villa Publishing

A CIP record for this book is available from the British Library.

In this work of fiction, the characters, places and events are either the product of the author's imagination or they are used entirely fictitiously.

ISBN 978-0-9561510-6-3

For Kathy, Claire, Tom and Emily, and my dear friends
from days gone by, living and dead

Acknowledgements

Thanks to JK for his invaluable insight into the organisation of the Thames Valley Police, and also to Louise Maskill, my 5 star editor.

Cover design:

Books Covered

'And I thought the dead ... more fortunate than the living ... but better than both is the one who has not yet been, and has not seen the evil deeds that are done under the sun.'
(Ecclesiastes 4:2–3)

Author's note

Creatures of Dust is the sequel to *Black December*, but it can still be read as a standalone novel, so don't worry too much if you haven't read BD.

I hope you enjoy Inspector Moran's latest outing.

SH, March 2013

Prologue

The dirty water gurgled its way through the city centre, carrying the odd beer can and other remnants of a more personal nature along with it. Simon Peters paid little heed to the canal's floating detritus. Oblivious to his surroundings he was lost in thought, struggling in vain to make sense of everything that had happened.

As he crossed the bridge the intensity of his feelings stopped him in his tracks. He leaned on the railing and rested his gloved hands lightly on the peeling metal. Physical pain he could learn to live with but emotional pain, he was beginning to realise, was infinitely worse. The latter was exacerbated by the knowledge that his yearning would never be satisfied. She was his deepest need, and he would never have her. Worse still, she loved him too. That was why it was all so wrong. What did it matter that she was a Muslim? To him, that was an irrelevance. To them, it was vital, and as a Westerner he was the ultimate persona non grata. To them, it was unthinkable that Jaseena should associate herself, romantically or otherwise, with an unbeliever. And that was why they'd taken her away.

He stepped off the bridge onto the canal path and stopped. Something wasn't right. He had a sudden conviction that he was being followed. There – by the street lamp at the entrance to the multi-storey. Male, female? He had a fleeting impression of short, blonde hair and a slender athletic build before the figure disappeared into shadow. He walked on. The light was beginning to fade and few people were about; only the occasional car headlight was reflected in the scummy water.

He stopped again. Was that a scuffle of trainers? He spun on his heels. Now he saw his pursuers clearly and his heart lurched. He'd been so caught up in his bitter reverie that he'd forgotten his number one rule: stick with the crowds. Ever since Jaseena's brothers had made a direct threat he'd taken great care not to expose himself to what he believed was a very real danger.

He quickened his pace as best he could, aware of movement in his peripheral vision. Fear tightened his stomach. They'd promised to 'fix him properly' if he ever went near Jaseena again. Ahead, the canal path telescoped into the distance. There were footfalls behind him now, the slap of rubber on the paving. He threw his bag away and tried to run. After thirty seconds he knew it was hopeless; of course they were faster.

They caught him eventually by the rusted struts of the next bridge and waded in – dark faces, fists, a blow to the side of his head. He felt well-aimed kicks find their targets in his rib, his groin. Sickening, agonising pain, and then he was being pushed, rolled, shoved towards the canal. The last thing he felt was the sudden shock of water closing over his head.

It was over.

But he was wrong. He regained consciousness in a blaze of sensation. Bright lights, a needle in his arm, blankets covering him; waves of nausea as the pain intensified. Water and vomit pouring from his mouth. Muted voices, a siren nearby.

"All right, matey, take it easy. You're going to be fine." The paramedic's face loomed over him, wavering and distorted. Before the darkness took him again a burning certainty overrode the sedation just long enough to raise the corners of his mouth in a defiant smile. It was the certainty that, one day, he would have his revenge.

He sipped the lukewarm hospital squash and swallowed with a grimace. After the first three or four days the discomfort of his injuries had lessened to the extent that he was able to focus his mind on his next steps. He had to admit the doctors had been efficient. He had apparently sidestepped the dangerous possibility of pneumonia, and apart from the severe bruising on and around his ribcage he felt almost human again.

"You've taken quite a knock on the head, Mr Peters," the consultant had told him. "Probably banged it on the canal wall. You've really been in the wars recently, haven't you? Jolly bad luck all round." He met Simon's eye and looked away quickly. "Anyway, you mustn't be surprised if you feel a little distracted for a while. It'll get better."

In fact Simon Peters' brain was crystal clear, and very busy. The planning was therapeutic, carrying the added benefit of distracting him from thoughts of Jaseena. There was no point living in the past. He knew what he was going to do. It was time they were taught a lesson. All of them, one by one. His sole regret was that he hadn't thought of it before; he could have saved himself a lot of trouble.

The last week in hospital had dragged interminably. He smiled at the nurses and exchanged pleasantries with the other patients, but inside he was boiling with excitement.

He was impatient to begin.

Chapter One

Detective Chief Inspector Brendan Moran of the Thames Valley Police was concentrating hard. He frowned at the seven irritatingly blank squares glaring up at him from the newspaper like empty accusations. Nine letters. *Also a man's role in medical discipline.* A something D something – Moran threw down his pencil in frustration as the door opened and Detective Sergeant Robert Phelps' head appeared, followed by the rest of his considerable bulk.

"What *is* it, Phelps? Don't people knock any more?"

"Sorry, guv – thought you were on your tea break." Phelps squinted at the newspaper. "Crossword?"

"Got it in one."

Phelps grinned. "Can't get the last clue, eh? Let's have a butcher's – hmm…"

Moran drummed his fingers.

"Andrology."

"What?"

"Andrology, guv. You know, the study of male medical conditions. Waterworks and all that."

Moran eased his chair back and studied his Sergeant. Phelps was a huge man, East End raised, solid as a rock, faultless intuition, but as far as Moran was aware, crosswords were well outside his areas of interest. He regarded Phelps with a new curiosity.

"Have you imbibed a dictionary, Phelps?"

"What's that, guv?" The broad features cracked into a smile. "Oh, right. No, it's not that. Just – well, I'm studying a bit. Part-time, you know." Phelps broke off sheepishly.

"Are you? Are you really?" Moran nodded appreciatively. "Good for you, Phelps. What is it – a degree in obscure medical terminology?"

"No, guv. English Lit. Open University. Bloomin' hard work. I'm enjoying it, though –so far, anyway."

"And who, might I enquire, are you reading?"

Phelps scratched his chin. Even though he shaved twice a day his blue shadow was rarely absent. "Conrad, Chaucer, some bloke called Shakespeare..."

Moran studied Phelps with rekindled fascination. "I'm impressed, Phelps. And not a little envious."

"You could do the same, guv."

Moran shook his head. "You're kidding. I wish I had the time. Come to think of it, when do *you* squeeze in time for study? With a wife and kids to look after?"

Phelps winked. "The midnight oil, guv."

"Ah." Moran nodded. "The insomniac academic."

"Has a certain ring to it, guv." Phelps looked pleased. "Don't you think?"

"I do." Moran shifted his leg with a grimace. Following the explosion at Charnford Abbey and his discharge from hospital he was gradually coming to terms with the fact that he would always walk with a stick. After a car crash that had almost killed him, bouts of narcolepsy, and a mild stroke followed by a near-fatal explosion, Phelps had remarked that with his track record Moran should have been born a cat, not an Irishman.

As if guessing Moran's thoughts Phelps narrowed his eyes. "How are you, guv? I mean, how are you *really*?"

Moran scraped his chair back and stood up. "Surprisingly well, Phelps, thank you." He walked stiffly to the kettle, found two chipped mugs and rummaged in the filing cabinet for coffee. When he looked up Phelps' eyebrows were raised in a disbelieving arc.

"I'm all right, Robert, *really* I am. Thanks for your concern." Moran unscrewed the coffee jar lid and was hunting for a teaspoon amongst the debris when the office shook as if it had been hit by a truck. Both Moran and Phelps spun on their heels, ducking their heads automatically as they zeroed in on the cause of the disturbance.

"Ah." Phelps said, straightening up. "Neads. That's what I came to tell you, guv. He's in to clear his desk. And he's not happy."

Moran looked through his office window at the tall young man, whose face was contorted in hatred, hands pressed onto the clear surface. In the centre of his palms they could clearly see the angry scars of crucifixion.

"Uh huh." Moran went quickly to the door. "It doesn't give him an excuse to behave like an animal, though."

The former Detective Sergeant Gregory Neads was at the other side of the door as Moran opened it. Behind him the inhabitants of the open-plan office were silent, heads craning, mouths gaping.

"Inside." Moran spoke quietly but firmly, squaring up to the taller man.

"I'll leave you two to chat." Phelps squeezed through the gap, giving Neads a warning nod on his way past.

"You apologise?" Neads snarled. "Is that it?"

Moran cleared his throat. Neads had got himself into trouble during the Charnford Abbey episode, falling prey

7

to the unhinged former abbot. The DC had been impaled through hands and feet, strung up as some kind of warped atonement sacrifice for the murder of a former kitchen porter. Months in hospital had followed. Since that time Moran's nights had been tormented by the sickening image of the crucifixion, but he knew that for Neads the fallout would be much, much worse. The boy would need some serious counselling.

"What's left for me now?" Neads' nose was an inch from Moran's. "I'm a *cripple. Pensioned off.* I'm twenty-four. And I'm *finished...*"

"Gregory–"

"Don't bloody patronise me!" Neads hissed. He waved his forefinger in Moran's face, grabbing the desk for support as his balance was compromised. "You were supposed to watch *out* for me. And did you? No! You sent me off on a wild goose chase and left me with that..." he took a harsh, gulping breath, "... that crazy lunatic who ... who–" Neads' facial muscles twitched as he fought to control himself.

Moran put his hand on the young man's shoulder. "Gregory. I'm truly sorry. Listen, have you contacted the Police Rehabilitation Centre? It's in Goring. I think it would be helpful. If there's anything–"

Neads shrugged Moran's hand away and limped to the door. He turned and raised his finger again. "You watch your back, Moran. I'm warning you. You just watch your back..."

The door slammed behind him. Moran slumped in his chair and buried his head in his hands. *Well, that went swimmingly, Brendan. Nicely handled...*

Later Moran eased himself into his car. Since the incident at the abbey he knew he was lucky to be alive. So was Neads – but then, Moran reflected, his own injuries were caused by an explosion, something remote, almost random in its destructive power. Neads' wounds were caused by the premeditation of a very sick mind. There had been ample time for Neads to anticipate his injuries, to listen to the preparatory carpentry work before the first nail was driven into his flesh. Moran felt his skin crawl with the familiar remembered horror of that December night. Neads had an uphill psychological battle ahead of him, that much was certain. What was more uncertain was the effect that his experiences would have on the young DC. *Ex DC*, Moran reminded himself. He sighed. If today's encounter was anything to go by, the signs were not good. Not good at all.

As for you, Moran, he thought, it's all about physical rehab from now on. As if to confirm his self-diagnosis his leg shot him a bolt of pain as he engaged the clutch and steered the car out of the police station car park. *A small price to pay, Brendan, all things considered.* Yes, he was definitely on the mend. His head felt clear; the narcolepsy that had plagued him over the past eighteen months seemed to have vanished without trace. Dr Purewal had been right. A little R and R, plus the odd crossword to keep the grey matter ticking over, had done the trick.

Apart from the Neads episode, his first day back had passed without incident. Mike Airey, the new Superintendent, seemed supportive – unlike his late predecessor. All in all, things were looking up. Moran conceded that he wouldn't be too discontented if, just to ease him in, his return to work turned out to be routine, and – dare he think it? *Dull...*

And for the first month, much to Moran's surprise, it was.

Chapter Two

Simon Peters moved purposefully, every nerve in his body tingling. Rain began to fall – gently at first, but it quickly intensified, hammering the pavement and provoking a mass unfurling of umbrellas. He tilted his face, allowing the water to pound his skin and trickle deliciously down his neck. It felt cleansing and invigorating. He slid his hand into his pocket. The knife was hard against his fingers; he felt the circulating blood surging beneath his skin and his excitement grew.

It was getting dark; rush hour would soon be over and only the stragglers would remain. The town centre was emptying fast as tired workers caught buses or returned to car parks for the drive home to their TV dinners, bawling babies or dysfunctional marriages. *Sad little lives* ... *pointless, pathetic existences...*

But *he – he* had a purpose. A *mission*. All he needed now was a target...

Moran turned the key in the lock after another uneventful day. He was, he admitted to himself, getting restless. Not that he wished for trouble, but something fresh to stimulate his mind would not go amiss. He thought he might ask Mike Airey for clearance to work on one or two of the cold cases they'd discussed the week before. For the time being, Moran had had his fill of the mundane.

He had no sooner settled into his sofa with a glass of Sangiovese than his phone rang. He toyed with the idea of ignoring it, but he finally admitted defeat. A missed call was always the vital one.

"Moran."

"Hello? Is that Brendan Moran? It's Shona."

Moran frowned, hesitated briefly, and then the penny dropped. Before he could open his mouth, though, the caller beat him to it. "We met at the funeral. Shona Kempster – Kay's sister."

With recognition came the pain of loss and guilt. Kay, his one-time 'special' friend, had died in an explosion in Moran's garage. The blast had also killed his brother, Patrick. Eight months had passed but the wound was still raw, And it didn't take much for it to start bleeding again.

"I – I'm sorry to call. I just needed to talk, I suppose."

Moran tried to remember Shona's face. Shorter than her late sister, thinner. Quite attractive, in an anorexic, waif-like sort of way. He remembered her as a little over-bubbly at the funeral, behaviour that he'd put down to the shock of her sister's sudden death.

"It's quite all right, Shona. Nice to hear from you. Fire away."

"Well, you did say to call, if I – you know–"

"Of course."

"Well–" An awkward pause preceded a nervous laugh. "How are you? How's things?"

"Oh, you know. Getting back into the swing."

"Yep. Right. Me too."

Moran realised that unless he steered this particular conversation it was going to peter out before it had even begun. "Are you all right, Shona? Is there anything troubling you?"

"No, nothing in particular. I think I just need to chew the fat. You know, about what happened. Maybe we could meet up?"

"Sure. When and where?"

"You say. I'm free most of the time."

Moran dredged his memory. He was positive that Shona had been introduced to him as a sports physiotherapist. "Not keeping you busy enough at the clinic?"

"I – I don't work there any more."

"Oh. Sorry to hear that. Anyway, you can tell me all about it when I see you."

"OK. Um, how about next Friday? Cherries wine bar? Eight o'clock?"

"I know the place. Right, well, looking forward to seeing you then, Shona. Bye for now."

"Great. Thanks, Brendan. Bye."

Moran ended the call, shook his head pensively, and returned to his Sangiovese.

Simon Peters found the young man beneath the street lamp, waiting, perhaps for a friend. Arms folded, dark hair plastered across his forehead. A quick check, left and right, but there was no one about – not within clear view of the corner, anyway. Now, let the cleansing begin...

The youth glanced up, unsuspecting. A glimmer of recognition, a stock phrase, almost a sneer: "All right?" He looked away.

This is it. The power Simon felt was a huge adrenaline rush. The youth wore an air of disdain he knew well; it was just like the one he'd worn the last time they'd met.

"Yeah, Anoop. I'm good." The knife came out easily, casually almost, nestling in the cradle of his fingers.

Then, just to be sure, the vital question, which he asked with a smile, knowing the answer already.

"By the way, are you a Muslim?"

Moran was dreaming. It was a pleasant dream, a far cry from recent nightmares in which the scene would shift from Charnford Abbey to some dystopian town centre where gangs roamed unchecked, killing and looting at will. The troubled Gregory Neads usually played a starring role in these disturbing scenarios, the ex-detective sergeant's recent mugging and hospitalisation playing on Moran's mind. How unlucky could a guy get?

But this dream was different. It was warm and sunny and he was relaxed – happy, even. Trouble was, someone was ringing a bell, harshly and insistently. He wanted to put distance between himself and the noise so he walked further along the beach, past the ramshackle bar and the smiling barman, past the topless girl with the blonde ponytail ... the bell followed, its jangling undiminished. He turned, tried to push it away, but the barman had left his station and now appeared beside him holding a ludicrously inflated telephone.

"For you, boss. Big news." His smile was ingratiatingly wide, the whiteness of his teeth gleaming in the sun. Moran made a grab for the phone but it moved just out of reach. On the third attempt he woke with a start. His much smaller but equally irritating mobile was vibrating on the bedside table.

"Moran."

"Brendan? It's Shona."

Moran squinted at the bedside clock. "Shona, do you know what time it is?"

"I'm really sorry, Brendan. I just needed to talk to someone."

Moran sighed. "Go on."

"Well, it's about Kay – of course," she added. "I keep thinking – you know, why? Why her?"

"I know. I wish I could give you an answer. It should have been me, but–"

"And your brother. They were getting on so well, weren't they?"

"Yes." Moran thought of the wrecked garage, the shell of his Land Rover squatting in the ruins.

He kept up the sympathetic responses for another ten minutes before Shona's voice slowed to a normal rhythm. Highly strung, that's for sure. Perhaps he shouldn't have been as free and easy with his mobile number. But, he reminded himself, she was Kay's little sister. He owed it to Kay to provide a listening ear. It was the least he could do.

He signed off with a promise to keep the Cherries appointment and fell asleep with the image of Kay's smiling face looping around the spools of his mind.

Seconds later, or so it seemed, the mobile was vibrating again. Moran raised himself on his elbow and smashed the pillow with his fist.

"Moran."

"Guv?" Phelps' barrow-boy growl grated from the phone's speaker. "We have an incident."

"Where?"

"Town centre. Outside Dixon's, Broad Street."

"Details?"

"A murder, guv. Stab wound."

"I'll be there in ten."

Moran ducked under the outer cordon and negotiated the metal stepping stones of the common approach path set up by the crime scene manager.

Phelps waved a welcome. "What do you reckon, guv? Gang killing?"

Moran peered at the corpse. It was a miserable scene: in the crepuscular early morning light, huddled in the shop doorway was a young Asian boy of around twenty-two, twenty-three perhaps, with a dark stain on his jacket and a surprised expression in his widened, lifeless eyes. Moran felt sick at the sheer waste of it.

"Mobile?"

"Negative, guv. Either he wasn't carrying one or the killer took it."

"ID?"

"Nope. Nada."

"CCTV?"

Phelps looked up and down the street and shook his head. "Dead spot."

Moran watched the hooded forensics officer swabbing the bloodstains and committing the results to his tamper-proof evidence bags. A bag of life – or death, according to how you looked at it.

"Ah, Moran. How goes it?" A familiar brogue came from behind them. Sandy Taylor, the police doctor, had arrived to certify the time of death.

"It goes the same as it always goes," Moran said flatly. "Another one for your record book."

"Don't be so morbid," Taylor retorted. "If I kept a record book I'd only get depressed, and I can think of better ways to spend the rest of my life than trying to engage with the world through a haze of sertraline."

Taylor's examination was swift. "Stab wound to the neck. Death probably within seconds. I'd guess that he was half-carried or dragged off the street and dumped in the alcove."

"OK. Strong assailant, then. He's a big lad."

"Indeed."

"Time of death?" Phelps prompted.

"Oh, let's see – I'd say somewhere between one and two in the morning, give or take thirty minutes." Taylor stood up, shaking his head. "Sad, sad, sad. Still, a little more straightforward than your last case, eh?"

Moran grunted. "They're never straightforward, Sandy, trust me."

Taylor clicked his tongue and snapped his briefcase shut. "I do, my dear Brendan. Implicitly."

He paced the flat, adrenaline buzzing through him as if he were a live wire. His hands were filthy with mud, his shoes were soaked through and his jacket was torn. He had made a mistake. Someone had seen him – a girl. To his surprise, she had chased him. He had let her catch up by the canal and she hadn't put up much of a fight in the end. It was all right now. He'd dealt with it, but he was shaking like a man with the ague.

He'd returned the car to the lock-up and walked home in a daze, legs trembling like a pair of rubber stilts. The car was well off limits now. Maybe he should burn it, trash the whole row of garages... *Calm down*, he told himself. *You've sorted it for now. No one knows it's there.* As for the woman, he didn't care who she was. The way she was dressed she could have been any Saturday night girl. Or maybe a professional, with a skirt like that.

Forget it, he told himself. Some collateral damage was inevitable. Stupid cow. What had she been thinking? What had she hoped to achieve? He shuddered; he could still feel her body folding into unconsciousness, pressing against him. He'd hardly touched her; she was probably drunk.

He kicked off his shoes and went into the bathroom. *It didn't matter*. What *did* matter was that he had made a start, and he should mark that somehow, shouldn't he? What he needed was a new name, something to complement his new identity. As the hot water gurgled into the tub he thought of Jaseena's brothers, remembered what they had called him behind his back.

Kafir...

He looked at his reflection in the half-steamed bathroom mirror. He saw a strong face and a look of fierce determination. Yes. *Kafir*. That had a ring to it.

Later, after he had bathed, he went to his laptop and looked the word up.

In Islamic parlance, a kāfir is a word used to describe a person who rejects Islamic faith, i.e. hides or covers [viz. the truth]. The word means 'unbeliever'. First applied to Meccans who refused submission to Islam, the term implies an active rejection of divine revelation.

He said the word slowly, savouring each syllable. Perfect. So be it. If he was a *kafir*, he would be *the* Kafir. Simon Peters popped a breath mint into his mouth and began to think about his next appointment. This time he would be more careful. Best avoid Reading, mix it up a bit. The location was irrelevant to him; there were Allah-worshipping Asians everywhere.

18

It was almost too easy.

Chapter Three

Cherries wine bar was tucked beneath the old Top Rank building near the railway station in a small parade of shops that included, nostalgically, a greasy spoon called *Rankin' Robin's*. Cherries was not busy. There were a few office workers knocking back a swifty or two before catching the next train home to the wife, one or two singles sitting at high stools by the window, and a dishevelled-looking woman at a corner table nursing a glass of red wine. *What story would you tell me, love*? Moran wondered as she glanced hopefully in his direction. Moran looked away. Everyone had a story, most of them tales of woe or disaster. Best not to know; disasters usually found their own way to Moran's doorstep without much prompting.

Moran drummed his fingers on the imitation brass tabletop and pondered his easy acquiescence to this meeting. He had a bad feeling about it – irrational, maybe, but a bad feeling nevertheless.

He was also troubled by the young Asian lad's murder. No apparent motive, no sign of a struggle. It bore all the hallmarks of an unprovoked attack. The boy had no marks on him except for the knife wound. A normal racist attack would have kicked off with a beating. Moran shook his head slowly. *Normal*. Was he so desensitised? There was nothing 'normal' about murder.

His reverie was interrupted by a new customer, a woman of around thirty-five with a short, blonde bob.

She cast about this way and that, checking each occupant of the bar in turn. With a jolt of recognition Moran realised it was Shona. The last time he'd seen her she'd had shoulder-length auburn hair and, he recollected, an excess of make up – no doubt to mask her distress. On the day of Kay's funeral her face had been drawn, but now she looked completely different. Attractive. *Very* attractive. Moran stood and raised his hand self-consciously. At once she smiled and walked gracefully towards his table, drawing covert admiring glances from the lone male clientele.

"Hi." Her smile was wide and her teeth, as Moran remembered from the first time they had met, were perfectly white.

"Hello. Nice to see you." Moran pulled a chair over and made a gesture of invitation. "What'll it be?"

"Hmm. A glass of Pinot Grigio, if they have it."

"I'm sure they do."

Moran returned with their drinks and settled into his chair. "Well, cheers." They clinked glasses. Shona took a delicate sip and placed her glass carefully on the 'Chill at Cherries' logo-embossed coaster. She looked briefly down at the table as if unsure how to begin, and then raised her chin and smiled again, apparently flustered. A pink stain appeared at her throat and spread quickly to her cheeks and ears. She chewed her bottom lip, a mannerism he remembered from their first meeting, and sighed.

"I'm sorry, Inspector Moran, you must think it rather odd that I called you the way I did."

Moran was thinking how like Kay she was. The eyes, the curve of her ears, the delicate, darker pigmentation of her lips... "No, no. It's quite all right. I'm glad you did."

"Even at three in the morning?"

21

"Yes." Moran laughed. "My sergeant called ten minutes later so my beauty sleep was interrupted anyway."

Shona frowned. "Oh dear. I hope he doesn't make a habit of it. I shan't," she added quickly.

"It happens–" Moran sipped his wine and grinned. "–actually more often than I care to think about. In this particular case it *was* an urgent call, though. A murder."

"Oh no." Shona's hand went to her mouth. "How awful. In Reading?"

Moran nodded briefly. "Yes. But I can't say too much at this stage, I'm afraid."

"Of course. I understand."

"But we're not here to talk about my problems," Moran prompted, raising his eyebrows in what he hoped was an encouraging expression. "Are we?"

"No," Shona agreed with a slight side-to-side movement of her head. "No, we're not."

"If it helps, Shona, there's not a day goes by that I don't think about Kay, and about how I could have done something – anything – to–"

Shona placed a cool hand on his wrist. "Stop. I don't blame you. Let's get that straight before we move on, OK?"

Moran let out his breath in a long sigh. "Well ... OK. Thanks."

The hand was withdrawn, but Moran could still feel the tingle of her fingers on his flesh.

"I suppose I'm just looking for ... closure – that's what they call it, isn't it?"

"I understand. When you receive bad news second-hand it's a common reaction. You weren't there. You wish you had been so that you could have done something to prevent it."

"Exactly."

"Well, that's how I feel, too," Moran said. "I lent her the keys. I had no idea – at that stage – that I had been targeted."

"I know."

There was a slight lull in conversation. Moran let the silence be, giving Shona time to compose her thoughts.

"Was she *really* happy the last time you saw her?" Shona blurted the question.

Moran nodded vigorously. "Absolutely. I've never seen her so animated, so optimistic."

Shona smiled, a sad little smile that made her appear childlike, lost. She nodded, mulling his words over. "That's good. It makes it a little more bearable, to know that she was happy." She paused. "But it must have been a bit weird for you – you know, her being with your brother, with your history..."

Now it was Moran's turn to feel discomfited. He'd had an on-off relationship with Kay for years, but he had never been able to commit. There'd always been something in the way – doubts, whatever...

"I'm sorry." Shona reprised her magazine smile which made Moran feel instantly better. "I didn't mean to embarrass you."

Moran laughed and ran his hand through his hair. "Not at all. It was a long time ago."

"I know, but nevertheless..." Shona smiled mischievously.

"I suppose I felt ... protective towards her," Moran said. "My brother wasn't in the best of health. He was unstable, unpredictable. Kay didn't need that. She needed someone solid and reliable."

"We all need that, don't we?" She held his gaze. Moran turned his eyes away, unsettled by her directness. Or had he misinterpreted the look?

She reached over the table and took his hand. "Brendan, I know you've lost someone close to you as well. Your brother had problems, but he was still family, wasn't he? And you and Kay ... well, you were old friends. I just want you to know that if you need anyone to talk to, I'm here, OK?"

Flustered at this unexpected role-reversal, Moran muttered his thanks.

"I mean, we can help each other, right?"

Moran cleared his throat and composed himself. "Right. Of course."

Shona sat back in her chair and studied him as if he were some kind of biological specimen. "You're such a typical man. You can't open up, can you?"

Moran coughed. "Well, I–"

"Of course you can't. Maybe when we know each other a little better?"

Moran inclined his head in acknowledgement. "Sure. I'm sorry." He shook his head self-deprecatingly. "Emotional stuff is not my forte."

"Hmm. You don't say. Can I buy you a drink?"

"Well, I was thinking perhaps a bite to eat?"

Shona made a cooing noise in her throat. "Now you're talking." She grinned. "I'm *always* hungry."

Moran made his way past the front desk, pausing briefly to ruffle Sergeant Robinson's carefully laid-out leaflets and pamphlets. Robinson was a lovely bloke, but he was completely obsessive about the reception area. Any small deviation from what Denis Robinson considered acceptable produced an apoplectic Jekyll to Hyde reaction. Which, of course, was what made provoking him so enjoyable. *It's the little things that make life bearable...* Moran whistled a tune as he took the lift to the squad room and found, as he had expected, a buzz of expectancy.

"So." Moran surveyed the team. "Come on. Let's have some ideas. We have, in no particular order, a body, no motive, no witnesses. Your thoughts, please."

"He was Asian, guv," a young DC offered. With his fresh face and sandy hair he looked as though he would be more at home in a classroom than a murder incident room.

"Thank you, DC Hill. Anything else wandered within range of your acutely-honed observational skills?"

There was a ripple of laughter and the young policeman blushed. However, despite his embarrassment he spoke up again.

"Well, guv, he was young, casually dressed. No ID, no money, no phone. Traces of a small intake of alcohol; the BAC reading was around 0.031. Plenty of bling – worth a bit, from what I've seen. Maybe he was hanging around waiting for a lift – or a customer."

Moran raised his eyebrows. "Pusher?"

"Pimp?" someone else offered.

"Right wing extremist group?" said someone else.

"Okay," Moran said. "Ifs, buts and maybes aren't going to get us very far. As no one has reported a missing person answering our friend's description we'll just have to go looking ourselves. He has family, somewhere. Friends, clients, girls – whatever. I'd suggest chatting to one or two of the Oxford road ladies to start with." He turned to his sergeant. "Can you take that, Phelps?"

Phelps nodded. "Pleasure, guv."

"But not too much, I trust," Moran said dryly. More subdued laughter from the assembled officers.

"And I'd like one of you to check out the town centre pubs. Chances are he was in one of them earlier in the evening. Maybe he'll be remembered."

"That'll do for me, guv," DC Hill piped up.

"Take your ID with you, son," one of the older officers advised.

"All right, all right. That's enough," Moran shouted above the hilarity. "Let's remember this is a murder investigation. I want concrete facts and I want them fast. We reconvene tomorrow at eight sharp."

The team began to disperse, some reclaiming their desks, others making for the canteen where a new coffee machine had reversed the facility's ailing fortunes.

"Hang on, hang on." Moran called them back. "One announcement before you get cracking. DI Pepper was due to join us this week but is apparently down with a dose of the summer flu, whatever that is."

Knowing grins were exchanged. One DC made a comic noise of disbelief.

Moran waved the laughter away. "All right, all right. Don't get any ideas – I don't want anyone else going AWOL, not while we have a murderer to track down. In DI Pepper's absence, Detective Sergeant Phelps here will be acting DI. If I'm not around for any reason you are to report to him and him alone. Any questions? Right, let's get on with it."

Slough town centre was teeming, but there were precious few white faces among the crowds. Empowered and enlightened by his new identity the Kafir felt like an outsider. *An outsider in my own country.* He walked through the shopping mall, watched the shoppers pass by. Young, old, sick, fit. happy, grim-faced – on they went, tunnel-visioned, trudging along their allotted pathway like automata.

He went into a Starbucks and ordered a frappuccino.Trade was good, conversation buzzing. An image flicked through his mind; a beautiful girl, dark-skinned, smiling. He shut her out with a brief shake of his head. He would make Jaseena a memory, lock her away in some cold corner of his subconscious where no harm could be done. He sipped the cold coffee, skim-read a discarded newspaper.

The Kafir sat in the corner, watching. Waiting.

Chapter Four

Oxford road. Dodgy area. Phelps homed in on his target. She was slim, smoking and smiling. As he got within spitting distance she threw the cigarette down on the pavement and ground it out with an exaggerated stamp of her high-heeled shoe. She gave him a knowing look.

"Copper, right?"

Phelps nodded. "Obvious?"

She held his gaze. "Right."

"I'm not here to hassle you," Phelps told her. *Much...*

"Really?" The girl drew out another cigarette and placed it between her bright red lips. She was pretty, of mixed race. Around twenty-five, Phelps guessed – mouths to feed at home, caught in the economic cleft stick which made the oldest profession seem like her best option.

She lit the cigarette and blew smoke in a thin stream. "What you want, then?"

"You heard about the murder in the town centre?"

She shrugged. "Maybe."

Phelps pressed on. "Asian guy. Young. All blinged up."

She shrugged again.

"Anyone you know gone missing? Any of your buddies short of work this week?"

"What are you trying to say, officer?" Her voice was mocking, poshed up for effect.

"Oh, come on, sweetie." Phelps felt himself losing his patience. "The guy looked like a dealer or a pimp, maybe both. It's a small world around here. You must have heard something?"

"You got a photo?"

Phelps showed her. She gave the image a cursory glance and shook her head.

"Nah. Not one of ours."

Another girl appeared across the road by the pub. Phelps' girl waved and received a greeting in return.

"Go and ask Zoë, big boy," she advised him. "She knows everyone. Even out-of-towners."

"Thanks."

Phelps crossed the road. The girl watched him approach with ill-concealed amusement.

"Hello there. What can I do for *you*?" she purred and sidled up to Phelps, ran a slim hand down his lapel.

Phelps removed the hand and flashed his ID.

"Ah. Shame." She placed both hands on her hips. "I was looking forward to getting to know you, babe."

"I'll bet. Did you get to know him?" Phelps repeated the photo-show.

Zoë peered at the image, rolled her shoulders. "Maybe. I seen him in the town centre once or twice." She pronounced it '*centah*'.

"Where and when?" Phelps pressed, trying to avert his eyes from her ample cleavage.

"The Retreat. And he was in Chameleon's once."

"The bar on Friar Street?"

"Yeah."

"Friend?"

"Nah. Mouthy little git. He came on to us but he was all talk, y'know?"

"Name?"

"Dunno."

"Nothing to do with your line of work then, Zoë?"

She gave him a look. "No way. He was just a kid."

Phelps tucked the photograph away. "Now he's a dead kid." He gave the girl a hard look. "I hope you're not telling me porkies, Zoë."

"Pleasure to meet you, *officer*." Zoë turned and sashayed away. A van passed and Zoë acknowledged the wolf-whistle with a casual wave. Phelps watched her retreating figure and lit a cigarette. She was lying, for sure.

Nice legs, though.

"Come *on*, Archie." Moran called his spaniel for the umpteenth time but the little dog was having none of it. He'd found a scent – of which there were plenty in Sulham Woods; squirrel or deer, probably – and he wasn't going to let it go without a thorough investigation. It began to rain, lightly at first and then more persistently. Moran squatted gingerly on a tree root protruding from the chalky soil and resigned himself to a lengthy wait. When Archie was in this kind of a mood it was best, time allowing, to let the cocker get on with it. At least it gave him a little more thinking time; the woods were perfect for that and this evening he was in no hurry.

He buttoned down his waterproof and allowed his thoughts to return to the dead Asian boy and the fact that no relatives had come forward. Why not? Perhaps they hadn't realised he was missing, or maybe they had closed ranks. He'd come up against that before; any closed community was likely to deal with a serious incident on their own terms – at least initially – because the police were considered outsiders. Charnford Abbey had been a classic example. And now perhaps the Asian community were playing the same game.

From the undergrowth came the sounds of snorting and snuffling as Archie homed in on the source of his obsessive quest.

No relatives, no friends. Too ashamed to come forward? Too scared? No ID, no useful prints or DNA. Moran sighed. He wanted a cigarette badly, but that would earn him Dr Purewal's wrath. He'd been 'damn lucky', the pretty GP had told him, and 'damn stupid' to have refused an ambulance at Charnford. Moran grunted at the recollection. She was probably right, but Rory Dalton was now well and truly detained at Her Majesty's pleasure, and Moran's stroke had been less severe than it could have been. "*This* time, Inspector Moran. Next time, not so lucky.' Dr Purewal had glowered through her designer spectacles.

Another dog appeared, a well-groomed Labrador with a chain collar. Moran recognised it. It belonged to Alison Miller, a neighbour and the only soul he'd had any real conversation with since he'd moved in. She and her husband were a nice couple; he was an architect and she ran some kind of sports injuries clinic.

"Max?" Alison's voice came from somewhere nearby. "Where are you?"

Max emerged from the undergrowth, snorting and dripping with mud. Moran did a double-take. A woman's handbag was dangling from the dog's panting mouth. Archie appeared, trotting along behind Max, sniffing at the ground.

"Oh *no*." Moran shot up from his seat of roots and zeroed in on the gap in the tangle of bush and foliage from which the two dogs had emerged. He squelched across the mossy woodland floor, ducking his head to avoid the wet, springy branches, scanning the ground for something he didn't want to find.

What he did find was Alison Miller. His neighbour was rooted to the spot, her expression one of sheer horror.

"Brendan. My God, I– I–" Alison's hands went to her mouth.

He followed her shocked gaze, at first seeing nothing untoward until he bent down to look more closely, and there it was: a woman's hand, black and caked with mud, half-hidden under a shroud of fallen leaves.

Moran squinted in the intense light of the murder scene. White-suited SOCOs moved back and forth under the glare, studying the ground for information, bagging samples, inspecting every centimetre of woodland as if mining for gold. Which, in a way, they were; as far as Moran was concerned a leading clue was infinitely more precious.

"Can't believe you turned this up, guv." Phelps shook his head in disbelief.

"If I hadn't, somebody else would have," Moran said. "This is a prime dog-walking area, Phelps. Whoever buried this girl knows nothing about dogs."

"Unleash the dogs of war, eh, Moran?" Sandy Taylor was at his side, brusque and breezy, briefcase at the ready, feet clad in Hunter wellingtons.

"A casual observer might conclude that you enjoy being dragged out at the witching hour, Dr Taylor," Moran observed dryly.

"Fresh air, fine health," Taylor replied with a wide grin. "Always glad to get out and about."

"Spare me the nocturnal bonhomie, Sandy," Moran told the pathologist. "Just tell me how she died."

Taylor bent to his task and Moran did his rounds, chatting to the scene manager, a tough Scot named Maclennan, and each SOCO in turn. There was general agreement that the woman had been dumped, not killed in situ. By the time he had finished Taylor had also concluded his examination.

"Strangled," Taylor announced. "Several broken fingernails. I'll prime Bagri to pay particular attention to those."

"Usual question, Sandy."

Taylor sucked in his cheeks. "Two or three days, I'd say."

"Right. Thanks."

"Poor kid," Phelps observed morosely as the body was bagged and the zipper closed over the tangle of hair. There was something final about that moment, Moran always thought, a precursor to the finality of the crematorium's closing curtain.

"Poor kid, indeed," Moran agreed quietly.

He dismissed Phelps and made his way back to his car. Two or three days. That would put the timeframe close to the town centre incident. It could be related – or maybe not. He glanced at the Rover's clock. Ten past one. He was dog-tired but he felt the old, familiar reluctance to go to bed. A snatch of Shakespeare came into his head: *to sleep, perchance to dream…*

Gregory Neads was also wide awake. He slipped the car into first and followed the Land Rover at a discreet distance. His head throbbed with the memory of the agony he had suffered at Charnford. His thoughts were cold, calculating, devoid of compassion. High summer it might be, but his soul inhabited a world that was forever winter.

Chapter Five

A pretty woman, blonde, sitting at the foot of his bed. Moran knew he was dreaming but somehow it didn't seem to matter. He looked again. It was Kay. She smiled and raised her hand.

"Hi," he said. It was warm, close but not oppressively so. Kay was naked. She came to him, pressed her lips to his, but then she stepped back, a warning finger raised. He frowned. What was wrong? There was someone else in the room, a fleeting, fugitive figure. He caught a movement in the corner of his eye. Kay backed away until she was standing by the bedroom door. Someone stepped in front of her – another woman. A girl with no face. Rotting leaves clung to her clothing and her hair was tangled and filthy.

Moran felt sweat seep from his pores and his feet turn to lead. The faceless girl advanced, step by step, arm outstretched. He tried to shout for help. Nothing came out. It felt like the stroke all over again, the paralysis, the helplessness. A car engine fired into life, noisily. The apparition faded. His eyes opened and a wave of relief flooded through him. *A dream, that's all. A dream.*

Wincing at the stiffness of his recuperating tendons, Moran swung his legs onto the floor and reached for the curtains. The tail lights of a speeding car winked as the vehicle screeched around the corner. From the other direction a milk float idled into view. Dawn was breaking. Moran limped to his bedside table and picked up his clock. Six minutes past five. He tossed the clock onto the bed. Another night prematurely over, another endless day ahead.

The M4 was pleasantly clear and the purr of the engine was soothing. The Kafir felt relaxed and refreshed. It was good to know what you were about, what your next job was. He was intrigued that, despite frequent headaches, his mind continued to provide him with fresh, challenging insights. He felt that the headaches were a small price to pay for this privilege. Since his discharge the only other troubling side effect from his beating was a persistent, but not particularly unpleasant, metallic taste in his mouth and throat. However, the doctors had forewarned him of such a possibility so he wasn't unduly worried. After all, he had weightier topics to consider than the vagaries of his own health.

This morning he was pondering the problem of fundamentalism, something which had troubled him long before his relationship with Jaseena. He wondered which particular flaw in human nature was responsible for prompting one culture to want to impose its belief system on another.

It was happening here in the UK, right now. Subtly, perhaps, but he had no doubt that the imposition would become increasingly blatant. In time, relentless pressure would force the government to make ever-greater concessions. The curse of political correctness would come into play; fundamentalists would be appointed more frequently into positions of power and influence. Was it not abundantly clear? Mosques were already replacing churches. Ghettoes were rapidly expanding, consuming neighbouring communities like a cancer. Soon, there would be no compromise. *The rot within...*

It had to be stopped.

He drove into the multi-storey car park and guided his car into a parking bay. He made a note of the level number and then headed down the urine-scented staircase to the main shopping area. Enough reconnaissance. Today was the day. He'd found another one, a relative. Not immediate family, but a second or third cousin who worked in some tedious financial institution as an IT specialist.

Jayesh.

Jayesh, who had pointedly failed to acknowledge his presence on the sole occasion he had attended a family function. Jay, who had turned his back, blanked him. And later, who had been laughing and pointing with her brothers. He could still see the hurt on Jaseena's face, her darting look of guilt and apology. As far as he was concerned it mattered little now, but Jayesh had hurt Jas, and so he deserved to die.

It was a quarter to five; almost home time for the Slough office workers. The windows of *Mukhandra International* glinted like mirrored building blocks in the afternoon sun. The Kafir found a bench, placed a mint on his tongue and settled down to wait.

"Got a sec, guv?" Phelps' bullish head appeared around Moran's office door.

"Always," Moran said flatly. "Come in, Phelps, and restore my faith in humanity."

"Guv?"

Moran removed his glasses and wearily pressed the heels of his hands into his eyes. Stars danced briefly in the blackness and then cleared. When he opened his eyes again Phelps was studying him with close concentration.

"I'm *all right*, Phelps. Stop looking at me as if I'm some kind of laboratory experiment."

"Sorry, guv. What's the problem with humanity, then?" Phelps settled into the chair opposite, which creaked loudly in protest.

"If you have to ask that question, Phelps, then I really do despair."

Phelps grinned. "Point taken."

"It's the insurers." Moran flicked a sheet of paper on his desk. "They're refusing to cover the cost of the damage to my property."

"On what grounds?"

"Exemption on the grounds that the damage was caused by a terrorist attack, for which I apparently need a separate policy. Which, of course, I don't have."

Phelps raised his bushy eyebrows. "You're kidding."

"I wish. Can you believe–?"

They were interrupted by a sharp knock on the door.

"May I?" A thin, balding man half-entered the room. There was a proprietary look about him, as if he were about to take ownership of Moran's domain.

"And you are?"

"Superintendent Alan Sheldrake. OCG. I–"

Phelps interrupted. "Ah. That's what I was about to tell you, guv. The girl in the woods–"

"Thank you, Detective Constable," Sheldrake broke in and made an ushering gesture towards the door. "I'll take it from here. If you wouldn't mind?"

"Acting Detective *Inspector*," Phelps growled.

"Go on, Phelps," Moran told him. "I'll see you in a minute." Something told him that Sheldrake was a man of brevity – and probably a pain in the backside to boot.

Sheldrake closed the door.

"Coffee, sir?" Moran rose to switch the kettle on.

"No. This won't take long, Moran. You've heard of Operation Kestrel?"

Moran sat down again, but Sheldrake remained standing. "Yes, of course."

"You found a body. The girl."

"Yes. I'm waiting for foren–"

"Don't bother. *I'll* take it."

"Sir?"

Sheldrake hesitated. His face had a pale, slightly yellowish hue and there were dark smudges under his eyes which suggested that he'd spent too many nights away from his bed. He gave a weary sigh. "She's one of ours, Moran. Her name is – was – DS Valerie Reed-Purvis."

"Oh. I see. But–"

"She was working undercover. Deep cover. She was meeting a local dealer – a useful contact. He was about to lead her to the next level."

"What happened?" Moran had a sinking feeling that he knew exactly what had happened.

"The dealer was attacked. It seems likely that DS Reed-Purvis saw it happen and tried to intervene." Sheldrake shrugged. "She got the worst of the encounter, as you know."

"Where was she last seen?"

Sheldrake shrugged. "One of the town centre bars, I believe. I don't recall which – DS Flynn can confirm the location. They were working on this together."

"And the dealer? He wouldn't by any chance be a young Asian, blinged up to the nines? No identification?"

"Yes, he would," Sheldrake acknowledged tersely.

"So," Moran said. "We're both looking for the same killer."

"No. *I'm* looking for the killer. You can move on and leave this one to me."

Moran felt a flush of anger. "How do you know for sure the attack was drug-related?"

Sheldrake leaned over Moran's desk. His eyes blazed. "Of *course* it was drug-related. Unless you know better?"

"Well, how about a standard mugging, a grudge killing, a *crime passionnel–*"

"Don't try to be clever, Moran. I know what this is about. Organised Crime has been working on this particular drugs ring for months."

"Sir, if I might–"

"That's enough, Moran. I've spoken to your Chief. You're off this one. Understood?"

Moran nodded, fuming. "Sir."

"Glad we see eye to eye. I want everything you and your team have established, and everything you're in the process of following up, handed over to me by Thursday at the latest. Got that?" Sheldrake gave him a lingering look and swept out of the office, leaving the door open behind him.

Moran picked up his empty coffee cup and flung it into the corner. It didn't make him feel any better.

Moran found Phelps in the car park. He felt slightly calmer, but not to the extent that he intended to lie down without a fight. This smelled wrong, and he was going to find out why.

Phelps looked up as Moran approached and gave him a wry smile. "I had a feeling he might rub you up the wrong way, guv. What'd he want?"

Moran outlined his conversation with Sheldrake. "The Chief is away until ... when?"

Phelps frowned. "Guv, are you sure–?"

"There's no direct evidence that Bling Boy's murder is related to Kestrel," Moran broke in tersely. "It was too open, too blatant. A drugs ring would deal with problems more circumspectly."

Phelps nodded. "I tend to agree, but this Sheldrake looks like a forceful sort of character. He won't like us poking our noses in."

Moran snorted. "It's the other way round as far as I'm concerned. Till Friday, wasn't it?"

"Guv?"

"Our illustrious leader's absence."

"Yep. He's at some conference in Maidenhead."

"That gives us an extra day, then.. To hell with Sheldrake's ultimatum."

Phelps shrugged. "If you're sure, guv." He took a deep pull on his cigarette.

"Sure? I'm as sure as eggs is eggs, DI Phelps."

Phelps grinned. "Saving the grammatical anomaly, that's good enough for me, guv."

Moran poured himself a glass of Sangiovese and settled into his settee. What he needed was some quality thinking time. He was sure, whether by instinct or some subconscious process, that Bling Boy's death was unrelated to Sheldrake's operation; that the killer hadn't necessarily been aware of the victim's involvement in drug dealing. The big question was whether the Bling

Boy killer had also murdered DS Reed-Purvis. Sheldrake's story suggested that was the case, but Moran had learned not to jump to conclusions. The answer, he hoped, would be supplied by the pathologist, Dr Moninder Bagri, tomorrow morning. The secondary question, one that always sent a shiver of anticipation down his spine, was whether this was a one-off, or whether they were dealing with a potential serial killer.

Moran closed his eyes. Strangely, the first image that came to mind was unrelated to the case. Shona Kempster had popped into his head unannounced in much the same way as her previous phone calls had done. He took another sip of Sangiovese and shook his head. *Here you go again, Brendan.*

The phone rang.

"Hello?"

"Hi Brendan. Shona."

"Hello. I was just thinking about you."

"Were you indeed? Nice things, I hope."

"Of course," Moran heard himself say.

A pause. "I love the way you say 'Hello'."

"Ah." Moran felt his heart skip a beat. "The accent's still there, then."

"To be sure." Shona's voice was silky, teasing. "How was your day?"

"Started well, finished badly," Moran said truthfully. "Yours?"

"Well, I had a few things to sort out, you know."

"How's the job-hunting?"

"Job-hunting?"

"You said you weren't at the clinic any more. I assumed you were job-hunting."

"Oh, right. Yes, of course. Nothing so far, I'm afraid."

"I'm sure something will turn up."

"Yes. Brendan?"

"Uh huh?"

"Could I ask you something in confidence?"

"Sure. Fire away."

"No, I mean, I think it should be face-to-face."

"Oh, OK. Would you like me to come over?" Moran felt his mouth dry and his pulse quicken a little. He took a gulp of wine.

"No. I mean, perhaps I can come to you? Or maybe–"

"What about dinner tomorrow evening?" *Woah, Brendan Moran. Steady, steady...*

Shona's voice softened. "That would be lovely."

"Great. How about I pick you up at eight? You'd better let me have your address."

"No, I don't want you to go to any trouble. I can meet you in town?"

"Sure. If you'd prefer."

"How about outside Nino's?"

"The Italian? Sure, good choice." He chuckled. "Absolutely irresistible to an Italophile like myself. See you then."

Moran signed off and replaced the receiver with a frown. He felt a nudge on his leg. "Hello, Archie. Time for a wee walk, is it?" He heaved himself up from the sofa and retrieved his stick, reluctantly as usual; its presence reminded him of his frailty, of how close he'd come to death. *So, what's wrong with living a little, Brendan? She likes you. Enjoy it...*

As he left the house a small voice whispered in his ear. *Yes, enjoy it. While you can...*

Chapter Six

Dr Moninder Bagri was Moran's favourite pathologist. Small in stature, big on detail and humour – his own brand of humour – he was also renowned for his ability to find and fit together the tiniest and most obscure pieces in any given forensic puzzle.

What Moran was after this morning was speed. He had persuaded Bagri to begin thirty minutes before schedule, before Superintendent Sheldrake turned up to oversee the examination of DS Reed-Purvis' remains. From behind the glass in the obs room Moran watched the preparations. Eventually the body was wheeled out and arranged on the examination table. Dr Bagri glanced up and made a gesture of invitation. When he spoke his voice was tinny and trebly through the loudspeakers.

"Come on down, Chief Inspector! We're all ready for you!"

Moran made his way along the corridor and into the sterile environment of the examination room, wondering not for the first time how Bagri could remain so cheerfully buoyant in his work. The waft of chemicals and the inescapable odour of death made his nostrils twitch. He'd skipped breakfast deliberately; it had proved a wise decision on many previous occasions.

"So, the early bird is catching the worm, is it?"

"Something like that, Dr Bagri." Moran smiled. "I have a little internal conflict with Superintendent Sheldrake."

"Ah. Say no more of it," Bagri chuckled. "I am completely understanding. As a matter of fact, I told the esteemed Superintendent that I would not be available until ten this morning."

"You're too good to me, Dr Bagri. I appreciate it."

Bagri wagged a thin finger. "And the favours I have received from your good self?" He grinned a complicit smile. "Too many to count." The pathologist selected an instrument from the tray and held it up for inspection. "Good," he announced. "Now then, a moment's pause, isn't it?"

Moran remembered this mark of respect from previous autopsies. It always brought him up short, focused his mind on the reality of the situation. Someone had lost their life in violent circumstances. In this case it was a young girl – young enough to be his daughter. He made himself look down at the pale form laid out on the cold steel.

Reed-Purvis had been very attractive; her lips were full and her nose delicate and shapely. Her hair was cut in a fashionably short style; her breasts were small but firm and her fingers were long and artistic, the unbroken nails well-manicured. Her belly was flat and toned, the product, no doubt, of regular attendance at the gym.

"We proceed," Bagri said quietly, more to himself than to Moran.

Moran peered closely at the detective sergeant's white body. Bagri began with the hands and arms, probing them gently, pointing out any anomalies and paying particular attention to a line of bruises on the upper arm.

"Fingers?" Moran asked.

"Undoubtedly," Bagri replied. "And judging from the spread and dimensions, fingers belonging to a male."

"What about there?" Moran wanted to know about some bruising he could see on the girl's forehead.

"Ah." Bagri frowned. "Produced by a hard, flat object. Very painful. See here as well–" Bagri indicated the bruising around the eyes. "All related, I am thinking."

"He nutted her," Moran said, his lip curling in distaste. "The scumbag nutted her."

"Ah, with the head, yes," Bagri agreed. "The marks are indicative that this is a possibility."

"And the force of the blow? Would it have been enough to render her unconscious?"

"Oh, indeed," Bagri said, looking up over his half-moon spectacles. "Very much so."

"OK," Moran said. "He spotted her, caught her and knocked her for six. Then into the car and off to Sulham Woods. I'd suggest a strong, fit assailant, Dr Bagri."

"Yes, yes." Bagri nodded several times in quick succession. "This is a young lady in her prime, muscular, fit indeed, a good strong runner I am thinking. To incapacitate her is a difficult thing." He continued his external examination, finally parting Reed-Purvis' hair and running his instrument along her scalp. A few seconds later he gave a triumphant exclamation. "Ah!"

"What is it, Dr Bagri?"

"A flake which is definitely not a dandruff," the little doctor held up his forceps.

"Then what?" Moran asked, trying to curb his impatience. Bagri loved to draw out his findings and conclusions for as long as possible, the only trait Moran found trying in the pathology expert.

"I am thinking maybe, paint?" Bagri cocked his head to one side. "We shall soon see once we put it to the test."

"Paint?" Moran was puzzled. "What kind of paint?"

"Perhaps she banged her head," Bagri suggested, "maybe in the town, yes? *Before* the burial, or maybe in his car? In the boot?" Bagri turned his attention to the fingernails of the right hand. Two were chipped and torn, in contrast to the neatness of the others. "Let us see what lies beneath – ah."

Moran bent closer as Bagri retrieved a tiny sliver from beneath a nail. "More of the same, I am thinking. Maybe the same brand of paint?"

"Maybe indeed, Dr Bagri." Moran was delighted. As usual, the hidden things had been exposed by Bagri's painstaking attention. "We'll see what the lab comes up with."

"We shall. And the toxicology report will also be available for you by the end of the morning."

"Thank you," Moran pumped the little man's hand.

There was a commotion in the gallery, a booming voice echoed in the corridor. "Damn," Moran said. "He's early."

A wiry figure bustled into view, accompanied by a thin, ascetic-looking female sergeant. Dr Bagri smiled his winning smile at the newcomers. A door banged at the far end of the examination room. By the time Sheldrake and his DS had taken up position at the pathologist's side Moran was in his car and on his way to forensics.

Leaving forensics and bubbling with impatience, Moran drove home to squeeze in Archie's walk before he reconvened the team back at the station. As he approached his house he noticed that there was something on his door. A note?

He snatched it from beneath the knocker where it had been wedged. It was a picture, a graphic of a knife with two large drops of blood dripping from its blade.

What on earth ...?

He turned and surveyed the road. There was no one in sight.

Moran entered the house cautiously, but Archie met him excitedly as usual and nothing else seemed amiss. Irritated and perplexed he crumpled the paper and fired it into the bin. His mobile bleeped.

"Moran."

"Guv?" Phelps' voice rasped across the network. "There's been another one."

Better, he thought. *Much* better. Cleaner, too. The elation had dissipated, bringing a deep sense of satisfaction and peace. If he'd been unsure at the beginning, now he was certain he'd done the right thing.

He had spent the morning disposing of unnecessary junk. The room in which he stood contained only a bed, a TV on a stand and a small table with an open newspaper spread across its worn surface. Everything else had been consigned to charity shops, skips, and for the heavier items the local dump. It felt therapeutic, ridding himself of his earthly possessions. What need had he for material things?

In any case, it was time to move on. He had so many operations to plan, and according to the newspapers the police were in the process of linking his local exploits. It would be good to move to a fresh location – somewhere simple, somewhere with good views. He would check out the estate agents first thing in the morning.

The Kafir yawned, stretched, picked up the newspaper and skim-read the headlines, paying particular attention to the photograph of the investigating policeman. DCI Moran's statement was copybook waffle which the Kafir read with amusement:

The Senior Investigating Officer, Detective Chief Inspector Brendan Moran, said: 'We have a team of detectives working on the case and we are committed to carrying out a full and thorough investigation into the circumstances leading to this tragic incident. We are renewing our appeal for any witnesses to come forward, as I know there were a large number of people in the town centre at the time of the incident who may have seen something, or who may have information which could assist our ongoing inquiry. We would ask them to call us.

Anyone with information can call the twenty-four-hour police enquiry centre on 101, or call Crimestoppers anonymously on 0800 555 111.

DCI Moran himself looked tired; his face in the photograph was lined and drawn. But there was something else...

The Kafir frowned, puzzled. It was as if something important had been mentioned which he had somehow failed to grasp.. Frustrated, he went to make a hot drink. No matter, he told himself. Anything of importance wouldn't escape his attention for long..

"Grim," Phelps said quietly. "My boy's about the same age."

Moran nodded. He had to agree that the victim looked very young, almost too young to be out on his own, but he was probably in his early to mid twenties. The corpse was squatting in a foetal position in the corner of Marks and Spencer's entrance lobby. Apart from the unnatural stillness of the body, a tiny smear of blood on the shop window was the only indication that anything untoward had happened. Which, Moran realised, was the reason people had just passed by without stopping to investigate. Just another homeless kid in a shop doorway. All that was missing was the dog on a length of dirty string. If anyone had stopped to look properly, though, they would have seen that this homeless kid was wearing a sharp suit – now stained and crumpled, but still recognisably a good cut. He pulled on a pair of plastic gloves.

Phelps blew his nose loudly. "Too young to be a local office worker, guv?"

"Maybe. Maybe not." Moran waved his stick in a wide arc. "Plenty of offices in and around the town centre. Could be a trainee." He paused. "I'm beginning to wonder about the racist angle now."

"Right-wingers?" Phelps made an inverse U with his mouth. "I've not heard of any particularly proactive group based in the Berkshire area, guv. Have you?"

"No, but that doesn't mean they don't exist."

"True. Or it could be that our killer is of the extreme right-wing persuasion himself. No backup, no membership, just a solo artist." Phelps spread his hands and indicated the body. "Or this lad could just be a pimp who got unlucky."

Moran bent and looked into the dead eyes. "No, Phelps, this is a good boy from a good home, with a good job."

"You think?"

"Look." Moran exposed the dead man's neck and fished out a fluorescent lanyard from which dangled a blank security card. "I'm betting he's an IT worker." He peered at the lanyard. "Sometimes these have company logos. Your eyes are better than mine, Phelps."

Phelps grunted and inspected the lanyard. "Aha. Spot on, guv." He read the name. "*Mukhandra International.* Our killer's getting careless – if it's the same one."

Moran stepped aside to let a forensics officer through. He winced as the glare of the superlite flashed across his path of vision. "Oh, it's the same killer, Phelps," he said grimly. "I can feel it in my bones."

Chapter Seven

Detective Constable James Hill was on a mission. He was sick of the endless stream of jokes and witty leg-pulling fired at him day after day. It was usually DS Banner who kicked things off with some comment about his hair or his baby-faced appearance. Then the scene would be set for the others to join in. He took it in good part, as far as they knew. He made a point of laughing it off, giving something back. But it hurt, and he'd had enough. Why couldn't they pick on someone else?

He couldn't help looking young. OK, so he did have to carry an over-eighteen ID card; otherwise he'd be refused service every time he went into a bar. Banner knew this, of course, and never missed an opportunity to bring it up. It was crushingly embarrassing; the worst time ever had been when he'd taken Helen out to a trendy bar. It was a busy Saturday night and the bar was packed with youngsters of his age. The barman had looked him up and down with a knowing wink. "Away you go, sonny. You'd better get your big sis to take you home."

Helen had smiled politely and told him it was OK, it didn't matter. But he could see it did. Hill sighed and rapped the steering wheel in frustration. He was a grown man; he had a man's needs, a man's thoughts, but he was invariably treated like some spotty teenager. Well he'd show them. He'd get respect if it was the last thing he did.

That's what his mission was all about, and so far he was on track. OK, so he should be sharing with the team – and he had done, to an extent – but the info he'd gleaned from the manager of the Zodiac club could solve both the case and his persecution problem in one fell swoop.

Hill jumped as the bar door opened and someone came out. The man paused to light a cigarette, then walked briskly down the street with his collar turned up against the light summer rainfall. Hill peered through the windscreen. It was him all right, the guy the manager had pointed out – the skinny Asian in the sharp suit who called himself Jag. Hill had produced a photo of the dead bloke and asked the manager if he knew him. "Twice a week, Tuesdays and Thursdays, regular," was the response. "Always sits in the corner, talks to the skinny geezer. Never stays long. Why? What's up?"

Hill had declined to answer, enjoying the unusual feeling of having the upper hand in a conversation with a barman. "Police business, I'm afraid," he had told the white-smocked manager. "Thanks for your time."

Hill had clocked the guy in the corner on his way out; he was alone, talking on his mobile. Hill had resolved there and then to wait until this Jag guy decided to leave.

Jag got into a silver Merc E Class saloon and gunned off down the road. Hill followed at a discreet distance, excitement pumping through his veins. As he negotiated the one-way system he tried to remember the rules for tailing a suspect. *Not too close, keep him in sight, get a car or two between you if possible...*

They hit the M4 and Hill was pleased to see that Jag had adopted a constant middle-lane speed; he wouldn't have to burn up the fast lane to keep him in sight. But where was he headed? Maidenhead? Slough? London? His question was soon answered as the Merc indicated at the sign for the turn-off to Slough West and pulled into the slow lane.

Hill maintained his distance as they crawled through Chalvey. One left and another left later the Merc pulled up outside a row of terraces. Hill parked behind a white van and waited. Jag approached the middle terrace, knocked and was admitted.

Hill relaxed. Now what? He looked at his watch. Ten pm. Early enough for something else to happen. In that case ... he flipped the backrest switch and settled down to wait. His thoughts drifted. He wondered what Helen was doing. Was it worth trying again? Why not? He'd talk to her in the morning. Hill closed his eyes and thought pleasant thoughts. Sleep took him unawares. The clock hands moved slowly around the dashboard display. Hill slept on.

He awoke with a start, the sound of a door slamming jolting him to wakefulness. For a second he had no idea where he was. Then, as he saw the thin man walking along the pavement towards him, it all came back in a rush. Someone else was coming out of the house. Hill watched him lock up and join Jag by the Merc. The two men got into the car and the engine fired.

What should he do? Follow? Hill racked his brains. Wait. The house could well be empty. Perhaps he would find conclusive evidence, or at least a lead of some sort. Something he could wave in DS Banner's smirking face.

He waited until the Merc had turned the corner and the street was quiet. He looked at his watch. Just before one o'clock. With a shock of guilt he realised he'd been out for the count for three hours. *Great surveillance work, Jimmy boy. Better not put that in the report...*

There was a side alley between the terraces. He checked the street, checked the other houses for curtain twitchers and quickly made his way to the rear of the block. The back garden was a rubbish dump, with overflowing bins, discarded papers, an overgrown lawn – hardly a lawn, more a patch of scrub. No lights. A back door, paint peeling. Hill tried it. Locked, of course. He fished in his pocket. The second key fitted. It usually did, unless the lock was an expensive one, which this clearly wasn't. Nothing to hide? *We shall see*, Hill whispered to himself, and prodded the door open.

Silence met his first step inside. He was in the kitchen. He fired up his mobile's flashlight app and held his phone in front of him. A circular table stood in the centre of the room; dirty plates and empty takeaway containers were scattered on its Formica top, on the draining board, on every available surface. The sink was piled with unwashed dishes.

A staircase loomed on Hill's right. Ahead, another room – the living room. Before it, another door; a cupboard maybe? Hill moved forward cautiously, tried the handle. A black space, stairs leading down. A musty, damp smell floated up from the depths.

He paused, listening, all his senses tingling. Had he heard something? He hesitated by the basement door, flicked off the phone's beam. He could hear his heart pounding. A minute passed. Another. Hill took a breath, composed himself and stepped onto the basement staircase.

Six steps and he was at the bottom. The floor was unfinished, covered with dust and rubble; a rectangular wooden table was the sole piece of furniture. He turned on the flashlight again and the beam played on the clear plastic bags stacked in a neat pile, the contents gleaming like snow in the moonlight.

Hill caught his breath, hardly daring to believe he'd hit a bull's eye with his first throw. He was deliberating whether or not to take a sample with him when the basement door above closed with a bang, followed by the unmistakeable sound of a key turning in the lock.

A voice called down. "Don't bother calling for help, Mr Snooper – no one's gonna hear you down there. I'll see you later, my friend. We're going to have a nice little talk, just you and me."

Hill heard the front door slam, footsteps receding, a car engine firing. He cursed himself for an idiot. They must have made him all along. He called up his contacts on the phone. No signal. *Damn.*

It was half past one. It was going to be a long night.

"So," Moran finished his espresso with a satisfied flourish, "What was it you wanted to ask me, Shona?"

It had been an enjoyable meal, the conversation a good deal less awkward than their previous meeting. Shona seemed more relaxed, more at ease. Were it not for the day's events Moran would have been feeling relaxed too, but he couldn't get the image of Reed-Purvis' face out of his head, nor the note pinned to his door. Forensics was also taking its time over the paint sample.

And there was something else, too; Bagri had called him with an update. He had found something in Reed-Purvis' stomach – fragments of glass and metal, the detailed analysis of which was also taking longer than usual, thereby adding to his frustration. The chief was back soon and Moran wanted evidence to support his hunch while there was still time. There was also something about Sheldrake; he couldn't quite put his finger on it, but it was there nevertheless, an uneasiness that had nothing to do with his being pushed off the case. *Well I'm not off it yet,* Moran thought to himself. *Not yet...*

"Brendan? Are you with me?"

He shook his head self-deprecatingly. "I'm sorry, Shona – it's been a long day."

"Lots on your mind?"

"As ever." He gave her a thin smile. "I'm sorry; I didn't mean to be rude. Please – tell me what's troubling you."

Shona fiddled with her napkin. A waiter arrived to collect the coffee cups. After Moran had assured him that their needs had been satisfied, Shona paused for a moment until she could be sure she was not going to be overheard.

"I have a problem," she began, "and I don't quite know how to explain it."

"Try me." Moran gave her a smile of encouragement. "I'll do my best."

"If you had a friend, and they were in trouble, you'd help them, wouldn't you?"

"Of course. If I could."

Shona nodded. "But let's say they didn't know what was best for them. Would you try to make them see sense?"

Moran poured a glass of water and offered the pitcher, but Shona waved it away. He took a sip and considered his response.

"I would, in all likelihood, yes. But it's difficult to say for sure unless I know the circumstances."

"But would you? Would you make sure they did the right thing?"

"Well, that depends on what the 'right thing' might be. As long as I wasn't treading on their toes, or being too heavy-handed, I'd–"

"Is that it?" Shona's cheeks had coloured. "You think I'm being heavy-handed?"

Moran held up both hands, alarmed at her reaction. "No, of course not. I don't know the whole story, so–"

"You think this is all *my* fault?" Shona had got up, pushed her chair back. Flushed and shaking with anger, she jabbed her finger at Moran. "You're just like the others, you haven't a clue!"

Moran was stunned. Other couples in the restaurant had turned to see what was going on. The buzz of conversation had died. The head waiter hovered by the bar, ready to step in.

Moran held up his hand. "It's OK," he said. "Shona, please, sit down. I didn't mean to–"

Shona glared at him; "Well, you should have thought of that before." And with this baffling riposte, she turned on her heel and stormed out of the restaurant. Moran saw her silhouetted figure walk briskly past the window.

Conversation resumed. The head waiter smiled sympathetically. Moran shook his head. What had he said? He turned the conversation over in his mind. There was nothing untoward. How could there have been? She hadn't told him anything – hadn't given him a chance.

After a while the waiter brought the bill. Moran took the opportunity to order a grappa and a second espresso. He winced as the fiery liqueur burned his throat.

Women. How were mere men supposed to understand them?

She was easy to follow and Gregory Neads was an expert. He tracked her across town feeling relaxed and confident. Of course she hadn't sussed him. He waited until Shona had parked and locked her car, and then he cruised by as though he was heading for another road or looking for a parking space. He watched her in the wing mirror. Which house? Shona walked quickly from her vehicle, turned and opened a small iron gate.

Neads estimated that he would easily reach her before she could get the key in the lock. He prepared to move, but then something surprising happened. Neads relaxed into his seat and shook his head in disbelief. *Well, well, well.* He hadn't been expecting *that...* His smile widened and soon became a fixed, contented grin. *So,* he thought happily, as he steered the car out of Shona's road and rejoined the dual carriageway. *That explains a lot...*

Chapter Eight

Phelps listened patiently to Moran's list of issues and problems. It was a long one. Moran tried to make it shorter but one seemed to follow another. Eventually he finished and let out a sigh of frustration.

Phelps chewed a biro thoughtfully. "You know what you're doing, guv?"

"Most of the time, Phelps. Not always."

"No, I mean all that stuff you've just come out with."

"Enlighten me."

Phelps leaned over and picked up Moran's coffee mug. "Two sugars?"

"Come on, Phelps, the suspense is killing me."

"You're catastrophising, guv." Phelps plugged the battered kettle into the wall socket and spooned coffee into his and Moran's mugs.

"Is that what I'm doing now, DI Phelps?" Moran smiled despite his mood. "And that'll be one of your candle-burning concepts, no doubt?"

Phelps splashed longlife milk into the mugs. "Since you ask, guv, I have touched on the subject during the course of my studies."

"Well, good for you. Thanks." Moran accepted the steaming coffee. His head would be grateful to have an ally in the war against the effects of last night's grappa. "Let's start with Hill. When did he last grace us with his presence?"

"Yesterday afternoon, guv. He said he had one bar left on his list."

"Being?"

"The Zodiac, Friar Street."

"OK. Anyone tried to knock him up?"

"Yep. Banner tried on his way to *Mukhandra*. Got a no show."

"Maybe he just didn't want to answer the door to Banner?"

Phelps gulped a mouthful of coffee. "Point taken, guv, but he wasn't in. Car wasn't there."

Moran sighed. What he didn't need right now was a member of his team going AWOL. Hill was sensitive, and Moran knew he took a lot of stick. Maybe he'd had enough, bunked off somewhere. Moran drummed his fingers on the desk. Then again, maybe not.

"Pop down to the Zodiac, Phelps, would you? See if he paid them a visit."

"No probs, guv. What's on your agenda?"

Moran knocked the coffee back. His headache was receding a little, being replaced by a not unpleasant caffeinated buzz. "Doctor's appointment first, then a spot of glass reconstruction – followed, I trust, by the faintest of lights at the end of our tunnel."

Phelps raised his eyebrows. "Sounds promising, guv, if a little cryptic. But you know what Arlo Guthrie says?"

"Arlo who?"

"Guthrie. The American poet. He says, you can't have a light without a dark to stick it in."

"True, Phelps, very true." Moran stood up and fished his coat off the hook. "But neither must we forget to turn our faces to the sun, that the shadows may fall behind us. Eh?" Moran retrieved his stick and shrugged on his raincoat, enjoying Phelps' perplexed expression. "Not heard that before, Detective Inspector?" Moran grinned. "Old Maori proverb."

DC Hill had given up trying to force the door. It was strong and the lock was a heavy, old-fashioned iron job. He had little choice except to wait and see what happened when his gaoler returned. He'd show his ID and put the fear of God into whoever this guy was. Surely they wouldn't detain a serving police officer any longer? But then there were the drugs; Hill knew the sort of people who were likely to be involved in trafficking on this scale. There was no point in deluding himself. He was in deep trouble.

Just don't panic, keep your cool...

He took a few deep breaths to chase the panic away. He needed a plan. Or a weapon. Preferably both. But apart from the table there was nothing useful to hand. Hill also had another problem: he needed to move his bowels. *Least of your worries, James...* but the stomach cramps were becoming more urgent. Hill tightened his buttocks. There was no way he was going to go down here, like some caged animal.

Then he heard the front door open and shut, the muffled sound of shuffling footsteps above. Fear coursed through his body like a live current, undoing all his disciplined restraint. With a sob of frustration he dropped his trousers and voided his bowels on the dirt floor.

Phelps had one hand on the door handle of his car when he happened to glance across at the parade of shops opposite. He growled under his breath as he recognised DS Neads – *ex* DS Neads, he corrected himself –

hovering outside the newsagents. Doing nothing in particular. Waiting.

Loitering...

Phelps strode across the dual carriageway despite its accident blackspot status; he wanted to get to Neads quickly, and if he used the subway it would take longer. The hot weather had produced its usual quota of loony driving, so Phelps took extra care as he wove between passing traffic, the action earning him a double blast of horns and one raised fist. Neads watched him approach, a humourless grin playing about his lips.

"Well, well. If it isn't faithful Sergeant Phelps, right-hand man extraordinaire."

"Look, Neads, I don't know what you think you're doing hanging around here. Take my advice and clear off."

"Subtle to a fault, Sergeant." Neads lit a cigarette with an unsteady hand and sucked in smoke. "I'm not breaking the law, you know."

"Don't play games with me, Neads. You know what I'm talking about."

"You don't like me, do you, *DS* Phelps?" Neads tapped ash onto the pavement. The day was windless and still. Passers-by hurried up and down the parade, the women showing off tattoos on shoulders, arms, cleavage, their men pale-legged in ill-fitting shorts and designer-copy sunglasses.

"It's not a question of *like*, Neads," Phelps said, mopping his brow with a spotless white handkerchief. "I'm sorry about what happened to you. I know you've had a hard time. It could have been anyone. It could have been me."

Neads laughed. "Could have been; should have been. Whatever. Makes no difference now."

Phelps could see the scar on Neads' hand as the young man drew on his cigarette. It was ugly. He felt a sudden wave of sympathy. "Look, Neads, take my advice: book yourself a holiday, a change of scene. Chase some women. Think about your future. Be positive."

"Oh, well, thanks for the prescription. I'll be sure to do that. Then all my troubles will be over, right?"

Phelps decided on a harder approach. "There's no point feeling sorry for yourself, Neads. It won't help."

Neads drew smoke and maintained eye contact. After a moment he exhaled and spat a gobbet of phlegm into the gutter. "Pleasure talking to you, Detective Sergeant Phelps. Must dash." Neads flicked his stub into the road and, with a final look of defiance, walked casually away.

"Don't let me see you hanging around here again," Phelps called to Neads' back.

A group of shoppers stared. "What're you looking at?" Phelps growled, mopping his perspiring brow with what was now a very damp handkerchief. He slung his jacket over the crook of his arm and wove back across the road to the car park. As he pulled out he saw Neads standing in the same spot outside the newsagents, one arm raised in mock-salute.

Chapter Nine

"**M**aybe." The Zodiac barman sniffed. "Hard to say. Get all sorts down here."

Phelps grimaced as the sound system crashed into life with a pounding bass line and a noise like a rupturing petrol tank. "Turn that racket *off*," he mouthed.

The barman reluctantly went to the end of the bar and fiddled under the counter. The thumping in Phelps' gut eased, marginally.

"He was a policeman, remember?" Phelps prompted. "You would have been able to tell by the nice shiny ID card he would've shown you."

The barman frowned and shrugged.

Phelps glanced around the bar. It was half full, but the clientele were clearly not on lunch breaks from town centre offices. Three unshaven youths in jeans and T-shirts leaned on the bar downing lager; two or three over-made-up girls nursed half-empty glasses, waiting desultorily for business. A couple of Big Issue vendors were arguing in raised, slurred voices. Phelps turned back to the barman.

"Yes, I think I probably could."

"Could what?"

"Bust most of your lunchtime clients," Phelps said reasonably. "And I could always pop down again tonight to bust a few more. Does that help your cognitive processes?"

The barman scratched his head. "Oh, yeah. I remember now. Baby-faced lad?" he grinned, his crooked incisors protruding like mandibles. His breath smelled of stale alcohol and cigarettes.

Phelps took an involuntary step back. "Time?"

"'Bout ten ish, I s'pose."

"And what did you tell him?"

"Nothin' much. He showed me a photo. Asked about the skinny bloke."

"And who might that be?" Phelps asked patiently.

The barman folded his cloth and reached for a glass. He pulled himself a half of Tennants. "Want one?"

Phelps shook his head.

The barman took a swig and grinned again. "He was just a bloke down 'ere last night. Can't say as I know who he was."

"You don't know why DC Hill asked about him?"

"Nah. Why should I?"

Phelps grimaced as another wave of halitosis-laden breath wafted into his personal space. "Because," he leaned across the bar, trying not to breathe through his nose, "you might have told DC Hill something about him which sparked his interest, that's why."

"Not me," the barman shook his head. "I don't know a lot to tell."

"Really?" Phelps scribbled his phone number onto a beer mat. "Well, there's no time like the present to build on your knowledge, as my mother used to say."

"Eh?"

Phelps pressed the beer mat to the man's chest. "You're going to find out all about this 'skinny bloke'. I don't care how, but when you have, you call me. If you don't, I'll be back. And I may not be in a very good mood."

Phelps glowered to make his point clear, took a last look around the bar and left.

"Ate it?" Moran's face creased in disbelief. "She *swallowed* a light bulb?"

Dr Bagri bowed his confirmation. "Yes indeed, Inspector Moran. A brake light bulb, if I am to be specific."

Moran was speechless with admiration. DS Reed-Purvis had been a very brave and level-headed officer; injured, drugged and trapped in the boot of her assailant's car, she had nevertheless found a way to improve the odds of tracing the vehicle. If anyone was deserving of a posthumous decoration, Reed-Purvis had to be first in line. Moran made a mental note to brief the Superintendent on his return.

Another thought occurred to him. "The paint, Dr Bagri?"

Bagri beamed. "Crystal Blue, they are calling it. A clear match for an Audi A4 2.0 TDi TDV SE, 2006. For which, I might add, the brake light is also a suitable fit."

Moran could have hugged the little pathologist, but he contented himself with a vigorous handshake. "You're a ruddy marvel, Dr Bagri. Thanks a million."

"And toxicology report is also done; the lab has been busy and so it has taken a little longer than I had hoped. But I think you will find it interesting."

"Oh yes?"

"Yes, for sure. Actually there is evidence of gamma-hydroxybutyrate in the blood."

Moran frowned. "The date rape drug?"

"Exactly so, but if it is administered in this high dosage it will lead to unconsciousness, and then eventually coma and death."

Moran was stunned. "How long before the drug takes effect?"

Bagri cocked his head to one side, an habitual mannerism when asked his opinion. "It will be actually be, for a normal person, between fifteen and thirty minutes."

"Good God," Moran said, half to himself. He refocused on Bagri's anxious face. "So, can we tell if the drug was administered *before* she was attacked, or afterwards?"

"Mmm. Difficult, Chief Inspector. I am thinking we would need to establish her behaviour in the time before the attack."

"What effects would you expect?"

"Ah. Nausea, maybe a little dizziness."

"But she would still have been mobile? I mean, for a quarter of an hour or so?"

"She was a fit woman, so yes; I would say that is very likely."

"You've been very helpful, Dr Bagri." Moran left the lab and hurried back to his car. This case was beginning to stink.

"I don't believe it," Phelps muttered under his breath. He was half way between the Zodiac and his car. Limping towards him was the unwelcome sight of ex DS Neads. Now what?

"Lost something, have we?" Neads looked Phelps up and down.

"You're going to lose something if you don't push off." Phelps felt his self control sliding away. "I'm busy. Go and find something better to do with your time."

Neads squared up to Phelps. "And you wouldn't call locating missing policemen a fruitful use of my time?"

Phelps froze. "*What* did you say? Do you know where DC Hill is? Now listen, Neads–" Phelps grabbed the younger man's arm – "you'd better fess up, boy, if you know what's good for you."

"Is that a threat, Detective Sergeant Phelps? I am a member of the public, you know. I wouldn't like to have to make a complaint – especially as you fellows do such a great job–"

Phelps resisted the urge to clock him and lowered his voice. "What have you done with DC Hill?"

"Me? I haven't done anything with him." Neads shrugged off Phelps's grip. For a man with a wiry build he was certainly strong enough.

Phelps tried a different tack. "OK, Neads; what do you want?"

Neads shrugged. "Nothing much. A job, a life. A new pair of hands." He held them up. Phelps almost recoiled at the sight; the palms were a mass of ugly scar tissue. Neads laughed bitterly. "Feet aren't much better."

"You do know where Hill is," Phelps said quietly. "How?"

"Simple. I followed him."

"So, where is he?"

"Ah. Now that would be telling."

Phelps squared his shoulders. "Neads, I'm going to arrest you for obstruction if you don't tell me, *right now*, exactly where I can find DC Hill. Understand?"

That was when both men heard the sickening double thump of a passing car making contact with human flesh. There was a moment's vacuum-like stillness, and then someone screamed.

"*Where* is DS Phelps, would someone oblige me?"

"Dealing with an RTA, sir. Outside the Zodiac. He's just called in. He said he had something on James – I mean DC Hill, sir." The young DC blushed and fiddled with the papers on her desk.

So *someone's* holding a candle for you, young Hill, Moran thought, repressing a smile. "Thank you, DC McKellar. ETA?"

"He said about thirty minutes, sir."

"Right. Anyone got anything else?" Moran roamed the no man's land in front of the whiteboard. On it were pinned various photographs: victims one and two, a new glossy of an Audi A4 2.0 TDi and Reed-Purvis' woodland grave. Moran scanned the incident room. "DS Banner?"

Banner stepped forward. He was a squat, muscular man of around thirty-three. Moran had never taken to him, but over the few months they had worked together he had proved himself to be a natural detective.

"Spoke to colleagues of victim number two. All very shaken up. Nice guy, apparently. Bit cocky, one for the ladies. Name of Jay Dass."

"Go on." Moran turned and began to write on the whiteboard. "Family?"

"Lives – lived – with his father and mother in Slough."

"You'll be talking to them, Sergeant?"

Banner nodded. "Yes, guv. I've made an appointment for six o'clock this evening."

"Right. Have a good sniff around, Banner. The parents might think their boy was squeaky clean, but we don't think the same until we've proved it to be the case." Moran turned and faced the room. "Do we?"

"No, guv," the assembled officers intoned as one.

"Guv?" DC McKellar's hand was up.

"Uh huh?"

"You were saying that DS Reed-Purvis was drugged, guv. How are we going to find out what happened?"

"Glad you asked, DC McKellar. I might need your services in that regard. Yours and Sergeant Banner's."

Moran noticed the glance exchanged between the two officers. No love lost there, by the look of it. In Moran's experience the best way to sort out an internal clash was to make the antagonists work together. After a while, provided all went well, professional respect eroded most of the bad feeling.

He looked at each officer in turn. "I'll tell you what I have in mind if you both come and see me first thing. Alright with you, Banner?"

"Guv."

As the team dispersed Moran saw Sheldrake pushing his way into the room.

"What do you think you're playing at, Moran?" Sheldrake was wearing a black pinstripe suit and a blue tie. He was freshly shaved and his thinning grey hair was combed back from his angular face. He looked like he was going somewhere important. *Good*, Moran thought. Sheldrake in a hurry was better than Sheldrake with time on his hands. Moran adopted an innocent expression. "Can I help, sir?"

"Don't play games, Moran." Sheldrake pointed to the whiteboard. "I told you to wind down your investigation into the town centre murders."

Moran pricked up his ears. "*Murders*, sir? I was under the impression that there was only *one* murder confirmed and attributed to Reading central?"

Sheldrake harrumphed. "You know what I mean, Moran. DS Reed-Purvis and the Asian boy."

"Ah. Yes, sir. But I have another incident in Slough. I believe they may be connected."

Sheldrake thrust his face into Moran's. The smell of aftershave was overpowering. "Listen to me, Moran. The Reed-Purvis case is mine, understand? If you think you've found a connection in Slough, you damn well filter it along to me or my sergeant. I thought I'd already made that clear."

"By Thursday, I believe you said, sir." Moran consulted the wall calendar. "That gives me another couple of days by my calculations. In the meantime, I'll be sure to inform you of any emerging links. We've almost completed our initial enquiries. Rest assured, I'll personally brief you on the details."

"You'd better, Moran. You'd better." Sheldrake turned on his polished heels and left, banging the door behind him.

Banner looked up from his screen. "Problem, guv?"

"Nothing I can't handle, Banner." Moran studied the board. An image of Gregory Neads came into his head – the anger in the young man's face; the terrible scars... Neads had been his responsibility, and so was DC Hill.

Come on, Phelps. Hurry up...

Moran drew a line between the photo of Reed-Purvis' shallow grave and Bling Boy's town centre shop front, adding a question mark above it for good measure. He muttered a silent prayer to any god that might be listening. *Please. Just please don't let me lose another one...*

"Well, stink-boy? Nothing more to say?"

DC James Hill clamped his teeth together in a combination of bloody-minded determination and an overriding desire to hide his fear. No way was he going to give this guy the satisfaction.

Hill was bound to a chair, very securely. Two of them had done that. After they had left him, someone else had come down into the cellar. Chinese; a big man with short black hair, receding at the front. His eyes held no compassion; empty windows, giving nothing away.

"Come on, copper," Chinaman said, lighting a cigarette. "Don't be shy."

Hill's face felt as if it had been through several rounds with Mike Tyson. He could taste blood and he knew that his nose was broken. He coughed as smoke was blown into his face and braced himself for the next pulverising blow. The pattern had been the same for – how long? He was losing track of time. He knew he had drifted in and out of consciousness two or three times at least, but each time he had been dragged back to uncomfortable reality by a hard slap on the cheek.

The blow came, heavier and more painful than the last. Hill cried out despite himself; his head rang like a badly tuned bell and splotchy stars danced before his eyes. He became aware of a low, moaning sound, and with a jolt he realised it was coming from his own mouth. He clamped his jaws shut and raised his chin. Chinaman blurred gradually into focus.

"How did you know?" his tormentor purred.

"Know what?" Hill braced himself. Nothing happened.

"You are young. And stupid." Chinaman took a contemplative pull on his cigarette. "That's why you followed us. Without backup."

"I have backup," Hill whispered, praying that it was true. "They'll be looking."

Chinaman studied him with narrowed eyes, as though trying to read his mind. After a moment he said, "I don't think so. Nobody knows where you are. I can take all the time I want. Now, tell me, please, about your busy little drugs op. What does your boss know? What does he think?"

"I don't work on drugs," Hill said. "I'm following up a suspicious death."

"Are you, indeed? So, you are telling me that you stumbled across my business by accident? By luck?"

"Lucky me," Hill muttered.

"Ha ha. Funny man." Chinaman forced Hill's chin up. "Who is in charge of your operation? What leads are they following?"

Hill shook his head and then regretted it. It felt as though someone had stuffed a skewer in each ear. "Confidential, I'm afraid. Do you have any tea? I'm rather thirsty."

The blow came immediately and although Hill was ready for it, the force of the impact shook him so hard it felt as though his brain had become momentarily detached from the rest of his body. The pain was followed by the sick realisation that this man would not hesitate to kill him. More than that; he probably intended to. His head swam and then gradually cleared.

Keeping his eyes shut he pulled gently against his bindings. There wasn't a lot of slack to play with, but if he could spin the interrogation out he might just be able to work an arm loose. But Hill didn't want to spin it out; he wanted it to stop. Even if he succeeded in freeing an arm, what then? It would be cramped, numb. He wouldn't be able to strike with the necessary power; Chinaman could simply take a step back. He fought against the sudden wash of despair.

Don't give up, James. Don't. They'll find you ... just hold on. Hold on.

Chapter Ten

"**D**amn," Moran said aloud, pacing up and down the length of his kitchen, watched with interest by Archie; every time Moran moved Archie was there at his feet, cocking his head expectantly with eyes like saucers, pleading for his outing. Moran's head ached, whether in anticipation of the CT scan Dr Purewal had recommended ('to be on the safe side') or as a result of the relentless humidity Moran didn't know. However, neither Archie nor the impending hospital appointment was responsible for his frustrated expletive; as usual, it was a combination of problems.

Phelps had been held up dealing with the RTA; some old boy had been knocked over in the town centre, but was apparently stable in the RBH. Phelps had promised to come straight over. He had something on James Hill. It had better be good...

The other niggle was Shona. He had resolved not to call her; as far as he was concerned he'd done nothing wrong. She had been overwrought, so it was best to let her calm down and get in touch. However, Moran had grudgingly acknowledged to himself that he was anticipating her call with something more than a desire to set things straight. He *needed* her to call.

He shook his head wearily and tossed a mental coin to choose a drink. Heads, tea; tails, a small Sangiovese. The

Sangiovese won, as it usually did. Moran poured a quarter glass and stood at the back door, looking out over his neglected garden. Six pm and it was still brutally warm.

The gentle buzz of a bee and the murmur of subdued conversation from a neighbouring garden brought its usual stab of guilt. Alison Miller apart, Moran hardly knew his neighbours; he supposed they would say that he kept himself to himself. And so he had. He had never felt the need for too many people in his life. Not since Janice. What had happened to her had changed him irrevocably. He had been to grief counselling, given it time, but the wound was still raw. How many years now? Thirty-four, but if he closed his eyes he could still see the opening car door, the gust of flame and smoke. Then, in slow motion, like a movie, a flat, eerie silence as particles of debris drifted to earth.

Since then his relationships had been cautious, unsettled. Kay had been the closest he had come to a long-term relationship, but he had stalled somewhere between love and commitment. It was a wall he had never managed to scale. Now Kay was dead and her sister was a puzzle, albeit a very attractive one. Why hadn't she phoned? Moran drained his glass. *Good God, Brendan, you're acting like a teenager...*

He deliberately shifted his thoughts back to work. Reed-Purvis and Hill. Two coppers, one dead, one missing. He toyed with the idea of calling in to see if they'd made any progress tracing the Audi. He had two DCs on it, poring over fuel station CCTV images. So far nothing had shown up.

He limped into the kitchen and considered a refill. Better not; Phelps was on his way and he needed a clear head. Archie placed a saliva-coated tennis ball hopefully at his feet and Moran bent to stroke the curly head.

"Later, boy. Later." The doorbell rang. Phelps.

Moran opened the door. It wasn't Phelps; it was Shona. He was completely taken aback.

"Oh, hello. Come in," he managed.

"Is it a bad time, Brendan? I can come back later..."

"It's fine. I'm expecting my sergeant so I may have to dash off, but–"

"No probs." She smiled. "I'll call back another time. I just wanted to say how much I enjoyed the meal the other night."

"Enjoyed–?" Moran was nonplussed. Had she forgotten how the meal had ended?

"Look, I know I overreacted. I'm so sorry, Brendan. But yes, I did enjoy it," Shona said brightly. "Is that OK?"

"Of course, but–"

A car drew up and Phelps got out. He waved a greeting and made an 'OK if I interrupt?' gesture. Moran waved him an affirmative.

Shona squeezed Moran's arm. "I'll leave you to it. Call me later."

"I will," Moran said. "For sure."

She turned and walked briskly to her car, nodding a greeting to Phelps on her way past.

Phelps grinned as he approached. "Such pulchritude as befits a man of your standing, guv. I'm impressed."

"I'm not in the mood, Phelps. Come on in."

"Right you are, guv." Phelps wiped his feet unnecessarily on the doormat; the evening was as dry as dust.

Moran led Phelps into the lounge. "So – Hill?" he prompted.

"Guv, it's Neads. He's been haunting me today. Reckons he knows where Hill is, but I don't know if he's winding me up."

"Didn't you apply pressure?"

"That was going to be my next move, guv, but then the RTA happened. By the time I handed over to the paramedics Neads had cleared off."

"Been to his place?"

"Moved out. Recently."

Moran groaned. "Great. Is that it? Did he say anything else?"

"Told me he'd followed Hill. Dunno whether I believe him or not."

Moran scratched his cheek. The hot weather made his beard itch. "D'you think Neads has him banged up somewhere?"

Phelps sank into Moran's sofa with a weary sigh. "Doubt it. He's pissed off, all right, but not *that* pissed off."

"OK. We'll bring him in. Put the word out."

"Already have, guv."

Moran sighed. "Of course you have."

"We'll get him, guv, don't worry." Phelps was eyeing him with ill-concealed anxiety.

Moran kicked the tennis ball and watched Archie scurry after it. His head was throbbing. "I have a bad feeling about this, Phelps. Come on. Let's make ourselves useful."

The Kafir rose from his cross-legged position, sweating lightly after his meditation. Although the apartment was at the top of the building the room was cool, the air conditioning purring efficiently, keeping the sultry heat at bay. He liked his new home. A lounge, a small designer kitchen, a bedroom, a bathroom. That was all. No bed. He had toyed with the idea of a futon, but the vivid dream of the previous night had changed his mind. Jaseena had come to him, caught him unawares. Although he knew he was dreaming he had been powerless to escape her flirtatious company, and he had been all too aware that he wanted her. *Still* wanted her. For the rest of the night he had sat up thinking, firming his resolve, concluding that if sleep was a weakness then he would not sleep at all; there was plenty to occupy his mind in the wee small hours.

He went to the sink and drew himself a glass of water. He would never use the state-of-the-art oven or microwave. He would eat at the various cafés and diners along the Caversham Road.

The Kafir stretched and rested his arms on the half-open Velux window. The view was pleasant. He could see the restless movement of the river and the spread of the town beyond. Lowry-like figures hurried to and fro along the busy pavements. From his god-like eyrie they all looked pitiful, scurrying around as if there were a purpose to it all.

What gave their lives meaning? *Religion.* It was all about religion. They all worshipped some god or other, the Kafir reflected; for most Brits it was materialism. For others it was a false God. Allah, the God of the Bible, whoever...

He recollected some vague Catholic connection from his past. Ritualistic mumbo-jumbo, that was all it added up to. Had he had been made to serve at Mass? Perhaps, although it was now a distant memory. In his mind's eye he saw a little boy in a white surplice following the priest along the altar rail as he dispensed communion – *no*, a dab of ash to the forehead. He frowned, trying to remember its significance. Ah, yes, Ash Wednesday. Ashes symbolised mourning, mortality and penance. The Kafir smiled. That was fitting. It summarised his new mission very concisely.

'Remember, O man, that thou art dust and unto dust thou shalt return.'

With these words the priest had made the sign of the cross on each expectant forehead. The memory was stronger now; he could almost smell the incense. *Yes*, the Kafir whispered to himself. *Creatures of dust, that's what you are. Small, insignificant creatures of dust...*

The Zodiac was buzzing. Moran's ears twitched at the low frequency assault on his faculties. The bass was so loud it was vibrating his rib cage. "How can they stand this noise?" he mouthed to Phelps.

Phelps shrugged and pushed through the press of bodies to the bar. It was manned by three harassed-looking girls, each dressed identically in hippy headbands and matching astrological T-shirts.

"Manager in?" Phelps yelled.

One of the girls shook her head. "Night off."

Moran signalled a thumbs down. No point in talking to the barmaids in this chaos. They were on their way to the exit when Phelps was approached by a slim woman in a leopardskin waistcoat and tight leather trousers. She winked at Phelps and pointed to the door. Moran frowned. Her profession wasn't hard to guess. They followed her outside.

"Well, well. Hello again." She drew out her cigarettes and offered the packet.

Phelps waved it away. "No thanks, Zoë."

"You remembered. I'm impressed. Who's your friend?" Zoë puffed smoke and looked Moran up and down. "Not bad. Nice eyes."

"This is DCI Brendan Moran."

"Ooh. A real Chief Inspector. How exciting."

"We're busy, Zoë. What do you want?" Phelps moved aside as the door opened with a burst of music and two youths joined them in the street to light up.

"It was what *you* wanted, love, remember?"

"Spit it out, Zoë." Moran was losing patience. There were other bars to cover, other contacts to chase up.

"First name terms already?" Zoë purred. "I like an assertive man."

"You won't like it in a minute when I bang you up. Is that assertive enough for you?" Moran growled. "Now stop wasting our time and tell us what's on your mind."

Zoë gave Moran a hard look. "Fair enough. So, what's the deal?"

Moran put his nose an inch from Zoë's. "The deal is, you tell us something useful and I don't lock you up."

"Like that, is it? Funny how you can go off people."

Moran saw Phelps shoot Zoë a silent warning. She registered it, pursed her lips and folded her arms.

"OK. I was in here the other day and I saw a young copper asking Dave about one of the regulars."

"How did you know he was a copper?"

She shrugged. "Bleedin' obvious, innit? You can always tell."

Moran conceded the point. "Go on."

"You was askin' me about the kid who got killed? Well, this geezer your mate was on about might tell you something. I know where you can find him."

"Name?" Phelps had his notebook out.

"He's known as Jag. Not sure about the surname. It's foreign, you know. Might be Ramadan, or Rana, or something like that."

"OK. Was Jag here that night? Did the young copper talk to him?"

She shook her head. "Jag was there earlier, but he left."

"And the policeman?" Moran asked.

She shrugged. "Dunno. I was busy after that. He left too, I suppose."

"So the barman definitely gave DC Hill this name?" Moran prompted. "Jag?"

"Yep." Zoë fished for another cigarette. "I don't know him that well – just, you know..."

Phelps nodded. "Yeah, we know."

Zoë drew her skimpy leather jacket around her thin body and shivered. "Nasty piece of work, I reckon. Creepy."

"And would you have an address?"

Zoë's eyes darted to right and left. "There's a place in Slough. I dunno if it's Jag's, but you might find him there. You know Chalvey?"

Moran and Phelps exchanged looks.

"Yeah, right. So, you go into Chalvey from the M4, take the first left before the railway bridge, then first left again. There's two rows of terraces. Second row, second house on the left. It's run down big time. You'll know it when you see it."

"No number?" Phelps' pencil was poised over the notebook.

"Like I said," Zoë stubbed her cigarette out and turned to go back into the Zodiac. "You'll know it. Hey–" she called to their retreating figures, "you owe me one now, right?"

Chapter Eleven

Hill spat blood and retched. When his vision cleared he saw that Chinaman had produced a knife. Fear shot through his veins. He was going to die; he knew it, but he wasn't going to give up without a fight.

The Chinaman sighed. "I don't like nosy people. Especially nosy policemen. Where I come from, the police do what we say. No trouble. You should learn the same lesson." The Chinaman rotated the point of the knife in front of Hill's face, an inch or so away from his left eye. "Hear no evil, see no evil, right?"

Hill watched the knife, ready to move his head at the strike. *Just a little closer, China, and I'll have you...* Hill knew it was his only chance. He had to use his head, literally. His arms and legs were no use, even if he could have freed them. They would take precious minutes to recover. No, his forehead was his only weapon, but the Chinaman's face was just out of reach, as if he knew what Hill was thinking.

The knife hovered to the left, then the right. His torturer was enjoying himself. Hill wondered briefly if there were others upstairs, ready to take over, to help in case of any trouble. *Can't think about that, James. Deal with this guy first...*

Hill cursed himself again for his stupidity. No one had a clue where he was. There would be no cavalry, no eleventh-hour rescue. It was down to him. He bit his lip. *Keep your concentration...*

Without warning, the knife flicked forward. Hill twisted his head at the last moment and the blade scored down his cheek. Chinaman's face loomed closer, following the knife's trajectory as Hill had hoped. *Now.* Hill brought his head forward in a single whipping motion and felt his forehead connect jarringly with Chinaman's nose. There was a satisfying crack of bone and cartilage. His tormentor howled and dropped the knife. Blood sprayed in Hill's face, his own or the Chinaman's – he couldn't tell. Hill ripped an arm free and flung himself forward, scrabbling for the weapon as the Chinaman pressed his hands to his face.

Hill's hand closed around the knife handle but the Chinaman lashed out with his leg, once, twice. Still attached to the chair, Hill twisted and turned to avoid the blows but a third one caught him hard in the ribcage. The pain was excruciating. He felt a foot crunch down on his hand, shattering bone. The knife skittered away.

Another impact, this time to the side of his face, and Hill was violently sick. The room receded as if it was being siphoned away through a huge, fibre-optic tube. The pain was sucked away with it until all that remained was a dizzying spread of darkness.

"Won't this thing go any faster, Phelps?"

"Foot's on the floor, guv," Phelps replied, his tone edgy. "I'd say we need back up."

"I know you would, but I don't want to go in like the proverbial bull. Nine times out of ten it ends in tears."

"You know best, guv," Phelps muttered.

"Observation, decision, action, right?"

"Right," Phelps said, overtaking a middle-lane crawler.

"In any case, Hill may not be there."

"True."

Moran watched the junctions flash past. Chalvey had a reputation. It was the kind of place where you wound your windows up before you drove through; where you tried not to tarry at traffic lights. He hoped Hill was indeed somewhere else, because if he was in Chalvey the chances of a happy ending were not as good as Moran would have liked them to be.

His mobile rang. "Moran."

"Banner here, guv."

"Tell me all."

"Not a lot to tell, guv. Or see. Nice couple, respectable. Proud of their son. He was a hard worker, nothing dodgy. They've taken it hard."

"No girlfriend, iffy associates?"

"There was one thing. The mother mentioned something about a black sheep, some cousin as far as I could tell. Husband cut her off. She'd have said more, but I reckon she was too scared."

"Of the husband?"

"Maybe. Not in a frightened way, more like a respect thing."

"Asian families are pretty hot on integrity and the respectability of the family," Moran said. "Might be worth exploring. Give them a day or so, then pop back. I might come with you."

"I can cope."

"I know you can, Banner. I just want to keep on top of this, OK?"

"Sure."

"Sure, *guv*."

"Sorry. *Guv*."

Phelps grinned and Moran allowed himself a brief smile. "Where are you now?"

"Just leaving the station, guv. Why?"

Moran hesitated. It wouldn't do any harm to have Banner on standby.

"I'd like you to stay put for an hour or so, Banner. Is DC McKellar still there?"

"Hang on."

Moran grabbed the dashboard as Phelps swung the car off the motorway.

"Yes, guv. She is." Banner sounded slightly irritated.

"Good. Tell her to sit tight for an hour as well."

"What's up?"

"Not sure yet. Might be a storm in a teacup, but then again..."

"Where are you headed? Guv."

"Chalvey. Left turn before the bridge. Left again. Second row of terraces."

"Fine. Keep us posted," Banner said peevishly, and rang off.

The high street was quiet. Phelps eased the car into second and indicated left. A few cars were parked along the street. None of them belonged to DC Hill. All was quiet.

"That's the one." Moran pointed. Zoë was right. It was tatty to the point of decrepitude.

Phelps passed the house and found a space a few metres past the property. The terraces had been constructed with a covered side passage. No lights were on as far as Moran could tell; it looked as though the entire row was deserted.

"Round the back, guv?"

"Round the back."

They approached the terrace. Moran gripped his stick hard. His intuition seldom gave him false alarms, and right now his internal radar was buzzing like a Fylingdales early warning alarm.

The grey council render was flaking and cracked, the replacement aluminium window frames tarnished and ill-maintained. As they approached the passageway Phelps stopped in his tracks. Moran had heard it too, a muffled thump, as if something heavy had been thrown down. They advanced more cautiously. Moran blinked to encourage his night vision as they entered the passageway.

The rear garden was a mess, a junk yard. Phelps motioned Moran closer. The back door was ajar. Phelps pushed it gently and stepped back. No reaction from inside.

He flicked on his Lenser and played the spot beam around the kitchen's tatty interior. A staircase to their immediate right led directly upstairs. There were two doors, one adjacent to the stairwell, probably a cupboard, and another directly ahead which was open, and led into the front room.

Moran stepped carefully across the kitchen floor and went into the front room. A car went by in the street, casting an orange flood of light over the threadbare carpet and peeling wallpaper. It was barely furnished, just an old three-piece and a low coffee table. No pictures, TV, stereo. A blank canvas. Moran rejoined Phelps in the kitchen.

"Smell something, guv?" Phelps wrinkled his nose.

Moran could. It was a familiar smell. Faeces and vomit – and something else. But where was it coming from?

Phelps motioned to the stairs and cocked his head. Moran nodded and slipped back into the living room. The smell receded. He heard Phelps' heavy tread creaking across the floorboards upstairs and checked the room again. There seemed to be nothing amiss.

Moran half turned to retrace his steps, but as he did so a figure exploded from the kitchen's middle door, the one Moran had mistaken for a cupboard. The door flew back on its hinges and hindered Moran's lurching return to the kitchen, catching his leg and his stick and knocking him off balance. A bulky silhouette appeared briefly in the rectangle of the back door and was gone.

Phelps thundered down the stairs, beating Moran by half a second. As they exited the passageway a diesel engine burst into life and a silver Mercedes ripped itself from the line of parked vehicles and accelerated away, fishtailing from one side of the road to the other before its driver regained control. It took the corner on two wheels and was gone.

Moran was on his mobile. He'd only got the first part of the registration, but it would do for pursuit. Passing the information to Banner he signed off and returned to the house. His leg ached where the door had caught it. *Damn.* Why hadn't he checked? *Not a cupboard, Moran, you Irish tosser – a basement...*

Phelps was already there, probing the darkness of the basement with his Lenser. The foul smell grew stronger until the powerful beam picked out the prone shape of DC Hill lying face down in a pool of blood and vomit.

"Bastards." Phelps held the torch steady as Moran bent and felt for a pulse. It was faint, but it was present. He cradled Hill's battered head in his arms.

"Don't die, son," he said in a harsh whisper. "Don't you even think about it."

As the ambulance tail lights disappeared into the night Moran sat on the low garden wall and wished for a cigarette. Hill had been stupid. He'd got his lead and followed it alone, the worst mistake in the book. Moran understood why, but that didn't help.

He watched as the terraced house was illuminated from within by the SOCO's harsh lighting. The previously silent street was now alive with police activity, although Moran noted that members of the public were conspicuous by their absence. This area of Chalvey was clearly out of bounds.

"I'm going to the hospital, Phelps," he told the acting DI. "I'm relying on you and Banner to bring in our runaway driver, OK?"

Phelps nodded. "Banner says they've got the Merc heading west, guv. Approaching Junction 11. I'm on it." The sergeant gave a brief wave and squeezed into a waiting car with an agility that never failed to surprise Moran.

He watched the blue light of the Battenberg-marked police car recede towards the M4 and wearily limped up the street to his own vehicle. Was he to blame for what had happened to Hill? On paper, no, but what did paper have to do with it? He sat quietly for a minute, and then ground the car into gear and pulled away. As he left Chalvey behind he wondered how he was going to break the news to DC Helen McKellar.

Chapter Twelve

Moran sensed the sombre atmosphere as soon as he entered the station. He nodded to the duty sergeant on his way to the lift and received a terse jerk of the head in return. Everyone knew about Reed-Purvis, and by now everyone would know about Hill. Although officers were keenly aware of the risks and demands of their job, the injury or death of a colleague never lost the power to shock.

Moran found Banner and McKellar waiting in the IR. They both looked drawn and grey-faced, especially McKellar. Moran didn't feel much better himself, having spent most of the night at the hospital.

McKellar stood up. "Morning, guv. Is there any–?"

Moran held up his hand. "DC Hill is still in the ICU, but the consultant is cautiously optimistic – his words. Hard to say any more at this stage. There's a touch of swelling around the brain..." Moran shrugged. "I can't shed any further light. I'm sorry."

McKellar gave a brief nod. "Thank you, sir. Coffee?"

"Thank you, DC McKellar." He gave the pretty DC a tight smile, impressed by her poise. She would be ideal for what he had in mind. He placed his stick against the whiteboard and threw his coat onto a nearby chair. A glance at the clock told him it was seven in the morning.

"Here you go, guv." McKellar placed the steaming drink on his desk.

"Thanks. Can you ask Banner to come in?"

"Guv."

When both officers were seated Moran asked for an update on the Mercedes pursuit.

"Caught up with him near Swindon," Banner began. Something in the sergeant's tone told Moran that the outcome had not been good.

"He went off the motorway, guv," McKellar picked up the baton. "Hit the central reservation and turned over. He was doing over a ton." She shrugged miserably.

Moran sighed. A wave of exhaustion washed over him. He reached for his coffee, but finding it too hot he contented himself with an inhalation of caffeine fumes.

"Dead, I suppose."

"Yes," Banner said. "But guess what else was in the car?"

"Don't tell me. A box of heroin or ten."

Banner and McKellar exchanged glances.

"Twenty-five kilos, guv." McKellar bit her lip.

"*Twenty-five?*" Moran whistled. "That'd be worth, what, two to three million on the street?"

Banner nodded. "Give or take."

"Does Sheldrake know?"

"We haven't heard from him," McKellar said. "But his DS was poking around here yesterday. I was going to mention it."

"Oh yes? What did she want?"

"Asking about the wrap up." Banner scratched his forehead. "Wants us to get a move on."

"We agreed close of play Thursday." Moran shook his head. "Bloody OCG."

"They seem very keen to hang on to this one, guv." McKellar shifted in her chair and Moran caught a brief whiff of perfume that stabbed at his memory. Tweed. Kay had worn Tweed; it had been her favourite fragrance.

He shook the thought away. "Keen? They'll be even keener when they find out what you were up to last night," Moran sipped his coffee with a grimace.

"Would you like some more milk?"

"No, I'm fine, thanks." Moran drummed his fingers on the desk in a marching tempo, a habit that he was hardly aware of. His team knew that it usually preceded a decision.

"Right," he said after a few seconds. "Not a word to Bessie about the heroin. I want it kept to ourselves for now. Clear?"

"Guv." They both nodded.

"Make sure it's safely under lock and key in the evidence room, please. Now, you two are going to spend a couple of days doing your favourite thing."

McKellar frowned and Banner raised his eyebrows.

"Hanging around in bars." Moran took a tentative sip of coffee. "Actually, one bar in particular."

"The Zodiac?" Banner asked.

"The Zodiac."

Banner let out a resigned sigh. "With *her*?"

"Oh, thanks," McKellar said, giving Banner a filthy look. "The feeling's mutual, I'm sure."

"Now now, children." Moran got up and walked around his desk, placing a benevolent hand on each officer's shoulder. "You're young. New to the area. Really into each other. You love a good time. Good at making friends. Got the picture?"

He bent so that his head was between theirs. "You're going to find out who carries a bottle of gamma-hydroxybutyrate around our happy little joint – and more importantly, why they picked on DS Reed-Purvis." Moran straightened up. "Was it our friends the dealers? Did they suss her out? Or was it an opportunist? If so, what was the motive? Any connection with Slough? Was it the same guy who killed Bling Boy, or someone else? Who was Reed-Purvis talking to before she left the Zodiac on Tuesday night? Where was DS Flynn? Sheldrake said she and Reed-Purvis were working together; she should have been somewhere in the vicinity. The quantity of the drug administered suggests that our bad guy wasn't interested in date rape. Far from it," Moran said grimly. "He was only interested in making sure DS Reed-Purvis was taken out of the picture."

"Because she found out something she wasn't supposed to?" McKellar said, almost to herself.

Moran downed his coffee in two large gulps. "Well, that's for you two lovebirds to find out."

McKellar made a face and Banner looked out of the window.

"Off you go, then." Moran clapped his hands. "You'll have lots to talk about. I'm sure DS Banner is capable of a modicum of gentlemanly behaviour, given a little encouragement."

"Anything else?" Moran peered through the shattered windscreen of the wrecked Mercedes. The interior had been painstakingly disassembled in the search for further items of interest. The case with its packed bags of heroin was under lock and key in the evidence room – and there Moran was determined it would stay, until he'd uncovered enough evidence that the Reading murders were linked to the heroin haul. From that point on Sheldrake was welcome to it.

"Not a lot," a weary forensics officer admitted. "A leather wallet." He held up the bagged item for Moran's inspection. "No money. No ID. Couple of business cards. Want a look?"

"Anything you've got is worth a look." Moran took the bag and carefully fished out the wallet. Inside he found two cards. The first was from a London financial advisor, the second a local physiotherapy practice. "Mind if I hang on to this?"

"Be my guest," the officer said. "I'll let you know if we turn up anything else."

"Thanks."

Moran examined the cards on his way to the lift. As he exited on the second floor and made his way through to the IR his mobile announced a new text message. Moran thumbed the text icon and did a double take. The sender was 'Neads, Greg'.

The text read: *Sorry to hear about DC Hill. Shame. Reckon you need some help on this one, Moran. Still, you know where I am. Oh, hang on, you don't, do you?'*

Moran's face was like thunder as he entered the IR. No one dared ask why.

Phelps entered the canteen to be greeted with the familiar waft of bacon and chip fat. The room was uncomfortably warm, the sun streaming in through two large plate glass windows which acted like a giant magnifying glass, bathing the breakfasting officers in a relentless pool of heat.

Phelps mopped his brow and searched the room for his friend, DS Chris Newland. He'd known Chris since training, a period of his life that now seemed impossibly distant, as though the events and people he'd met in those youthful, carefree days were part of someone else's life, not his own. He and Chris had kept in touch, even worked in the same team occasionally when circumstances had conjoined favourably to bring them together. Chris lived in Maidenhead. He was a family man like Phelps himself – golfing at weekends, holidaying in France at the same campsite each year, content with his role, his career, his friends and his attractive blonde wife. Chris was rock solid, the one person – apart from Brendan Moran – whom Phelps would trust with his life. Not to mention a few discreet questions about certain key associates in Organised Crime.

Chris saw him first, raising his fork aloft and waving Phelps to the table he was sharing with two other men Phelps didn't recognise. As he approached the two unfamiliar officers rose simultaneously and made off with their trays and a cursory nod of acknowledgement in Phelps' direction.

"Something I said?" Phelps grinned and pulled up a chair.

"Still look like trouble, even in your old age," Chris observed through a mouthful of egg and toast. "Good to see you, Bob. What brings you into the hallowed confines of OCG?"

"Just wanted a chat, really." Phelps declined Chris' offer of a slice of toast. His stomach was playing up this morning and the canteen smells had made him feel a little queasy.

Chris cocked his head in a familiar gesture and reached for his coffee cup. "Oh yes? What about?"

Phelps hesitated. It was always awkward, asking questions about fellow officers. Had to be done, though.

He felt another spasm of nausea wash through his stomach. Something he'd eaten? Unlikely; he'd only had a plain cheese salad for tea last night. Probably just the heat.

"Are you OK, Bob? Your face is as pale as the canteen wall."

"Fine – just bit tired, that's all. Do you know a guy by the name of Sheldrake?"

"DCS Sheldrake? Yes. As a matter of fact I worked with him last month. Some house-to-house, a bit of surveillance."

"What did you think of him?" Phelps took out his handkerchief and dabbed the sweat from his forehead.

"Hard-nosed bugger. No sense of humour, But good at what he does," Chris conceded. "One thing, though."

"What's that?"

"He likes to keep his team on a leash. Once you're with him, you generally stay. I was an exception."

"So how did you escape?"

"I was only on loan, for three weeks. It was enough."

Phelps pushed his chair back as a canteen lady clattered by with a trolley. He caught a fresh waft of grease-laden air and had to stop himself gagging.

"Are you sure you're OK?"

"Not really. This weather; it's too damned hot."

"Make the most of it. Winter is just around the corner." Chris buttered a fresh slice of toast and spread marmalade liberally over the browned surface.

"You sound like Michael bloody Fish." Phelps winced as a dull pain pulsed in his left arm. He massaged it distractedly and poured himself a glass of water from the corrugated plastic jug on the table. "D'you know Sheldrake's DS? Sharron Flynn?"

"High-flying Flynn?" Chris shook his head and grimaced. "She's a nightmare."

"Really? Why?"

Chris finished his toast and wiped his mouth with a napkin. "Too ambitious for her own good, that one. Total pain. But," he interlocked his fingers, "her and Sheldrake, they're like that."

"Is that so?"

"Too right." Chris leaned over the table and lowered his voice. "The rumour machine is on overdrive with those two. Sheldrake's married; Flynn isn't."

"Reckon he's skiing off piste?" Phelps raised his eyebrows.

Chris scraped his chair back, stretched his legs under the table and yawned. "Could be. But you know what the rumour machine is like." Chris wiped his brow with his napkin. "You're right, it's stifling in here. Shall we have a wander outside?"

Phelps followed Chris into the car park. His arm still ached but the nausea seemed to have passed. He reached automatically for a cigarette, frowning at the depleted packet. Had he really smoked fifteen since yesterday afternoon? He had to cut down. After this pack.

They found a seat on the entrance foyer wall and enjoyed the spectacle of a red-faced sergeant attempting to manoeuvre his car into a ridiculously tight space.

"Car park still a nightmare, then." Phelps blew smoke and shook his head. You could never get a space here unless you were on nights. Same old same old. He turned to Chris. "Still on the bike?"

Chris grinned. "Only way to travel."

"Even in this?" Phelps waved vaguely at the cloudless sky and shook his head. "You must feel like a well-done joint of beef after twenty-five miles in all that leather gear."

"You never did get it, Bob. It's the freedom, the convenience—"

"And the budget," Phelps offered morosely.

"That too." Chris nodded. "Damn sight cheaper than running a car. Anyway, why the interest in Sheldrake and co.? Come on, spit it out."

Phelps shrugged and flicked ash towards the shrub border. "In a nutshell? He's trying to muscle in on our murder enquiry."

"Who's the guv?"

"Brendan Moran."

"Ah. Now, Moran I like. He's been out of it, though, hasn't he? The explosion at Charnford?"

"It'll take more than that to keep DCI Moran off his feet for any length of time," Phelps said with conviction.

The humid air hung closely around the two men like heavy water as an airliner droned a cotton vapour trail across the perfect blue of an otherwise empty sky. The car-parking sergeant scuttled by with an embarrassed dip of the head on his way into reception.

"Tempted to wear shorts today," Chris said. "Bloody posties are allowed to. Don't see why we can't."

Phelps turned his head to reply, but when he opened his mouth nothing came out. His arm felt strangely numb, as though it were no longer a part of his body; seconds later the numbness was superseded by an acute pain that left him gasping for air. Gradually the sensation spread to his chest; it felt like a giant claw squeezing his insides, then releasing, then squeezing again. He clutched at his shirt, ripping the buttons as he tried to stand. He was vaguely aware of Chris' voice in his ear, calling for help.

By the time the paramedics arrived Phelps was flat out on the paving stones surrounded by a gaggle of police officers. His breath was coming in short, stabbing gasps as he clung to consciousness, but he was fighting a losing battle; soon the airliner's puffed-out vapour trail smeared the surrounding sky into a wide, all-encompassing shadow which fell slowly earthwards until it spread its darkness over him.

Chapter Thirteen

Moran rubbed his eyes and tried to concentrate. Traffic was bad, the heat wave shortening tempers and lengthening journey times as Berkshire's working population were forced to compete with carloads of coastbound holiday makers. The perennially cheerful Chris Evans grated in Moran's ears as he searched for the turning to West Reading Physiotherapy clinic.

Returning a burst of horn-blowing from a stroppy Tesco lorry he slipped past the gesticulating driver into the service road where, miraculously, there appeared to be a few parking spaces left. Cursing the clinic's owners for electing to site their practice in one of the busiest areas of Reading, Moran shoe-horned his car into a space and withdrew the business card from his wallet. *Smile at someone today, make a difference,* Evans was burbling. Moran, however, had little to smile about; he'd just received a call from the hospital informing him of DC Hill's death at ten past seven that morning from 'catastrophic brain trauma'.

The waiting room was half-full and the receptionist greeted him as if she'd been listening to Chris Evans as well. He presented his ID and asked gruffly to see the practice head.

"I'm afraid he'll be in clinic all morning," the receptionist told him. She was a pretty twenty-something with a dusky, lightly made-up complexion, shoulder-length black hair and slim, articulate hands.

"I'm afraid I'll have to interrupt clinic," Moran told her. "I'm conducting a murder investigation."

"Oh. I see." She looked him up and down briefly as if satisfying herself that he was the genuine article, and then asked him to wait.

Moran scowled at the waiting room and hovered at the reception desk. Why did Hill have to die? *Why*? Was it his fault? If he'd teamed Hill up with the more experienced Banner it would never have happened. By now they might have the Chinese in custody and the case well on the way to being wrapped up. Hill and McKellar would probably have started dating, Sheldrake would be a distant memory and–

"What can I do for you, Inspector? My name is Sandeep Suri. I am the practice manager."

Moran jerked his head up. The owner of the silkily smooth voice was a tall, handsome man in his early thirties. His skin was testimony to his Asian origins, his accent to the upper echelons of the British education system.

Moran shook the proffered hand and showed his ID. "Perhaps we can talk privately?"

"Of course. Please follow me." Suri led him through a narrow corridor to a door marked *Sandeep Suri BSc MSc MCSP HPC ACPSM AACP*.

"Please, Inspector." Suri invited Moran to sit and took his place behind the plain walnut desk. The desk was uncluttered, holding a framed family photograph, a PC and monitor, a blotter and an old fashioned twin-potted brass inkstand. "So what can I do for you, Inspector?"

Moran produced a Photofit picture of the dead Chinese driver. It was a skilfully realised image, created at Moran's request due to the disfiguring injuries sustained by the Chinaman in the fatal RTA. "Seen this man before?"

Suri took the picture and studied it. He made a negative side-to-side motion with his hand and returned it. "No, I am afraid not. Why do you ask?"

"Because we found your business card in his wallet."

Suri shrugged. "That is no crime, surely? We are a reputable practice, all legal and everything." He made a half-hearted attempt to inject humour into his statement by holding up his hands in mock surrender.

"I'm quite sure you are, Mr Suri. Are you positive you've never seen this man before?"

"Completely sure. I am sorry I cannot help. I hope very much that you will find him."

"Oh, we've found him. That's not the problem. The problem is that he's unable to answer our questions; that's why I'd like to talk to someone who could perhaps identify him for us."

"I see. I see. Perhaps I can ask our receptionist? She is quite new, but really on the ball, you know?"

"That's very helpful. Thanks."

"Please make yourself comfortable," Suri said. "I will also ask my partner."

Suri took the Photofit and left the room. Moran waited a few seconds before carrying out a more thorough inspection of the office. There was little to see: a locked filing cabinet, a small occasional table supporting a vase of fresh flowers, a single metal-framed painting of a Third World rustic scene adorning one of the tastefully sponged walls. The room was uncomfortably warm, the windows shut and security-bolted in spite of the heat, and Moran felt his head beginning to pound as he sat down and waited for Suri's return. As he took out his mobile it began to vibrate. He didn't recognise the number.

"Moran."

"Ah, Brendan. Mike Airey."

Moran groaned inwardly. The Superintendent. The last person he wanted to speak to. He took a deep breath. "Sir."

"I've had a call from Superintendent Alan Sheldrake. Chap from Organised Crime."

"I thought he might call you, sir."

"He's not very happy, Brendan. What's the story?"

Moran explained. When he'd finished there was a brief silence at the other end. The door opened and Suri appeared, but when he saw that Moran was on the phone he discreetly withdrew.

Airey cleared his throat with a metallic sounding cough in Moran's ear, and then continued in a slow, deliberate tone Moran understood to imply that he'd better be listening, and listening well. "You can't tread on this chap's toes, Brendan. He's a very high profile officer. He tells me they've been working on Kestrel since the operation's inception. You must know how big this is."

"I do, sir, but I'm not convinced that Reed-Purvis' murder is drug-related."

"How can you be so sure? It seems to me that she was in it up to her neck. Someone sussed her out and she was deliberately targeted. Makes perfect sense."

"It's too neat, sir."

"I like things neat, Moran. So does the chief."

Moran noticed the switch to his surname, but he was in no mood to be patronised. "Sir, with respect, I have cooperated fully with Superintendent Sheldrake. I've already confirmed that we'll hand over the case by Thursday evening."

"See that you do, Brendan. If you please." Airey cleared his throat again. "By the way, I was very sorry to hear about DC Hill."

"Yes, sir. Thank you."

"You'll be in touch with the parents?"

"Of course."

"I'll deal with the press," Airey went on tersely. "It's critical we don't upset the Kestrel applecart. I don't want alarmist headlines all over the shop. I'm sure the parents will understand. Tell them we'll see that justice is done." A moment's hesitation, and then Airey added, "And Sergeant Phelps. Damn shame about that. I know how close you two are."

Moran's brain shuddered as if under fire. "I'm sorry, sir?"

"Haven't you heard? In that case, I'm so sorry to be the bearer of bad tidings. Robert Phelps suffered a serious heart attack earlier this morning. He's been rushed into the Royal Berks. DI Pepper has been told to report to you ASAP."

Moran hardly heard Airey signing off. As he flung the office door open and left the clinic he threw a promise in Suri's direction that he'd be in back in touch before the end of the day.

The Catholic church was situated by the roundabout on the Tilehurst Road, just as the Kafir had remembered. He'd deliberately picked a quiet time of day, so he was confident that few parishioners would be around to interrupt his work. He noted with satisfaction that only two other cars occupied spaces in the church's expansive car park.

He briefly debated whether he should wear his jacket, but the wave of heat that struck him as he left the comfort of his air-conditioned vehicle made the decision a no-brainer. There was nothing unusual about the way he was dressed; T-shirts and chinos had become *de rigueur* while the weather held.

He twisted the large wrought iron door handle and stepped into the church's gloomy interior. At once the all-pervading smell of incense provoked rapid-fire snapshots from his memory; the discomfort of a surplice, the sick terror in his stomach as he walked from the vestry into full sight of the packed congregation...

He hesitated on the threshold. The stench of Catholicism began to evoke a more terrible memory, a feeling so powerful that his mind could scarcely articulate the fear. He shuddered. For a moment he wondered if he could go on, whether he could even physically enter the building.

You have buried the past, said the voice in his head quite clearly. *You are not what you once were.* ***You*** *are the Kafir.* Now, *do what you must...*

Yes, he nodded, *you're right. Someone has to pay...*

As his eyes became accustomed to the reduced light he saw that the queue for confession was, as he had hoped, down to just a handful of patient sinners. He took his place behind the last occupied pew and bowed his head. The feeling of sheer *rightness* intensified. He was *supposed* to be here. It was as if he was driven by some external force, animating his senses and filling him with assurance. He felt the need to respond, so he made a solemn vow: while the rot of religion existed, he would be there to stamp it out, to be its nemesis. His name would be spoken with reverence and awe by future generations. He knew this with certainty. It was as inevitable as the setting sun or the waning moon. He would not be stopped, not by the policeman Moran, not by *them*, not by any human intervention.

He winced as a stab of pain lanced through his head. For a moment his vision blurred, as if a migraine were about to strike. Then, as abruptly as it had arrived, it cleared.

The Kafir looked up at a slight noise, the creak of some roof timber expanding in the heat perhaps. He was alone in the church; all the penitents had gone. Then he realised that the noise he had heard was the click of the confessional door as the priest checked to see if any souls still awaited absolution.

The Kafir rose to his feet and the priest withdrew into his cabinet of contrition. The interior of the confessional was just as he remembered from his boyhood – musty, claustrophobic. The curtained grille, directly in front of him as he knelt, masked all but a faint outline of the black-garbed priest. For a moment the Kafir was tongue-tied, a boy again, struggling to remember his lines. Then they came to him and he heard himself recite in a low monotone. *Bless me father for I have sinned...*

Moran drove soberly and sadly back from the hospital. It had been a pointless visit, as he had known it would be. Phelps was in ICU, still fighting – and no, the duty registrar (who looked to Moran as though she should still be studying for her A-levels) was unable to say which way it was likely to go. In his favour, Robert Phelps was a strong man. Stacked against him was a lifetime of smoking, a penchant for malt whiskey and all-too-infrequent exercise. The doctors were doing all they could. Moran had thanked the registrar and the ICU staff and asked them to keep him abreast of any developments, positive or otherwise.

When Moran got back to his desk he found a brief note in DC McKellar's precise handwriting tucked into the corner of his blotter. *Call Marie Alder ASAP Time: 3.45pm.*

Moran sank into his chair and rested his head in his hands. Marie Alder was the senior manager at Monkfields nursing home in Newbury, where his elderly mother was one of the oldest residents. A call from Mrs Alder was not going to be good news. Moran's mother had been a bright, intelligent woman until premature senility had struck her down at seventy-one. He had been forced to watch her decline, helpless to intervene, until she had reached the point where she could no longer look after herself. The transfer from Cork to Newbury had been painful and traumatic. Even now she still asked when she was going home.

For this reason among many others, visits were an emotional trial for Moran, but at least she was in good hands – or so he hoped. The home enjoyed a good reputation, even though in Moran's opinion staff interaction with the residents often seemed cursory and abrupt. He found that he could not bear to extend his visits beyond thirty minutes, and sometimes, guiltily, he made his exit after only twenty. Sure, the home was materially comfortable; all kinds of events and outings were planned, but he could never shake off the feeling that the residents' foremost occupation was simply waiting for the inevitable. They'd lived their lives, and now they were at the front of the queue for departure. Sitting in the overheated lounge for any length of time made him feel as if he too had reached the front of the queue.

When he got up to leave his mother would always say, 'Are you going already, James?' which made him feel even guiltier. James, his youngest brother, had died tragically young in a boating accident. His mother had put on a brave face for many years, but Moran often wondered if the strain of grief had contributed to the eventual loosening of her grip on reality. For this reason he hadn't told her about Patrick, his elder brother, who had died in Moran's land rover along with Kay barely eight months ago.

He took a deep breath. Having just come from the hospital where Robert Phelps was fighting for his life Moran had no desire to make Monkfields his next port of call, but it had to be done. Reluctantly he dialled the number.

After a brief conversation he replaced the receiver. His mother had fallen – no broken bones, but a badly sprained ankle and some severe bruising. She was very confused and agitated. Could he come immediately?

On his way out of his office he almost collided with a young woman poised to knock on his door. She took a step back in surprise as Moran emerged, clearly in a hurry.

"Oh! Sorry," she followed up with an apologetic smile. "DCI Moran? I'm DI Charlie Pepper. DS Banner told me you'd just got in."

Moran was taken aback. He'd assumed that DI Pepper would be a male officer. Automatically he looked her up and down, noting her trim figure, her almost Mediterranean complexion and her short, spiky blonde hair. Moran guessed her age to be around the early thirties. When she offered her hand, Moran noted initially that she was a leftie and secondly that her fingers bore no traces of rings, wedding or otherwise.

He took her hand and squeezed gently. "Nice to have you with us, DI Pepper. I'm afraid I have a personal problem to attend to, but DS Banner will update you. I'll be back by six, all being well."

"Thank you, sir. See you then." She smiled again and stepped aside to allow him to pass.

Moran turned, remembering her illness. "You're fully recovered?"

"Pretty much, sir. Trust me to pick up the 'flu during my summer hols," she added with a self-deprecating snort of derision.

"It happens." Moran smiled thinly. "Look after DI Pepper, would you, Banner? Or perhaps you'd care to brief our new DI, DC McKellar?"

"Sure, guv," McKellar answered brightly.

Moran noted Banner's aggrieved expression, but his face also betrayed something else – a look Moran recognised. It was a look of carnal interest mingled with the oldest human emotion: hope.

You'll be lucky, Banner, Moran thought to himself as he took the stairs two at a time. Pretty as she was, DI Pepper had her work cut out; Robert Phelps was a hard act to follow.

Chapter Fourteen

"What's he like, then?"

"The guv?" DC McKellar looked up from her perusal of her alter ego's back story. She had elected to become Gill McShane, unemployed, into dubstep, men and dope, not necessarily in that order. She had been concentrating so hard she hadn't heard DI Pepper approach. Banner looked up and leered in her direction, distracting her. DI Pepper half-turned, but Banner quickly put his head down and his pencil back in his mouth. McKellar would have liked to stuff it down his throat, given the opportunity. She was sick to death of his sexist attitude. He belonged in an episode of 'Life on Mars', not in the twenty-first century.

DI Pepper read her expression and grinned. "Ignore it," she mouthed and made a conspiratorial face. "He's not the first male DS to make a prat of himself, and he won't be the last, neither," she whispered *sotto voce*.

McKellar giggled. DI Pepper's accent had a slight trace of the Midlands about it which appealed to her. Her blue eyes and blonde hair made McKellar wonder if there was Nordic blood in her family. At any rate, she looked and sounded as if she knew how to take care of herself. *Good at her job too, I'll bet*, McKellar decided as Pepper drew up a chair.

"Go on, then. Spill," Pepper prompted again.

"Oh, right, the guv. Hmmm. Well, he's great to work for – fair, you know. He can seem a bit preoccupied, but he's got a *great* sense of humour when you get him going."

"You trust him?"

"Totally."

"That's all I need to know." DI Pepper nodded, satisfied. "Now, what can I get stuck into?"

McKellar gave her a rundown on the Reading and Slough murders, spending a few minutes on Reed-Purvis before moving on to the attack on DC Hill. Pepper listened intently, interrupting occasionally with pertinent questions concerning the MO and commenting perceptively when McKellar told her about Sheldrake's imposed.time limit and the haul of heroin.

"DC Hill," Pepper asked. "Was he a close friend?"

McKellar started to speak but then found herself welling up. DI Pepper produced a packet of paper handkerchiefs and gave them to her. McKellar didn't trust herself to say any more, but after a moment she had a go.

"Thanks. I'm sorry, DI Pepper. I knew him quite well. I mean, we were friendly, but–"

"You were hoping to get friendlier? I'm so sorry. I really am." DI Pepper's concern was so obviously genuine it made McKellar weep all the more. DS Banner got up and hurriedly left the office.

"Men," DI Pepper said, shaking her head. "Emotional cripples, the lot of them."

That helped. McKellar found herself laughing and crying at the same time, and then somehow she was just laughing.

"And you don't have to call me DI Pepper, OK? Charlie's much better."

McKellar blew her nose loudly and made them both laugh. "Right. Charlie it is, then. I'm Helen, by the way."

"Nice to meet you, Helen." Charlie Pepper stuck her hand out with mock solemnity and both women laughed again. Out of the corner of her eye Helen McKellar caught DS Banner scowling as he returned to his desk with the coffee he hadn't really wanted.

Macho idiot, Helen thought. Judging by Charlie's expression, she was thinking exactly the same thing.

"Treat you to our canteen's famous speciality?" Helen suggested.

"Namely?"

"Cappuccino with extra cream topping. It's the best."

Charlie Pepper licked her lips. "What are we waiting for?"

"So, you're fresh from Warwickshire and Coventry?" Helen asked, sipping her coffee with relish. Since the new machine had arrived the canteen had trebled its trade. In the past the dingy eatery had been shunned, but now a lengthy queue was the norm. As Moran was fond of reminding her, a police station's efficiency was based on a plentiful supply of quality caffeine, and for a change someone in admin had actually ticked the right box.

"I'm not sure 'fresh' is the right word." Charlie made a face. "The 'flu really zonked me out."

"You don't look bad on it," Helen told her. She couldn't help noticing Charlie's flawless complexion, which, unlike her own, looked as if it had rarely, if ever, been troubled by spot or pimple.

"Thanks. It was pretty miserable, though. I'd just moved in and wham, down and out for ten days. All on my tod as well."

"Don't you know anyone down here?" Helen frowned.

"I have a friend in Bracknell, Anna, but she's a busy girl – travels a lot. Also – well, the move was a quick decision. I'd have lost out if I hadn't jumped at it."

"You're very brave. I don't think I would be able to put myself out on a limb like that. I need my family and friends around me."

A brief hint of melancholy passed across Charlie's face. "I'm an only child. Mum and Dad died years ago, so there's not much to miss on the family side." She brightened a little. "But I do have some great friends in Cov. I knew I'd miss them, but … well, they'll still be there when I go back. And I'll make new friends here, so no probs." She smiled.

"What was it like in Coventry?"

"I really enjoyed it. The team was brilliant. I couldn't have asked for better, really. Especially my boss – he was great to work for and we all wanted to pull our weight, you know? Not let him down, like. There was a lot of trust between us. We looked out for each other." Charlie took a sip of her drink and made an appreciative murmur. "You're right. This is almost Costa quality."

"Told you." Helen smiled triumphantly. "A quarter the price, too."

"So, what about you?" Charlie asked. "How long have you been with DCI Moran?"

"Just over six months," Helen said. "But it feels like longer. It's my first posting as a DC."

"And you're a Reading girl?"

Helen laughed. "No. I'm from Essex originally, but I try to keep that quiet."

They both laughed and then Charlie pointed out a blob of cream on Helen's nose, which made them laugh even more.

"So, what's the deal with the nightlife then?" Charlie's eyes sparkled. "Where's the action in Reading?"

Helen looked down at her mug. "I'm not much of a one for clubbing," she admitted. "I'm more into eating out, country pubs, walking, that kind of stuff."

"Me too," Charlie agreed, "but I need a bit of a boogie now and again, if you know what I mean?"

Helen grinned. "Well, OK, maybe now and again."

"You can give me a tour sometime," Charlie said, draining her coffee. "Show me the sights."

"I'd love to. Reading itself is a bit grim, but the countryside is lovely. There are some great pubs out in the sticks."

"Sounds perfect. Let's do it."

By the time they finished their coffee Helen felt as if she'd known Charlie for years. She hoped some of Charlie's exuberance – not to mention her confidence – might rub off on her.

The Zodiac was full to brimming. Helen McKellar, aka Gill McShane, followed DS Banner (aka Rob Giles) into the throng. It was around half past nine in the evening and Helen felt a tingle of excitement, the way she always did when she was working in the field. The only downside was Banner, but even if she didn't trust him to keep his hands to himself she trusted him as a copper, and with DI Charlie Pepper keeping an eye on things she felt secure. Moran hadn't showed up back at base – some problem with his elderly mother, apparently – but Helen knew that with DI Pepper in the background she was in safe hands. That made all the difference, especially with Rob Phelps temporarily out of the picture. She could hardly believe that the big, tough sergeant was flat out in the RBH cardiac unit, but at least the latest news was positive. He was through the worst, and by all accounts he should make a full recovery. That was a huge comfort; she couldn't have coped with the death of another close colleague so soon after DC Hill's murder. The knowledge that she was helping to catch his killer only sharpened the edge of her excitement.

The music hit her in the gut as the DJ cued another song. Banner made a sign and headed for the toilets while Helen found a bench seat in a quieter corner and squeezed onto the end.

She casually scanned the clientele; the club was a melee of male and female, young and not-so-young. She was aware that they had precious little time to nail a result. Sharron Flynn's cover name was Ann Hooper. Moran's instructions had been simple: mingle fast and drop the name into the conversation to see what fell out.

A heavily made-up girl sashayed up and sat next to her. "All right if I sit here?"

"Sure." Helen tried to smile through her tension. The girl looked like a street girl, but then so did a lot of kids in the town centre clubs these days. It was hard to make a judgement.

"Club's OK, isn't it?" Helen began, immediately realising how lame she sounded.

The girl shrugged. "I suppose." She tapped a painted nail on the table in time with the music.

"I'm trying to find someone." Helen had to shout as the track reached a crescendo. "She promised she'd be here."

The girl was sitting back with her eyes half-closed, letting the rhythm wash over her.

"Her name is Ann," Helen persisted. "Ann Hooper."

"Oh yeah." The girl opened her eyes and took a pull at her bottle of lager. "The ice queen."

"Ice queen?"

"Cold cow."

"Oh, I see. You know her, then?"

"Most people do. If you get my meaning." The girl laughed and made an exaggerated smoking gesture.

"Right," Helen said, forcing a smile. "That's the one."

"You want to watch it with her," the girl said. "She's bad news."

"Oh. Why?"

The girl put down her bottle and studied Helen's face. "You don't look like you belong here, love."

Helen thought quickly. "You're right; I'm not really a clubber. My boyfriend and I are new to town. We're just having a look see, you know? This Ann Hooper told Rob she could get hold of some good smoke. Said she'd be here tonight."

The girl gave Helen a measured look. "Yeah? Oh, by the way I'm Zoë, if you want to know."

"Gill." They shook hands.

"You're after some hash, then." Zoë looked Helen up and down again. "You don't seem the type."

Helen shrugged. "It's for Rob really. I usually stick to beer or wine."

Zoë nodded doubtfully. "If I see Ann around I'll let her know, all right?"

"Thanks." Helen was getting worried about Banner. He'd been gone fifteen minutes at least.

Zoë got up and smoothed down her skirt. "You're a nice kid. Do yourself a favour, love. Walk away. You let your bloke deal with Hooper. I don't know how you ran into her in the first place, but she's bad news down here. Take my word for it."

"What do you mean?"

"Look." Zoë leaned in close and Helen caught a whiff of some pungent perfume. "Ann Hooper keeps bad company, know what I mean?"

"Not really." *Play dumb, Helen, play dumb...*

"She deals, sure. Always has done, but she had a kid a while back, right? I've seen her with it. So she's upped the ante. Brought all sorts out of the woodwork. I'm not sayin' no more."

Before Helen could reply the DJ had cued up another song and Zoë was walking away.

"Hi." A young emo appeared out of the crowd and winked through a gelled sweep of dyed black hair. Helen repressed a smile. He looked way too young to be drinking, but Helen supposed the Zodiac management were too busy to pay much attention to under-agers tonight.

Helen smiled and looked away in the time-honoured 'no thanks' signal. As she did so she caught sight of Banner weaving his way towards her. Thank goodness for that. But where had he been?

The DS had covered half the distance between them when Helen saw him wince, as if he had stumbled or had had a sudden attack of cramp. Two men moved alongside and Helen thought they were trying to help until they grabbed Banner by the shoulders and frogmarched him in the opposite direction. She called out, but the throbbing drum 'n' bass track drowned her voice.

She half-stood in a froth of indecision. Who were the men? How did they know who Banner was? Then it struck her. *If they know his face, they probably know mine...*

Even as the thought flashed through her mind she saw a couple moving purposefully towards her, a man and a woman. The man was a hefty, muscular type and the woman was wiry and thin-faced. They didn't look like punters. They looked heavy.

Helen thought quickly. She reached over to emo, whose mates had taken over the remaining seats on her table, and tapped him on the shoulder. The boy's face lit up. Helen motioned for him to sit closer, which he did with alacrity. Without hesitation, Helen leaned over and kissed him full on the lips.

Emo's mates began cheering and whistling, audible even over the sound system. All eyes swivelled in their direction. Helen came up for air and risked a glance across the dance floor. The two escorts had vanished. Grabbing emo's hand she pulled him to his feet.

"Take me outside. Quick." Eyes widening with a mixture of pleasure and confusion, emo obliged to a reprise of thunderous cheering from their table.

Outside the air was dense and sultry. A few smokers hung around chatting and laughing. Helen retrieved her ID card. "Look, I'm really sorry. I'm a police officer." She showed the card and the boy's face fell. "I'm in a spot of trouble. I can't say much more. Can you wait with me a minute?"

Emo shrugged. "Sure."

Helen dialled Charlie Pepper's number. "Charlie? It's Helen. Banner's been rumbled. I'm OK; I'm out of the club but I need back up. What do you want me to do?"

Charlie Pepper's voice in her ear was calm and precise. "Stay put, Helen. Keep your eyes peeled, especially round the back; they might try to get him out and away. Make a note of any cars leaving the premises. I'll be there as soon as I can."

Moran turned the key to his front door and felt in his pocket for his mobile. The battery had died a few hours previously and he'd forgotten his charger. Hopefully no one had needed him. Nevertheless, he always felt a moment of dread when he plugged back in and the list of missed calls appeared.

Archie the spaniel bounded into the hall, a well-chewed toy clamped between his jaws. "Hello, boy." Moran wrestled the toy from the dog's grip and threw it the length of the hall, enjoying Archie's skidding pursuit and retrieval. He propped his stick against the wall, plugged his mobile into the charger and went into the kitchen. The wall clock told him it was just after a quarter to ten. He'd been out of the loop for four hours. He poured a generous glass of Sangiovese and shrugged off his coat.

His mother was not good, not at all. She had seemed weaker, thinner, more confused than ever. All in all, the signs were not hopeful. Moran draped his coat over the chair by the telephone.

His daily had left the day's post on the kitchen table. A letter from the RBH confirming his CT scan: nine forty-five on Friday morning. A couple of bills, an official-looking letter, a card. Female handwriting? He opened it. It was from Shona.

Hi Brendan – get together soon? Be nice to get a call now and again. S x

And when had he had the chance to do that? Moran threw the card down with a muttered expletive. There was nothing he'd like better than to spend a quiet evening with Shona, to smooth over the dinner date misunderstanding, but right now his time was not his own. *Right now? And the rest...* a small voice whispered. A lyric from a song on one of his old LPs came to mind: *'...and then one day you find, ten years have got behind you. No one told you when to run. You missed the starting gun...'*

"That'd be right," Moran muttered to himself and tore open the letter. It was from the insurance appeal committee. They had heard his case, but they regretfully had to inform him that his appeal had been turned down. The insurance company policy was quite clear regarding acts of terror, having fully taken all circumstances into consideration etc.

Moran topped up his wine and contemplated a chaser. The failure of his appeal meant he was in hock to the tune of around £25,000. The explosion had caused extensive damage and he'd had no choice but to take out a loan pending the appeal result. His pension lump sum, which he had earmarked for paying off his mortgage, would instead have to pay the repair bill.

From the hall his mobile gave a bleep. Archie reappeared and dumped the toy at his feet. Moran stroked the spaniel's head while he drained his wine. The mobile bleeped a second time. *All right, all right...*

Archie followed him into the hall and then stopped, ears twitching, alert. A low growl began deep in the dog's throat and emerged as a series of short barks.

"What is it, boy?" Moran went to the front door and opened it. Nobody there. Archie continued barking until Moran showed the spaniel the empty doorstep and drive. "False alarm, Archibald."

Moran examined his messages. Two from the station, one from a mobile he didn't recognise. Not good. He dialled the unfamiliar number and waited.

"Hello? DS Snook speaking," a familiar voice said. Brian Snook, one of the current night shift officers.

"Brian? It's DCI Moran."

"Yes, sir. We have a serious incident, I'm afraid. I can't get hold of DI Pepper so I called you – sorry, sir, I know you're officially off duty."

"No such thing, Brian. What's up?" Moran didn't want to ask. It wasn't likely to be good news.

"St James' Catholic Church, sir. Tilehurst Road. On the roundabout, you know it? There's been a fatal stabbing."

"I'll be there in fifteen minutes, Brian. Tell them to keep the scene nice and tidy."

"It's pretty self-contained, sir," DS Snook said. "By all accounts," he added in a slightly more subdued voice.

"Thanks, Brian." Moran signed off and checked his other missed calls. One from DI Pepper. He decided to leave them for later; Pepper would have to rely on her own initiative for now. That wasn't a bad thing, Moran reflected, given her recent arrival; she now had a golden opportunity to prove herself before she'd even got her feet properly under the desk.

As Moran's car pulled away, Gregory Neads emerged from the shadow of the bus stop three doors away and sauntered towards his ex-DCI's house. As he reached the gate he heard a dog barking. Neads tutted to himself. He'd have to sort that out before he did anything else.

His hand was on the gate latch when he heard footsteps approaching. He walked on until the pedestrian had passed by. Neads stopped at the corner and glanced back. The hooded figure was loitering outside Moran's house. Neads ducked out of sight. When he looked again a few moments later the pavement was empty.

Chapter Fifteen

DI Charlie Pepper was at the Zodiac in five minutes flat, which was damn good going from the other side of town. By that time Helen had recruited two uniforms from a nearby patrol car and was impatient to move in.

"This has to be subtle," Charlie told them. "We can't just charge in like the cavalry and turn the place over. Not with the OCG interest."

"But Banner–"

"Will be OK, Helen. Trust me." She gave Helen a look which said, *I can handle this. Support me and everything will work out...*

Helen bit her lip and nodded.

"Any cars left the car park?"

Helen shook her head. "No."

"OK. Round the back, then," Charlie told the first uniform, a fresh-faced mid-twenty-something. "Nice and easy." She addressed his female partner. "Taylor, you stay here. Try to look like the Zodiac isn't even on your radar, OK? Anyone leaves in a way you don't like the look of, let me know immediately."

"Ma'am." WPC Taylor moved away from the glass-fronted club door and crossed the road.

The Zodiac's rear entrance led directly into the club's small car park, which was about half full. Most people didn't bother to try to squeeze their cars into the awkward spaces, primarily because of the brand new multi-storey immediately behind but also because no one wanted to get boxed in by double-parkers. Beyond the multi-storey lay the canal, and looming over it the elevated section of the Inner Distribution Road, or IDR as it was known locally.

Helen followed Charlie and the young PC into the car park. The muted pulse of the Zodiac's sound system grew louder as they approached the rear entrance. It was officially a fire exit and was locked from within, but an adjacent frosted-glass window stood partially open.

"Toilets." Charlie turned to the young PC. "Feeling athletic, PC Keohane?"

"Ma'am."

Helen watched as PC Keohane heaved himself up to the ledge and fiddled with the window catch. After a moment he had it fully open. They watched as he disappeared inside. Thirty seconds later the fire door opened and Keohane beckoned. "It was the ladies," he told them. "Fortunately unoccupied."

"What about the gents?" Helen had to raise her voice to be heard. Even out here the volume was gut-thumpingly loud. "Worth a check." Her heart was pounding as she remembered what had happened to DC Hill. OK, Banner was a pain, but he was a colleague too.

Charlie motioned to PC Keohane. The PC cautiously pushed open the door of the gents. They heard him rapping on cubicle doors. "Police. All right in there?"

Two punters appeared through the connecting door from the club, both girls. Charlie showed them her ID and told them to wait. The girls exchanged looks and retreated.

Keohane's head emerged from the gents. "One no reply, ma'am."

"OK, let's have a look." Charlie followed Keohane and Helen waited half-in, half-out of the doorway, ready to turn away any male clientele.

"Police." Charlie rapped hard on the cubicle. "Can you respond, please?"

Two seconds passed. Nothing. Charlie nodded to Keohane. The PC put his shoulder to the flimsy panelled door and it flew open.

"Damn." Helen heard Charlie's muttered expletive. "Helen?"

Helen was at the cubicle in two strides. "Oh no . . ."

Banner was sitting on the toilet, his head lolling on his chest. A note was pinned to his stomach, scrawled in red felt tip pen. It read, *Next time, dead.*

The church was a lofty, high-ceilinged building, unlike others Moran had visited which were usually modern, characterless halls. Diffused light from a large stained-glass window spread across the interior as he made his way to the centre of activity, to the right of the nave by the confessionals. A fretful young man in a dog collar was pacing up and down between white-suited SOCOs as they milled around photographing, videoing and scouring the area for tangible – and not so tangible – evidence. Patrick Maclennan, the scene manager, welcomed him with a gruff "Moran."

Maclennan led him to the first confessional, a two-door cupboard-like structure which enabled priest and penitent to face each other in complete anonymity. Outside the box Maclennan paused.

"Hope you're not a religious man, Moran. Not a pretty sight, I'm afraid."

Moran followed Maclennan's gaze. The second door, the priest's door, was wide open and floodlit. It was occupied by an older man, also dog-collared and clearly dead. A savage knife wound had opened his throat, and his black shirt was shiny with the blood which had splattered the woodwork and the gauze-curtained grille separating the two partitions. The grille was slashed and torn, as if the attacker had ripped his way through with the knife.

"God," Moran muttered.

"Absent, I'd say," Maclennan replied darkly. "Or not paying attention to what one of his own was up to." The big Scot gave Moran a humourless grin. "You taking this one on as well, or are you still tied up with the others?"

"One at a time, Patrick, that's the way it works. Unless there's a clear link." Moran peered into the confessional, wrinkling his nose at the sickly smell of blood.

"Same kind of slash to the throat as the town centre boy," Maclennan observed. "Tenuous connection, though. Blinged up Asian lad to parish priest?" He laughed grimly. "Good job it wasn't the local mosque or there'd be a political Hiroshima on top of us."

Moran straightened up as if he'd been stung. "What did you say, Patrick?"

The Scot frowned. "Just that an attack like this in the mosque would produce a much bigger backlash in the local community – all the way up the ladder. We'd never hear the end of it."

"I wonder," Moran said quietly. "Maybe this isn't some personal vendetta. Not against anyone in particular, anyway."

"Meaning?"

Moran looked the Scot straight in the eye. "Maybe it's about *religion*, Patrick. The second Asian boy was a Muslim; Bling Boy too, I'd bet. Now we have a Catholic victim."

"You reckon? What next? The Freemasons? The Quakers?" Maclennan looked sceptical, but Moran didn't wait to hear any more. By the time Maclennan had ticked off the Methodists, Baptists and Seventh Day Adventists Moran was already on his way out, stick in one hand, mobile in the other.

Maclennan shook his head and went back to his laptop to upload the crime scene photographs to the fingerprint bureau. They probably belonged to the victim, but you could never be sure. As he entered his password he wondered if Father Peter Jeffries had had time to make his own confession before his life had been so abruptly terminated.

Banner looked like crap. Not surprising really, Moran thought, considering the dose of Ketamine he had received. It said something for Banner's iron constitution that he was fit enough to attend the midmorning briefing at all, given last night's incident in the Zodiac's toilet – an incident that Moran knew the detective sergeant would struggle to live down, especially given the stick he habitually dished out to his colleagues. Wouldn't do him any harm, Moran concluded. He was just relieved that he didn't have to announce the death of another serving officer.

Moran had assembled the team both to update them and to find out more about what had been going on during his afternoon absence. Nothing good, by all accounts. Although DI Pepper had done the right thing in keeping the lid on Banner's rescue from the Zodiac, Moran was not best pleased that they had been sussed out so easily, and he wanted to know why.

"Right then, first things first." He addressed the tired but attentive faces. "You'll all be pleased to hear that acting DI Robert Phelps is doing well. He's out of immediate danger and is expected to make a good recovery, although it will be some time before he can resume active duty. DS Banner has been restored to us, albeit in somewhat sickly shape, by DC McKellar and DI Pepper, who I'm sure all of you have met by now. DI Pepper will be filling Robert Phelps' shoes in his absence, so hers is a timely arrival. DI Pepper, can I take this opportunity to formally welcome you to the team?" Moran looked at each officer in turn. "I'm sure you'll all give DI Pepper your full support." Murmurs of agreement. "Good. Secondly, DC McKellar is going to fill you in on tonight's events at the Zodiac."

Moran stood to one side as Helen McKellar described Banner's sudden abduction and her suspicion that she had also been targeted. When she finished Moran thanked her and resumed his position in front of the whiteboards.

"It doesn't take a great deal of head-scratching to realise that someone knew they were coming. Which means in turn that someone leaked not only the information that two coppers were going under cover, but they also got hold of some mug shots to make the job a simple one. Thoughts?"

Banner raised his arm. "I'd go for Neads, guv. Just the sort of thing that sick sod would enjoy."

"But how would Neads know what was going on, unless someone told him?" Moran appealed to the gathered officers.

"Does he still have network access?" Helen McKellar asked.

"Nah." One of the DCs shook his head. "All access is switched off on an officer's resignation. Or termination," he added quickly.

"Are we sure?" Moran frowned. "Neads was highly IT literate. We need to make sure those doors are closed. Can you check it out, DC Harding?"

"Will do, guv. I can check the stats to find out the last time he logged on."

"Thank you." Kenneth Harding was a bright boy – West Indian parentage, and a way with computers that was no less dazzling than his often visible smile. But was it really likely to be Neads? Sure, Neads was unpredictable but Moran didn't reckon he'd stoop so low as to expose his ex-colleagues to danger. But then, there was the mocking text, the way he had hung around the station...

Moran's eyes traversed the room. "DI Pepper. Any ideas?"

"Well, guv," she hesitated, "I don't really want to suggest this, but it's a possibility."

"Go on," Moran prompted. The room hushed.

"Isn't it possible that DC Hill talked – under pressure obviously? Maybe he was forced to spill info about the team."

A ripple of discontented muttering passed around the room. Charlie Pepper shrugged. "I'm sorry, but it's possible."

"But the Chinese died thirty-five minutes after Hill was found. He wouldn't have had time to pass on any info," Helen McKellar argued. Moran saw a slight flush of colour rise on the whiteness of her throat. There was a chorus of agreement from the other officers, and Charlie, tight-lipped, looked down at the carpet.

"DI Pepper is right." Moran quietened them with a wave of his hand. "Let's get this straight. DC Hill was under extreme pressure. We're not here to pass judgement. He was a fine detective, in spite of his youth. His integrity is not under question, but under the circumstances it is entirely possible that he may have reluctantly provided information, which could have been texted, emailed, whatever, even in such a short timeframe."

More mutterings and head-shaking from the floor. Moran paused, allowing the team to express their objections. No one wanted to think badly of an officer killed on active service, but he had to factor in the possibility and he was glad Charlie Pepper had been brave enough to suggest it. It told him a lot about the way she ticked, and so far he liked what he saw.

"OK. The threatening note left on DS Banner has been sent off for analysis, but I doubt it'll help us much. For the time being, excluding Neads as a suspect, I'm assuming that the perpetrators have some connection with the drug ring. We'll need to work out how to approach the Zodiac with a little more subtlety. DS Banner and DC McKellar, we'll get together after this to do a little brainstorming. If DS Banner is up to it?"

Moran waited for the catcalls and one-liners to subside. He knew that behind the ribbing lay relief and not a little concern. Banner raised his hand weakly and tried to laugh it off. A hard man, yes, but not immune to feeling a little shaken up. Moran raised his voice and the hubbub died down.

"OK, let's move on. You'll all have heard about yesterday's 's incident at St James' Church?"

Moran briefed them and floated his theory regarding the religious connections. "That means we have three separate murders, all of which have a similar MO, namely the victim's throat pierced with a thin knife and multiple bodily stab wounds. The exception is DS Reed-Purvis, who was doped and strangled. Question: does she prove the rule, or is her murder unrelated?"

"Have the path lab come to any conclusions about the weapon, guv? Was the same knife used?" someone asked.

Moran shook his head. "No word yet regarding the St James' incident; we'll have to wait for the autopsy. But Bling Boy and Slough Boy were killed with different weapons, that much we do know. Slough Boy's wound was more ragged, wider–" Moran pointed to the photograph pinned to the whiteboard. "And Bling's is neater, a sharper, thinner blade."

Charlie Pepper shrugged. "Doesn't rule out the same killer."

"Agreed," Moran said. "The killer isn't stupid. He hasn't left us much to go on at the crime scenes so far. No one saw anything untoward either before or after the attacks."

"Guv?" Banner's hand was up.

"Yes, DS Banner?"

"I guess that Father Jeffries' murder rules out the drug connection?"

Moran nodded. "I think so. Even taking into account the haul we found in the Chinaman's car, my belief is that we're dealing with a serial killer. He's moving in the same circles as the drug syndicate, but he's not actually involved with them – not directly, anyway. There's a connection of some sort, but exactly what that connection is – well, that's down to us to find out.

"Forgive me for stating the obvious, guv, but, well–"

"Go on, spit it out, Banner."

Banner hesitated, scratching his ear with his pencil. "Well, we reckon the Jeffries murder has Neads written all over it, guv. I mean, after Charnford Abbey, you know, and the guy was mugged recently wasn't he? Might have sent him over the edge…" Banner trailed off and, reading Moran's expression, began to examine a scuff mark on his shoe.

Moran exhaled deeply. "OK, let's put this one to bed. As I've said before, Gregory Neads may well be an awkward little so-and-so, and yes, he's been through the kind of traumatic experience I hope none of us ever have to endure, but I can't bring myself to believe that he's capable of multiple murders. I accept that he's a bit of a loose cannon, but I'm also convinced that his current game plan is to irritate and harass, not to kill. As I said before, I think we're dealing with a serial killer on some kind of religious agenda." He paused but no one challenged his opinion. All eyes were looking elsewhere – the floor, the window, the whiteboards. "OK, let's have some updates from you lot. What about the Audi? Any joy?"

DC Harding spoke up. "ANPR's been on a go-slow the last day and a half, guv. Something to do with IT maintenance work."

"In other words, they screwed up," another officer said to a burst of knowing laughter from the room. Harding carried on through the noise.

"But we've got an interim result anyway, guv. Came in just half an hour ago. A Crystal Blue Audi of the type we're after stopped at Tilehurst Service Station at five thirty-five the night Bling Boy was killed. We've got a positive ID via the station's CCTV. I've just sent the registration to the DVLA for matching.

"And Sulham Woods is down the road."

"Yes, guv. Around half a mile."

"Thank you, DC Harding. My desk as soon as, OK?" The news made Moran feel slightly better. It might not be the vehicle they were after, but then again, it might. At least they had something tangible. And then there was the fact that Reed-Purvis had been found in Sulham...

"Are we still on a short timescale, guv?" Helen McKellar asked.

"Very," Moran confirmed. "Today is half over already. We only have until tonight, strictly speaking. Maybe I can stretch it to close of play tomorrow. After that it's out of my hands and into OCG's. He clapped his hands smartly. "OK That's it for now."

"Are you joining us later, guv?" Helen stopped him as he turned towards his office.

"Later?"

"We're going down the Falcon. For a drink. You know, for James..."

Moran spotted the slight tremor in her voice and felt a wave of empathy. He nodded. "Of course. Eight o'clock?"

"Eight o'clock sharp, guv," she replied in a passable imitation of his own well-used phrase. "See you there."

Chapter Sixteen

The Falcon was the favoured watering hole of TVP, not on account of the quality of its beer or its outstanding ambience, but primarily because of its proximity to the station. That, and a long, friendly history with one of Reading's longest serving landlords, Brian Carroll. Brian was a huge, barrel-chested man with the most magnificent Jimmy-Edwards-style moustache Moran had ever seen. There was a long-running, apocryphal rumour that Brian would be awarded a full police pension on his eventual retirement, which, given his age, couldn't be that far away. He'd seen officers come and go, laugh and cry, argue and celebrate. He had dispensed and presided over the disputes, the birthdays, the engagements and, on occasion, as tonight, the wakes.

"What'll it be, Brendan?" Brian's eyes creased. "The hop or the grape?"

"Pint of Brakspear's please, Brian."

"Good choice." The landlord selected a glass and expertly pulled the pint. "Sorry to hear about Robert. How is he?"

"Holding his own." Moran sipped the pint. "I thought he was indestructible."

"Like you?" Brian laughed. "How's the leg, by the way?"

"I'm fine." Moran shrugged. "Physically, at any rate. The grey matter needs a little attention."

Brian leaned over the bar. "About the boy – don't take it personally, Brendan. I've heard you give that advice yourself."

"True. But he was so young. What am I going to tell his parents?"

"Tell 'em the truth. That's what they'll want to hear. Hard, yes, but it's the right thing to do."

"Brian," Moran smiled, "you've missed your vocation. You should have been a counsellor."

"I think not." Brian's eyes twinkled. "Suits me here just fine."

"Buy you one, guv?" Helen McKellar was at Moran's side.

"Allow me." He ordered for her, and they moved off to allow Banner and a few other team members access to the bar.

"Did you invite DI Pepper?"

"Yes, guv. She said she'd be here around half past."

"Seem OK to you so far?"

"She's really nice. And pretty quick off the mark, too."

"Good. She'll need to be with Rob Phelps out of the picture."

"Excuse me, guv." Helen indicated a group of colleagues at a nearby table. "I owe Jim a tenner."

"Sure." Moran sipped his pint. "Carry on."

Truth be told, Moran thought to himself as he watched Helen join in with the laughter and mounting din of conversation, his home and his bed appealed to him infinitely more than a night in the Falcon, but it was important for the team that he showed his face.

Did they blame him? No, he felt sure that wasn't the case. It was young Hill's enthusiasm that had led to his downfall. Or rather, the way in which he'd chosen to channel that enthusiasm with his accurate but misguided solo effort.

Moran looked over to where Banner was holding court, surrounded by his mates, cracking jokes and knocking the lager back as if there were no tomorrow. Was Banner to blame? He had taken every opportunity to rile Hill, to goad and belittle him. Is that why the young officer had gone off the rails? To prove himself? Moran drained his pint. What could you do? There were Banners in every police force. They had their plus points but had to be handled carefully. Even so, the high maintenance overheads generated by the Banners of this world invariably proved to be a complete pain in the gicker.

Moran squeezed his way to the bar to order another pint. Last one for the evening, he promised himself. It had been a frustrating afternoon without any tangible progress. Strictly speaking, he knew, his time was up; but as Sheldrake had been conspicuous by his absence Moran had every intention of continuing the investigation until he was forced to stop. If Sheldrake had been sidetracked by some other commitment, so much the better. As Moran waited to be served he allowed his eyes to traverse the pub, pausing for a moment on each animated, smiling face. A reaffirmation of life, that's what this was about. They weren't here to be sad; they were here to celebrate being alive. James Hill would be remembered in those quiet moments at home, in the small hours, when the suppressed fears and anxieties had free rein over the drowsy, semi-conscious mind. But overriding the fear, one guilty, uninvited thought would surface again and again: *I'm glad it wasn't me...*

"Hello, sir."

Moran started at the voice in his ear. "Ah, DI Pepper. Welcome to our five star policeman's watering hole. Drink?"

"I'll have a Beck's, please, sir. Thanks."

"A pint of Brakspear's and a Beck's, please." Moran placed his order with a young barmaid he didn't recognise. Another one of Brian's Polish protégés, no doubt. "Oh, and you can forget the 'sir', DI Pepper," Moran told his new DI. "In my book, 'sir' is for Superintendents. 'Guv' suits me much better."

"Right you are." Charlie Pepper gave him a cheeky smile. "And I'm Charlie, OK, guv?" She accepted the bottle, top off and foaming, and took what Moran considered to be a very unladylike swig.

"Glass?" Moran queried.

Charlie wrinkled her nose and gave him an odd look. "No way. Tastes better from the bottle. You should try it."

Moran took the head off his beer and made a satisfied noise in his throat. "Really? I think I'll stick to the tried and traditional method, if that's OK with you." He smiled self-deprecatingly.

"You sound like my Dad." Charlie grinned. "He's always on about tradition and the 'proper', old-fashioned way of doing things."

"Don't." Moran made a face. "You've no idea how old that makes me feel."

Charlie's forehead creased in concern. "Oh, I didn't mean *you* were old–"

"No? Come on." He took Charlie's elbow. "Damage done. Time to meet a few of my favourite renegades, some of whom even go as far as to call themselves detectives. You'll have to deal with them daily from now on, so you might as well make a start, eh?"

Charlie laughed and raised her bottle. "Lead me to them."

Moran turned into his drive just before one in the morning. He was exhausted. There was so much going round in his head he knew that sleep would be a long time coming, if it came at all. He tried once again to mentally order the chaos by his usual process of prioritisation, but fatigue jumbled his thoughts.

Two dead officers. Three dead civilians. What was the link? The more he pondered, the more he doubted his religious theory. But who would want to murder a Catholic priest? Drug-related crime he could understand, but this latest development made no sense. Perhaps Father Jeffries' murder *was* entirely unrelated to the slaughter of the two Asian lads? If so, what did that mean?

It means you have nothing, Moran, that's what it means. It means there are more crazy people out there than even you can account for...

He turned off the ignition and wearily pulled himself out of the car. As he approached his front door he noticed immediately that it was slightly ajar. Had he forgotten to lock it? Surely not? His senses went into red alert. He slipped past the dining room window and through the wooden gate leading to the garden. From the edge of the patio he could see that the lounge light was on. He never left the lounge light on.

Moran returned to the car and retrieved his Maglite from the glove compartment. He approached the front door obliquely, edged onto the porch, eased himself through the front door and crept towards the lounge. There was a faint rustle of paper, as if someone had turned a page or folded a newspaper. Where was Archie? The little dog would inevitably greet him at the door whatever hour of the day or night Moran returned. Full of dread, he reached the lounge door and pushed it gently open.

"You're late." Shona rose from the sofa as he entered and smiled a greeting.

Moran felt the tension rush out of him. "*Shona*. What on earth? How did you get in?"

"The door was open. I assumed you were in, but when I found the house empty I thought I'd better stick around just in case. Did you forget to lock up?"

"I don't think so. How long have you been here?"

"Oh, let's see." She consulted her watch. "Since around eight, I suppose." Her face fell. "Do you think you've been burgled? I didn't see anything out of place."

"My dog. Have you seen him?" Moran began to search, calling Archie's name and whistling. Something felt *very* wrong.

The doorbell rang. Moran was there in seconds. It was Alison, his neighbour. She was holding a long lead, at the end of which a panting and straining Archie was doing his best to pull her into Moran's hallway. She grinned.

"Hi. I found Archie on my doorstep. We gave him something to eat – I suppose he got locked out?"

Relief pumped through Moran's veins. For a moment he'd thought the worst. "Thanks, Alison." He looked at his watch. "I'm sorry it's so late; I kept you up..."

Alison shook her head. "We're mostly nocturnal, Brendan. It's not a problem. I did pop over earlier but there was no one around." Her smile faded. "Is there any news on the–"

"Not yet, Alison. We're still looking into it."

"That poor woman." Alison bit her lip. "I'm frightened to walk Max now." She hesitated. "You *will* find the murderer, won't you?"

"Yes. I'll keep you posted. You mustn't worry." He thanked her again and closed the door.

"All OK?" Shona came into the hall, arms folded.

"Yes. And no." Moran let Archie off his lead and the spaniel bounded away into the lounge. "Why are you here, Shona?"

Shona cocked her head to one side. "If the mountain won't come to Mohammed, then Mohammed must go to the mountain."

Moran shook his head wearily. "This particular mountain is in no fit state to be conquered tonight. Look, Shona, I've been wanting to catch up, I really have, but I'm up to my neck in it at the moment."

"OK. No problem, I understand. How's it all going?" She took his arm and led him back into the lounge. He belatedly noticed that a bottle of Sangiovese and two glasses had been placed on the table along with a fresh vase of flowers.

"It's going badly. Yes please." Moran acknowledged the poised bottle and gratefully accepted the glass.

"How badly? Talk to me." She slipped onto the sofa beside him.

"Usual badly. A lot of unanswered questions. It's always like this."

"Like what, exactly? Go on, I want to know."

Moran leaned his head back on the sofa. "Like a huge, scattered jigsaw puzzle. You pick up one piece and try to make it fit. Sometimes it does, sometimes not. That reminds me." He felt in his pocket and retrieved the physiotherapist's card. "This is your line of work, isn't it? Have you heard of this lot?"

Shona leaned over so that he could smell her perfume. It made him feel slightly light-headed. She took the card and looked at it closely.

"Nope. Don't know them."

"Just a thought."

"Sorry." Shona made a downcast face. "Keep talking. It'll make it better. You'll see."

So he did, and she was right – it did make it better. When she kissed him, that made it better too. After a while, nothing else mattered. They lay in each other's arms.

"Brendan?"

"Mm?"

"Tell me about yourself."

"What do you want to know?"

She stirred and poked him in the ribs. "That is *such* a male response."

"Well, I'm a male. I'd hate to disappoint."

"Come on," Shona cajoled. "Tell me all."

Moran wondered later how long it had been since he'd opened up so much to someone. It all poured out: his childhood, his father's alcoholism, his brother's accidental death, his engagement to Janice, the bomb...

"And you were happy?" Shona asked when he had finished. "With Janice, I mean?"

"Very," he said. "We fitted, hand in glove. It was just like that. A rare thing."

"Yes."

They fell silent for a while, but presently Shona spoke again, rousing him from the edge of sleep.

"Brendan?"

"Uh huh?"

"Don't you sometimes *ache* for the past? You know, for those days when everything was–"

"Uncomplicated?" He mulled the question over. The youthful years, when Janice was still alive. When his heart was free.

After a while he said, "I do, yes. But I can't allow the yearning to get in the way of the here and now. If I did, it would drive me mad."

Shona snuggled closer. "That's what I thought you'd say. You're a survivor, like me."

"More sinner than survivor."

"Hmmm. Same, I suppose. I used to be such a good girl, too. I don't suppose the church would have me back now."

"Does that bother you?" Moran mumbled sleepily.

"Sometimes. When I'm feeling guilty."

Moran's eyelids grew heavy. When he stirred much later to the gentle sound of the dawn chorus, she was gone.

Later still, the phone was ringing, shrilly and insistently. Moran's eyes opened slowly. The last thing he remembered was birdsong. *Damn.* He'd intended to get up no later than six. He reached for the phone.

"Moran."

"Guv. It's DI Pepper. I thought you'd want to know that we have a name for the Audi owner. It's Ranandan,

Ms Jaseena Ranandan. A physiotherapist and freelance chiropractor.

"Ranandan? You're sure? Do we have an address?"

"Yes, guv. Up by the Uni."

"With you as soon as."

He brewed a quick coffee, grabbed a banana and left, locking the door carefully behind him.

The house was unprepossessing, a typical Victorian semi in a well-to-do area of Reading near the University. Moran parked and turned to Charlie Pepper.

"Nice and steady, Charlie. The last thing I want to do is get anyone rattled. Gently does it, and we'll see what she has to say for herself."

"Right you are, guv." Charlie unclipped her seatbelt and nodded briskly. Moran caught a brief glimpse of her shapely legs as she got out. Very attractive indeed. But then, so was Shona...

As they walked up the drive Moran scolded himself. *Concentrate on the job, Brendan.* It was a tough call. Last night felt like a dream – a very pleasant one, for sure, but where it would lead was another story. No relationship was going to be straightforward given his history. He doubted whether he had it in him to even consider anything long-term. *One step at a time, Brendan...*

"No shortage of money here, guv," Charlie observed, taking in the size of the house and the two cars parked outside the double garage – the first a BMW, the second a sporty Mercedes.

"Indeed not." Moran rapped on the door knocker. "But no Audi."

The door was opened by a young Asian in his early thirties. Moran showed his ID.

145

"Good morning. We'd like to speak to a Ms Jaseena Ranandan, if that's possible?"

A guarded look appeared on the man's face. "My cousin. She's not here."

"Where might we find her?" Moran asked in a reasonable tone.

"She's in India."

"I see. When is she expected back?"

The man shrugged. "I don't know. She might not come back."

"Oh? Why is that?"

Another shrug. "She might stay in Mumbai. We have family there."

Moran tried another tack. "I understand she was practising as a physiotherapist?"

"Something like that."

"Could you tell me where she practised?"

"I don't know. I never went there."

"Never?"

"No."

"Do you have the address? Of the practice?"

"Wait."

The man disappeared. Charlie gave Moran a quizzical look. They heard voices from inside the house. The man reappeared.

"No. We don't know where it was."

Moran frowned. "How odd. Perhaps we need to have a longer chat. May we come in?" he made as if to step over the threshold.

The man didn't move, blocking the doorway. "We're going out now. It's not convenient."

"Well then, I wonder if you can tell me what your cousin did with her car when she left the country?

Perhaps it's garaged? Or maybe you're looking after it for her?"

"I don't know anything about her car. It's her business."

Charlie spoke up. "When did she go to India?"

"Couple of weeks ago."

"May we have the Mumbai address?" Charlie asked sweetly.

The man's face darkened. He disappeared again and returned with a slip of paper. "Here."

Moran took it. "I'd like to come back for a proper chat, Mr–?"

"Kumar."

"First names?"

"Atul."

"And when would be convenient?" Charlie asked.

"Saturday, maybe."

Moran shook his head. "I'm afraid that won't do. We're investigating a murder."

"A murder?" Now the face was animated. He took a step forward. "Has anything happened to Jas?"

"You told us she was in India, Mr Kumar," Charlie said. "With her family."

"Yeah, but, you know. We're family. I like to keep tabs. What's Jas got to do with all this?"

"That's what we're trying to establish, Mr Kumar." Moran said reasonably. "We just want to rule her out of the investigation."

"I'm in tonight."

"Good. Half past six, then."

The door closed.

As they walked back to the car, Moran felt the first stirrings of optimism. Mr Kumar was hiding something, that was clear, but something told Moran that when they came knocking at half past six they'd find that their bird had flown.

He voiced his thoughts. "Rob Phelps and I spoke to a girl called Zoë at The Zodiac club. She told us that the man DC Hill wanted to speak to went by the name of Rana, or Ranandan. Sound familiar?"

"Jaseena's surname."

"Right. I have to nip up to the hospital now, unfortunately. It's a two-minute walk. I'd like you to stick around and wait for Mr 'Kumar' to go walkabout. It won't be long. Keep tabs on him, and keep me informed. I'll get Banner to pick me up from the RBH when I'm done."

"Will do, guv. Are you sure I can't give you a lift?"

Moran shook his head. "I might look like a geriatric, DI Pepper, but I'm not so decrepit that I can't manage a two minute walk. Besides," he added, "I wouldn't want you to miss Mr Kumar's exit."

Moran put his head around the door of the side ward and found that he'd picked the right one. Sergeant Phelps was propped on a tower of pillows, tubed and wired up to all manner of machines and monitors. His eyes were closed and his face was a pale, yellowish colour, an effect not enhanced by the sheen of sweat glistening on his cheeks and forehead. Phelps' unshaven chin was blue with stubble. He looked awful. Moran took a breath and dug deep to find his cheerful hospital visitor alter ego.

"Hello, Robert. I won't ask how you're feeling on the grounds that you might hit me."

Phelps opened his eyes and managed a weak grin. "I couldn't hit a bloody paper bag at the moment," he said. "You're safe to abuse at will, guv."

Moran found a chair and pulled it alongside the bed. "Very inconvenient time to go sick, Sergeant." His tongue was firmly in his cheek. "But I have to say that your stand-in is rather attractive, so it's not all bad."

Phelps grunted. "Silver linings abound, guv. Everyone's entitled to one now and again."

"I'll make the most of it, then," Moran chuckled.

"Do that. I'll be back before you know it."

Moran shook his head. "You're not coming anywhere near work until you're one hundred per cent. And that's going to take a while."

"You sound like my doctor."

"Well, it makes a change from you going on at me all the time. Allow me my revenge."

Phelps laughed and finished with a bout of coughing. A nurse breezed in, collected several items from the table and went out. Phelps rolled his eyes.

"No peace in here. Day and night, it never stops. Tablet here, injection there. I feel like a sodding pincushion."

"You'll be home soon enough," Moran sympathised. If Phelps hated hospitals half as much as he did, he'd have to be a very unhappy bunny indeed. "Family been in?"

"Yep. They've been great. The boys think all this gear is 'well cool'." Phelps described a sweeping motion with his arm, taking in the buzzing and beeping machines. "Jane's been brilliant. Keeping her pecker up, you know?"

Moran nodded. "If I know Jane, she'll have everything well under control."

"Including me, if I ever get out of this place."

"You will. All in good time."

Moran pushed his chair back as a dinner lady wheeled a trolley into the room. She plonked a tray on the side table and clattered away. The smell of cabbage permeated the room.

"Smells like the Charnford kitchens." Moran sniffed and wrinkled his nose. "Remember?"

"How could I forget?"

Moran paused. "Robert, I'm sorry to talk shop, but I have to ask. Did you manage to talk to anyone at OCG?"

"Yep. I spoke to an old mate. He told me that Sheldrake and his DS were ... well, you know, pretty close."

"Oh yes?"

"He's a married man. She's a single girl."

"A bit spiky, I've been told."

"That's an understatement. She's the archetypal pain in the butt. Good copper, though."

"Right," Moran said thoughtfully. "Anything else?"

"My mate said he'd keep a weather ear open for us. His name's DS Chris Newland. Good bloke. If you ever need an extra DS, he's your man."

"OK, Robert. Thanks. Listen, I'll leave you to your cordon bleu. I've got an appointment up the corridor."

Phelps took a wheezy breath and raised a betubed hand. "Bloody old crocks, the pair of us."

"What music would you like?" the receptionist asked with a weary 'I've done this a hundred times today already' air about her.

"Music?" Moran was perplexed. "What, during the scan?"

"Yes," she replied. "The machine makes a lot of noise. It'll help relax you."

"I see." He thumbed through the proffered catalogue. "Not much I like here," he told her honestly.

"Well, you'll have to pick something."

"OK. I'll go for Enya."

She snatched the booklet from him. "Number 35? Fine. Take a seat."

As Moran waited he found himself wondering for the first time what he would do if the scan picked up anything amiss. Like a tumour, or brain cancer, or–

"Mr Moran?"

A white-coated medic was standing over him with a clipboard. He followed her into the scanning room.

"Done this before?"

"No."

"Nothing to worry about." She smiled brightly. "Bit noisy, but pay no attention. Try to relax and think about something else."

"Right."

"Take off your watch, please, and the chain around your neck."

Moran removed his watch, chain and crucifix as bidden.

"Lie down. Here are the headphones. Keep your finger on this button. If you feel uncomfortable, just press it and I'll stop the scan. OK?"

"Terrific." Moran lay back and the scanner lid slid over him. He felt as though he was being buried alive. The feeling was compounded when the angelic, ethereal voice of Enya began to filter through his headphones.

Moran began to wish he'd chosen Springsteen or even Led Zeppelin as alternatives, either of whom would have provided some earthy reassurance that he was still alive.

The machine began to bang and clatter as the scan progressed. 'A bit noisy' was proving to be an understatement. He tried to ignore the racket, instead turning his thoughts to Atul Kumar. The young man had clearly been rattled at the mention of murder, immediately concerned for his cousin, and yet he had told them that she was visiting relatives in India. Moran had a pretty good idea which physio practice Jaseena Ranandan had worked for; Mr Suri would be receiving a rather more thorough interrogation at the first opportunity.

As the scan progressed, and despite the random banging of the machine, Moran found himself dozing. He dreamed that he was lying in a graveyard, in an open coffin. Faces looked down at him: Shona, black-veiled and tearful, Phelps, dark-suited and sober, DI Pepper, strangely clad in a long evening gown. He felt the gentle sprinkle of rain on his face. The coffin lid closed abruptly and clods of earth began to thump on the lid. He couldn't push it open; it was stuck fast. Somewhere in the distance he heard the mourners singing a familiar hymn. *Now thank we all our God, with hearts and hands and voices...*

Moran woke with a stifled cry.

"All finished, Mr Moran." The scanner lid opened and the operator leaned over him with a smile. "Up you get. Don't forget your watch and chain."

Moran blinked and gratefully clambered to his feet. Mumbling a quick thanks to the scanning technician he made a hurried exit through the clinic doors, back to the land of the living.

Chapter Seventeen

The Kafir sipped a lemon tea and folded his newspaper. He wanted to feel the satisfaction he had so keenly anticipated, but instead he felt only a gnawing sense of unease. He had been so careful. He had taken all possible precautions, and yet he was quite sure that he had been followed. But by whom? Certainly not a policeman. They were nowhere near working out what was going on, he was quite sure of that as well. Someone was playing a very dangerous game – but who? And why?

He had of course considered the possibility that it was *them*, Jag and Atul, but if they had known where to find him they would have confronted him by now. No, this was more sinister, as if someone was playing cat and mouse, keeping just out of sight but nevertheless following his every move. The Kafir was deeply unsettled. He had to deal with this proactively, and soon.

He went to his kitchenette and reboiled the kettle, pondering his options as he waited for the water to cool. The temperature had to be just right for lemon tea, not too hot, not too cold.

When he had made and tested the tea to his satisfaction he went to the window and looked out at the river. The sun blazed in an empty sky. The newspapers were comparing it to the summer of seventy-six, when the heat wave had lasted all summer until the weather finally broke over the Reading Rock Festival weekend. A few boats were lazily moving up and down river and the larger shape of the Caversham Princess, the popular pleasure cruiser, was moored at its usual point of departure by the rowing club boathouse. People were in a holiday mood, making the most of the weather. *The pitiful, sad nobodies.*

The Kafir finished his tea and sat down cross-legged in the centre of the room. He needed to decide on the best way forward. If this *follower* knew what he had done, he would never be safe. It was time to turn the tables – and, whoever his stalker might be, they were going to regret their actions for the rest of their lives, a period of time he intended to make as short as he possibly could.

Had he forgotten to lock his front door last night? Moran racked his brains as he drove across town to his delayed appointment with Suri, the physiotherapist. *Maybe I am going nuts...* Moran was a careful man – not pedantic, but he liked things in order. He couldn't remember a previous occasion when he had failed to secure his house.

So what did that mean? Had Shona broken in? Ridiculous. The door had been unlocked, not forced. She had arrived to find it ajar, which explained why Archie had gone walkabout. Why would she want to break in, anyway?

After last night, however, Moran found he could forgive her almost anything. He put his worry on hold for a moment, savouring the recollection. Then he frowned; the door incident was still a niggle, especially taking into account that anonymous note.

The prime suspect was, of course, Gregory Neads; after all, he had delivered a direct threat. Moran didn't believe Neads capable of any real harm, though.

Harassment and mischief, perhaps, but not to the extent that he would plan some injurious revenge.

Moran overtook a dawdling Nissan and put his foot down, half tempted to switch the squad car's blue light on. That'd get the idle dawdlers out of his way. *Damn holiday traffic...*

Despite Moran's best efforts to think of other things, the problem of Gregory Neads lingered in his mind for the rest of the journey. He could still see Neads' twisted expression, hear the bitterness in his voice: *Watch your back, Moran...*

He shook his head, as if by doing so he could clear some space to think. He had enough mental balls up in the air at the moment without Neads troubling him as well, but he couldn't help the nagging feeling that he was missing something important.

Mr Suri was at the reception desk when Moran walked in. As he glanced up his expression clouded.

"Inspector Moran. I was expecting you yesterday evening."

"Something came up. But I'd like to have that chat now, if you have a few minutes?"

"Certainly, Inspector."

Moran was led once more into Suri's office. When they were seated Moran asked if the receptionist had recognised the man portrayed in the Photofit.

Suri spread his hands. "Unfortunately not."

"Have you ever employed someone by the name of Jaseena Ranandan?"

Suri frowned. "No, not to my knowledge."

"And how long have you worked here?"

"For five years now, since the practice opened."

"I see." Moran studied Suri's face. Was he lying? If he was, he was good at it; there was no trace of discomfort, no tell-tale beads of sweat on his forehead. The smile was easy, unwavering.

"May I see your employer records?"

A slight hesitation. "I will need to consult the administration manager. She is away this morning."

"But as the practice head you must know where they are kept, surely?"

"Indeed." Suri smiled again and Moran was struck once more by the perfect alignment of his teeth. "But Vina has the key to the filing cabinet."

"And you don't have a spare, in case Vina is off sick?" Moran asked, keeping the irritation out of his tone with difficulty.

Suri frowned. "Perhaps Barinder has a set. One moment."

Moran waited patiently. After a minute or so, Suri bustled back into the office. "I'm sorry, Inspector. It is a shortcoming, I'm afraid."

"When will the information be available?"

"When Vina returns from our other clinic." He consulted his watch. "I expect by midday."

"You have another clinic?" Moran raised his eyebrows.

"The chiropractic clinic, yes. Vina works between the two, but for practical day-to-day business we run pretty independently."

"I see. Why didn't you mention this before?"

Suri shrugged. "I am sorry; I did not think it important."

"Could the chiropractic clinic have employed someone called Jaseena Ranandan?"

Suri pursed his lips and leaned forward, resting his arms on the polished walnut. "I cannot be certain, Inspector. I have few dealings with the other clinic – only in terms of the administration, budgets and so on, rather than individual employees, if you understand me. They have had quite a high turnover in the last year or so, that is all I can say. Freelance staff come and go. You will need to speak to Mr Virjii, the senior partner."

"Address?"

Suri opened a drawer and passed a card across the desk. Moran thanked him and took his leave.

The thing about surveillance was that you could never afford to relax. Take a breather, stretch your legs, doze off for a minute and you could miss *the* significant incident, the moment that cracks the case wide open.

Charlie Pepper knew all about the boredom of surveillance work. Been there, seen it, done it, got the T-shirt – and the stickers, poster and mug to boot. That's just how it was: nine tenths mind-numbing boredom, one tenth adrenaline rush and action. Right now she was somewhere at the wrong end of the tenths scale.

She looked at her watch. Half past four. She'd been stuck here for hours, and so far nothing. Moran had called her at lunchtime, not that she'd been able to eat anything. There was a deli just down the road, but she knew that if she succumbed she would run the risk of missing the moment Atul Kumar decided to make a move. The guv was on his way to a chiropractic clinic in the hope that he could find out something more about Jaseena Ranandan before they knocked on her cousin's door a second time. If Mr Kumar was indeed her cousin.

Charlie sighed. *The glamour of detective work, eh Charlie?* Still, she was content enough with her new posting. Moran seemed like a good guy, and the rest of the team were friendly enough – except maybe DS Banner, but she'd win him round in the end. She wondered how her old team in Coventry were doing. Her promotion had been hard-won over five eventful years. She'd earned her stripes and got her DI after another two. Sure, she missed her old mates, but it had been time to move on. She had no ties in Cov. Her last relationship had ended a year ago, by her decision. So it was time to start afresh.

It *felt* right to be here in Berkshire. Reading itself wasn't much to write home about, but Helen had promised to show her the countryside and she was looking forward to sampling those Tolkienesque pubs she'd heard so much about. She'd also been up to London with a friend, Anna, and an Oxford Street shopping trip was already planned for the summer plus another outing to the West End to catch a show. Maybe she could invite Helen as well; her new colleague looked like she could do with a bit of nightlife. Charlie smiled to herself. For the short time she'd flat-shared with Anna it had felt like she was on some kind of extended holiday and it was only when she'd moved into her own place and fallen ill that reality had kicked in.

At that moment the front door opened and Atul emerged, followed by another young man of similar age and build. They got into the BMW and reversed out of the drive in a style that wouldn't have pleased a driving instructor. Charlie waited until the car had sped past and then gunned her engine and swung the car in a wide U-turn. She just caught sight of the Beamer as it made a left turn onto the main road by the hospital. Charlie settled into gear three cars back and kept her eyes fixed on the speeding vehicle.

Which way were they headed? *Not into town*, she muttered to herself, as they continued along the London road towards Southcote. Charlie wound her window down in an effort to cool the car interior; the aircon was rubbish. But then it was an old police vehicle, so what did she expect? TVP's budget was clearly as limited as West Midlands'. DCI Moran, she deduced, wasn't much of a petrol head.

The BMW hurtled onto the Bath road and continued west. By the time they reached the Theale roundabout and turned off to the right Charlie's limited knowledge of the local geography was beginning to fail. Up until now she had always had Anna in the car with her, so she hadn't paid a lot of attention to where she was going.

On they sped through villages Charlie had neither heard of nor visited: Tidmarsh, Pangbourne, across a quaint toll bridge for which Charlie had to ransack Moran's glove box for the forty pence toll, on into the middle of nowhere and a world of twisting, narrow country lanes delimited by tall hedgerows. She held her breath as the BMW slowed, thinking she'd been spotted, but it was only a horse and rider up ahead, languidly waving the traffic on. There was now a blue Transit between them so she was comfortable that the two men were still oblivious to their tail.

A few minutes later the Beamer turned off onto a raised farm track and disappeared. Charlie found a suitable spot on the verge which wouldn't obstruct the sparse traffic that was likely to pass by, and wondered whether to put in a call to Moran. Deciding against interrupting her new guv's appointment, Charlie got out and walked cautiously up the track, keeping close to the hedge.

The rutted ground was baked hard beneath her soles and she stumbled once or twice before the track flattened out and she found herself alongside what appeared to be a collection of farm outhouses. Several cars were parked in a line by a wire and wood fence, one of which was the BMW.

The outhouses formed the perimeter of a yard; empty save for a raised shed-like structure in the farthest corner. Even with her limited knowledge of farming Charlie recognised the building as a granary, differentiated from the other buildings by the six mushroom-like stone supports upon which it squatted. It was from within this building that Charlie could hear the sound of raised voices.

She crept forward, alert for any sign of movement from the adjacent buildings. Now she could see that the farmhouse was hidden away behind another hedgerow to her right. Next to the house a painted sign advertised fresh farm eggs. As she reached the granary she could see the hens' coop and wire enclosure to the farmhouse's left.

Somewhere close by a diesel engine fired, missed and fired again. Charlie's heart also missed and fired again. Not a car or a lorry ... a tractor eased slowly into view. It must have been tucked in behind the farm drive. Another metre and the driver would see her.

She moved quickly around to the back of the granary. A wooden ramp led up the side of the building past an open window which looked out onto open fields beyond.

The tractor crawled away along the path Charlie had just walked up. As the engine noise faded she heard voices again, but she could hear them clearly now because she was crouched just below the line of the window. A female was speaking, interrupted every so often by a male voice Charlie recognised as belonging to Atul. At each interruption the woman simply railroaded through until Atul was bludgeoned into silence again.

"I've told you. It's sorted. There's nothing to get het up about." The woman's voice was getting louder, and Charlie realised she must be standing right beside the window. Charlie flattened herself against the woodwork and prayed that she was out of the woman's line of vision.

"How can it be sorted if the cops have just come knocking?" Another voice, deeper and with a more pronounced accent.

"Will you just shut up and listen to what I'm telling you?" The woman again. Charlie pressed her ear to the woodwork. "Tonight is bust night. After that you'll be off the hook."

The second man responded. "We wouldn't have been on the hook in the first place if you'd done your job properly. And what about the two snoopers at the Zodiac? How much does this new copper know already? It's getting messy."

"The mess will be cleaned and bagged by tomorrow morning. They don't know anything."

"You'd better be right," Atul said. "What are we supposed to tell them when they come with their questions and all that?"

"Make sure you're not around when they come, you retard. Think you can manage that?"

A pause, and then Atul started up again; this time Charlie could hear the fear and anger in his tone. "And what about Jay, huh? Who did for him? The police don't know. *You* don't know. Someone did this thing, and how do we know they are not coming for us next?"

"It's probably just random. Nothing to do with you." The woman spoke dismissively.

"Nothing to do? He is family. And so was Anoop. OK, not close, but still family. Two killed. It cannot be coincidence. Random is rubbish."

"You told me you knew who it was. Jaseena's mental boyfriend."

The deep voice broke in. The owner sounded calmer, more self-assured. "OK. It *might* be him. But he has bloody disappeared."

"We should have made sure of him the first time," Atul said miserably. "Finished the job properly."

"We don't *know* it's him," deep voice said patiently. "It could be any bugger, who knows? We must be careful, right? Not jumping to conclusions all the time."

"Right." Atul reluctantly deferred to the other man's due care and diligence policy.

This seemed to close the subject and the conversation moved on to topics Charlie couldn't get a handle on. She made a note of a few names that cropped up and was considering making a cautious withdrawal when the granary door opened and someone came out. She moved quickly out of sight as footsteps clattered down the ramp. *Don't come this way...* Charlie prayed, holding her breath.

The footsteps receded and she risked a peep round the corner. The woman was walking briskly towards the farmhouse. She was of medium build with fair hair gathered into a loose ponytail, casually dressed in jeans and yellow T-shirt. Charlie craned her neck to catch a glimpse of her face as the woman reached the farmhouse gate but she was too far away to get any detailed impression. Inside the granary Atul and his friend were arguing again, but this time in their native language.

That's enough for now, girl ... time to be off...

Charlie felt her shoulders tingle as she made a dash across the yard towards the path. When she reached her car she realised how tense she had been. Her shoulders slumped with relief and there were dark wet patches under her arms. She realised that she was gripping the steering wheel like a lifebuoy, and breathing deeply, she gave herself a minute to let the tension ease.

When her breathing had returned to something approaching normal she retrieved her mobile and dialled Moran's number. Nothing. Then she noticed the network display read 'No Service'. Great. Now what? *Back to base, Charlie.* She had to let Moran know about this, and pronto.

In her haste she fumbled and dropped the keys. Charlie muttered a mildly rude word and eased her fingers gently between the seat's plastic trim and the gearbox. *Gotcha.*

She straightened up and her heart missed a beat. A misshapen face was peering in at her through the driver's window, and it didn't look friendly.

Chapter Eighteen

Another blank, Moran thought, turning the car into the HQ car park. Not that he believed what he'd been told, but he was frustrated that he had yet to find an excuse to search the premises. The chiro practice's senior partner had never heard of Jaseena Ranandan, or so he said.

The receptionist, a young girl called Nalini, had kept her head down while the conversation was in progress. On his way out he had smiled and thanked her. Was it his imagination, or had he seen fear in the tightness of her expression, the strain of knowing that something was being withheld but being powerless to do anything about it? He would have to think of a way of enticing her to share that knowledge – maybe find someone to get alongside her and put a reassuring arm around her shoulders.

Moran was confident he had someone to fit that particular bill, but time was short and he also wanted to reinterview the Slough family, Jay Dass' parents. Banner had had a feeling they were holding out on something.

He turned off the ignition and sat quietly, listening to the engine cool and tick. After an afternoon in the caned squad car Moran was looking forward to being reunited with his old Rover 75. Which reminded him; Charlie Pepper hadn't been in touch. He checked his mobile again. No missed calls. He dialled her number, but it went straight to voicemail. No matter; he was sure she'd call when she had something to report.

He found DS Banner and DC McKellar deep in conversation around Banner's PC.

"Ah, guv. Glad you're here." The sergeant looked up and cocked his head as Moran approached.

"Glad to see you awake, sergeant." Moran pulled up a chair. "What have you got?"

"Take a look. The boffins have cleaned up the forecourt film, given us a lot more clarity."

Moran squinted at the screen. He recognised the Tilehurst garage forecourt. Two vehicles were filling up, and the closest was an Audi. Moran pointed. "That the one?"

Helen McKellar nodded. "Look at the back end of the car."

Moran leaned in closer. "It's moving."

And it was. The Audi rear suspension was minutely but visibly bouncing, as if someone was pushing the rear of the car up and down.

Or if someone trapped in the boot was struggling to break free...

"Reed-Purvis," Moran said quietly. He felt a lump in his throat. It was one thing dealing with the death of a colleague after the event, but quite another watching their last moments on film. "That settles it. We have to find this Audi. *Now.* DC McKellar, you come with me. Banner, see if you can get hold of DI Pepper. She's staking out a house in Earley, or she was a few hours ago. Keep me posted."

"Guv."

Moran felt a fresh determination. He was close, very close. The chiro clinic was the key, he was sure of it.

"What's the plan, guv?" Helen McKellar asked as she trotted along in Moran's slipstream.

"We wait for a young lady called Nalini to leave work for the day. You have a little chat with her; see what she has to say. If all else fails, it's over to me."

"To do what, guv?" Helen frowned as Moran unlocked the car.

"To scare her to death," Moran replied grimly. "Let's hope it doesn't come to that, eh?"

"Hello. Can I have a quick word?" Helen tried to make her voice unthreatening. "My name is DC McKellar. You spoke to my boss this morning – DCI Moran?"

The girl slowed but didn't stop. "What about?" She frowned. "I answered all the questions."

They were a few metres from the bus stop where a line of silently perspiring workers waited for their transport home. Nalini was clearly on her way to join them. Moran had parked at the side of the road, far enough away not to be visible from the clinic, and Helen could see him impatiently tapping his fingers on the steering wheel.

"It's very important," Helen told her. "You know that we're investigating a murder?"

"Yes." The girl glanced anxiously up the road where a double-decker had just come into view. "I'm sorry, it's my bus. I have to go."

Helen opted for a direct approach. "Do you know Jaseena?" she asked, watching carefully for the reaction.

Nalini's eyes went to the pavement and she shook her head vehemently. "I don't know her. I told your friend already."

"Nalini." Helen caught hold of the girl's shoulder and stopped her in her tracks. "You're scared. I understand. I won't let anything happen to you, OK? I won't tell anyone you've told me. I promise." Helen injected her voice with as much sympathy and persuasiveness as she could muster.

Nalini searched Helen's face, weighing up her words.

"You *do* know Jaseena, don't you?" Helen said. "You're worried about her, aren't you?"

Nalini bit her lip and lowered her head. When she looked up again Helen could see moisture in her brown eyes. Imperceptibly she shook her head. "Yes. I am worried."

Elated, Helen put her arm around the girl and guided her towards the car. "Tell us what you're worried about, and we'll give you a lift home, OK?"

The girl nodded and allowed herself to be led away. Helen felt her heart beating with excitement. The guv had been right. They were one step closer.

"She is my friend." Nalini said quietly. "Always helpful for me. I have only been in the UK a few months. She found me a place to live, where to get what I needed. Always kind. But she was unhappy, I knew."

"Why was she unhappy, Nalini?" Helen asked gently. Moran sat quietly and listened. No need to butt in for now; Helen was doing fine. He let his eyes wander around the tiny bedsit. Not much of a place for a young girl to make a life for herself, but then he found himself wondering what sort of life she had left behind.

Nalini looked down at her hands. "Her family. They were always a problem for her."

"In what way?" Helen prompted.

"She had a friend. A man. She liked him so much. But he was not like them. Like us."

"Did you meet this man?"

Nalini nodded. "Yes. He used to come to the clinic to meet her. Mr Virjii was not happy about it. He told her brothers." She looked up and combed her hair nervously with her fingers. "She lived with them, you see."

"And their names are?"

"Atul. And–" Nalini hesitated, her eyes darting from side to side as if satisfying herself that no one was within earshot. "Jagdip," she whispered the name so quietly Moran opened his mouth to ask her to say it again then thought better of it. *Zip up, Brendan. So far so good...*

"I take it the brothers disapproved of this man? Of their sister having a relationship with him?"

Nalini nodded. "They were angry. Used to come here and shout. One day the man was here, and they fought. They threw him out. It was horrible. Mr Virjii was also very angry with Jagdip for causing such a bad thing at the clinic."

"And what was Jaseena's boyfriend's name, Nalini?"

"It was Simon, I think. I don't know his last name. I'm sorry."

"That's OK," Helen smiled. "You're being very helpful. Can you tell us when Jaseena went back to India? Did she leave suddenly?"

Nalini chewed her lip. "She didn't say anything to me. But we had arranged to do some cooking together. It was two weeks ago, and she never came to work that morning. No one will tell me where she is, but I don't think they know."

Helen frowned. "Who doesn't know? Mr Virjii?"

"And Jagdip. He came here looking for her. Mr Virjii refused to let him into the clinic. There was a lot of shouting again." Nalini began to sob, covering her face with her hands.

Helen gave Moran a look. Atul had told them Jaseena was in Mumbai. Lie number two following lie number one. Not cousins, brother and sister.

Helen took Nalini's hand. "So, what you're saying is that she just disappeared?"

Nalini nodded. "I miss her. I'm worried that something has happened, but I'm not allowed to say anything."

"Mr Virjii told you to keep quiet?"

Nalini shook her head. "No. Jagdip. He came here and said if I told anyone he would kill me. He didn't want anyone else to know he was looking for her." Nalini began to cry again and Helen shot Moran a look which said, 'Leave this with me for a bit'.

Moran took the cue and went outside. He dialled Charlie Pepper's number and cursed under his breath as it went to voicemail again. *Come on, Pepper. Where are you?* Moran rapped his stick on the pavement in frustration; he wanted to be sure the chameleon-like Jagdip Ranandan – or Kumar, or Rana – was at home when he came calling.

Chapter Nineteen

DI Charlie Pepper wasn't the kind of girl who scared easily. At least, she hadn't thought she was. She supposed it was an indication of how keyed up she'd been that she'd nearly jumped through the car roof when the llama had poked its head through the window.

A herd of escaped llamas wasn't the sort of eventuality she'd been prepared for, but the harassed farmhand had been pleasantly apologetic, explaining that a badly managed re-fencing project had given the herd the opportunity to explore pastures new. Still, her fright had been worthwhile in that she now knew who owned the farm and the surrounding land; it belonged to the Elm Grove Estate, a sprawling chunk of Thameside England owned by one Lord and Lady Emerson. Good landowners, the farmhand had told her, but they had their work cut out to maintain the estate in these days of austerity. Many of the buildings on and around the farm were rented to private tenants. It was all managed by the Estate Office – and yes, he could give Charlie their number.

All in all, not a bad afternoon's work, Charlie thought to herself as she followed the signs to Pangbourne and found herself back at the toll bridge. Her mobile played the first few notes of 'Postcards from a Young Man' by her favourite band, the Manic Street Preachers, which she interrupted with a brief tap on the iPhone's loudspeaker icon.

"DI Pepper."

"At last. Where have you been?" Moran's Irish lilt was laced with irritation.

"Long story, guv. Good news, though. The Kumars aren't at home, but I know where they are."

"Not Kumars, nor Jaseena's cousins either, DI Pepper. Brothers. Atul and Jagdip Ranandan. So, where are they?"

Charlie briefed Moran and was told to get back to the squad room asap. He sounded different, and Charlie guessed why. She'd got used to recognising the vibe; it was an indefinable thing but unmistakeable nevertheless. You could hear it in a colleague's voice, or just feel it in the air – that moment when a case finally begins to open up and reveal its secrets. Charlie put her foot down; no way was she going to miss any of the action...

It was almost time. Simon Peters rinsed his face and inspected his reflection. The Kafir returned his gaze. A confident, assured young man, With a strong chin, dark brown eyes and an intelligent brow. Perhaps a touch of Slavic ancestry?

The Kafir brushed his hair and wondered whether he ought to visit the barber. No. He rather liked his change of image. He had transformed himself from lean and smartly-presented professional to rakish, arty bohemian. He laughed aloud at the thought. But then the mirror shifted and blurred and Jag Ranandan's mocking face appeared right in front of him, grinning, shaking his head dismissively. The Kafir smashed his fist into the bastard's face. Shards of glass splintered and fell, tinkling into the basin. Blood dripped freely down the tiles.

The Kafir felt no pain. It was time. Time to pay back Jag Ranandan for what he had done.

He felt a sudden certainty that he was being watched. Had the mirror been a warning? Had Ranandan come for him? The Kafir went into his living room, fists raised, bloodied knuckles leaving a spotted trail on the carpet. No one. But he could *feel* a presence.

"Who are you?" he shouted. "Show me who you *are...*" His head thumped with a steady, pulsing beat. He went from room to room – kitchen, living room, bathroom. His flat was empty.

But he knew he was not alone.

"OK. This is what we know." Moran ticked off the first point on his forefinger. The congregated officers in the squad room fell silent.

"Number one. The murder of DS Reed-Purvis is forensically linked to an Audi which we need to trace as a matter of urgency. Number two. The owner of this vehicle, a Ms Jaseena Ranandan, is missing. Number three. She is linked to a chiropractic clinic, which in turn is linked to a business card found in the Chalvey Merc. Tenuous, maybe, but a link nevertheless. Number four. DI Pepper has identified that Ms Ranandan's brothers are up to no good, and I have a pretty good idea what that is. We also know that there is a connection with a farm on the Emerson estate."

One of the officers gave a low whistle.

"Yes, *the* Emerson estate. But the farm buildings are privately let, so it doesn't necessarily mean that the estate owners are aware of – or responsible for – any dirty dealings, whatever they may be."

"There's something else too" Moran went to the whiteboard and hovered his marker over Helen's neat diagrams representing the Zodiac, the Chalvey house and Jaseena's registered address. "DC Hill was given the name 'Jag' – or at least someone of this name was pointed out to him by the bar staff at the Zodiac." He drew a connecting line between Chalvey and Jaseena's house. "Earlier we met a young man at this address who identified himself as Atul Kumar and told us that Jaseena was his cousin. We've since checked the registration of the car parked in Mr Kumar's drive, and the DVLA confirms that it's registered to one Jagdip Ranandan." He paused to let it all sink in.

Moran stepped back a pace. "Right. Charlie, can you give us a quick rundown on your farm outing?"

They listened in silence as Charlie recounted the conversation she had overheard in the granary. When she had finished, Helen McKellar raised her hand.

"What sort of bust do you think they were talking about? It sounds druggie all right."

"It does." Charlie shrugged. "But when, where and what are questions we can't answer right now."

"Banner's good with drugs," someone said in a low voice.

"Only if he's got time to sleep them off." Another officer grinned at Banner's discomfort.

"OK, that's enough." Moran raised his arm. "Action plan. Number one, we pay Mr and Mrs Dass a visit. I'll take that. Number two, we stake out the farm and keep a close eye on developments. DS Banner, perhaps you or Helen can deal with that? Number three, we bring the

Ranandan brothers in for questioning. Charlie and I will conduct the interview. For the rest of you, it's all hands on deck to find that Audi. Any questions?"

"Any news from forensics on the St James' murder, guv?" Helen asked.

"Somehow I have to fit in Father Jeffries' autopsy this evening." Moran passed his hand wearily across his forehead. "I'm sure Dr Bagri will come up trumps for us. He usually does. He'd better, or Airey's going to take me to the cleaners when he gets back."

"Still think it's related, guv?" DS Banner asked as the team disbanded noisily.

Moran leaned on the nearest desk and cast his eye over the whiteboard for the umpteenth time. Four deaths, two suspects, a missing car, a missing woman, a fatal RTA and a forensically unforthcoming house in Chalvey. Moran suddenly felt overcome with exhaustion.

"I don't know, DS Banner. I just don't know."

"It's good of you to see me, Mr Dass." Moran followed the tall Indian into a large family room which was occupied by two young girls Moran guessed to be in their twenties, one comforting a crying toddler, the other laying plates on a wide dining table. The peaceful domestic scene was presided over by a smiling old lady seated in a brightly patterned armchair.

"My nieces, Daksha and Seema," Mr Dass beamed. "My nephew, Rajeev. And my mother." He bowed formally to the old lady. "This is Chief Inspector Moran. He has come to ask us about our poor boy. Do have a seat, Inspector."

Moran cleared his throat as Mr Dass fought back tears. "Thank you," Moran said. "I won't intrude on your time for very long."

"Anything which will help find out who did this terrible thing, I am happy to speak to you about," Mr Dass said, bringing himself under control. "My mother has persuaded me that I must tell you everything we know which may help you. When your Sergeant Banner came before I was reticent, but this I now realise was wrong. Mother's wisdom shall prevail." Mr Dass' mother inclined her head and made a quiet noise of affirmation. Mr Dass went to her side and she took his hand, squeezing it gently, reassuring her son. Moran was moved by this display of support and affection; to hide his discomposure he allowed himself to be distracted by the toddler at his feet, bent to accept a toy train the boy was holding up for inspection.

"Ah, a train fan just like me. The best toys are the traditional ones, eh?" Moran smiled and patted the boy's head.

"True," Mr Dass said. "And we are a traditional family. We try to do things right, don't we, Navpreet?" He stiffened with pride as an attractive lady in her late forties entered bearing two trays of food.

"Daksha, will you help me bring in the tea?" Mrs Dass gestured and the young girl followed her meekly out of the room, returning a few seconds later with a third tray on which rested a teapot, six cups, saucers and accompanying teaspoons.

"Please, Inspector. Help yourself. My wife's vegetable samosas are famous all over Slough."

Moran smiled and placed two of the delicacies onto his plate. "Thank you." He pressed on quickly, wanting to get the interview under way. "First of all, let me say how sorry I am for your loss. My team and I are doing all we can to bring the culprit to justice, but I do need to ask you some personal questions. It will be hard, but there is no easy way through this, I'm afraid."

Mrs Dass nodded and glanced at her husband. "We understand, don't we, Mahmood?"

"And your mother–" Moran began.

"She is family," Mr Dass interrupted. "My mother is the head of our family now that my father has gone. She is very much a part of us."

"Very well," Moran conceded. "Let's make a start."

By the time he left the Dass' household, his belt straining under the pressure of many samosas and an unwise second helping of chocolate cake, Moran had built up a clear mental picture of what had probably been going on. He felt buoyed up by the mention of Jagdip and his brother, Jayesh's first cousins. Mr Dass had spoken of their profligacy, their bad influence on Anoop. They had had money, a great deal of money, but no discernable means of earning such large sums. Mr Dass had no regard for Jagdip's claims to be a good businessman. He had suspected all along that they were crooks. He had warned Jayesh not to get involved, and still believed his son to be innocent of such involvement. His murder was unjustifiable, illogical. But Jagdip had the answers, of that Mr Dass was sure.

At last Moran felt he had some ammunition with which to justify bringing the Ranandan brothers in for questioning at least. Moran would never have described his state of mind as light-hearted, but he felt a growing conviction that the metaphorical dark clouds were finally giving way to, if not blue sky, then at least the distant prospect of a warmer front.

"So what do they call you oop north, then?" Banner mimicked a Midlands accent, badly. "Hot stoof?" He leaned back in his chair to watch for Charlie's reaction, grinning like an idiot.

"Don't be more of a tosser than you've managed to be already, Banner," Helen McKellar called over from her desk. "Why don't you do something useful instead of trying to impress the new DI?"

"Me?" Banner showed his palms. "It's my natural tendency, that is."

"To be a tosser?" Helen raised her eyebrows.

"Naw. Being impressive." Banner scratched his cheek and burped loudly.

"It's OK, Helen." Charlie stopped typing and looked up briefly. "Let DS Banner enjoy himself. Children need to wear themselves out before bedtime so they're tired enough to sleep."

"Aha. Is that an offer?" Banner swivelled his chair towards Charlie's desk.

"You wish." Charlie made a face and carried on sifting through the ANPR data. Now that the system was back up and running at full capacity it should be possible to check the entire Reading area during the timeframe before and after the Audi was spotted at the Tilehurst service station. And so far it was looking good: two matches, the first on the Tilehurst road, the second on the IDR. A third was yet to appear, if indeed there was a third. The Audi might have been parked up before it hit the next camera in the chain.

She drummed her fingers on the desk. Another hit. London road. OK, it was heading out of town now, towards Cemetery Junction and the motorway.

"Are you going to show me where this farm is or what?" Banner said. "I've got two DCs standing by, you know. At this rate it'll be teatime before we get cracking."

"Don't worry on my account, Sergeant," Helen called across. "I've told Mummy I'll be late for supper. Maybe you should call home too?"

"I'm nearly done, Banner," Charlie said distractedly. "Anyway, haven't you got any big boys' toys in your car to help you find the Emerson estate?"

"Who told you I was a big boy?" Banner smirked.

"Who indeed." Charlie muttered under her breath. At that instant the data mining query completed. "That's it," Charlie flushed with excitement. "No trace at the Thames Valley Park roundabouts or the Wokingham road."

"So what?" Banner got up and sauntered over.

"So, the Audi disappears somewhere between the King's Road and Cemetery Junction."

"Sounds like a possible Mandela Court destination to me." Helen had joined them at Charlie's desk. "That's Reading's drug capital," she explained for Charlie's benefit. "Not much space for integral garages around there, though. How about council renteds?"

"I'll take a look." Banner returned to his desk. A minute later he was back with a printout. "Gayles Road. Eight lock-ups in a row."

"What are we waiting for?" Charlie got up and pulled her jacket over her shoulders. "Come on, Sergeant; you can protect me with your big strong baton."

Banner's mouth opened and closed as he groped for a suitable riposte, but Charlie was already half way across the office. He shrugged and grabbed his jacket. There was only one thing worse than a clever woman, and that was two clever women.

A crowd of bored teenagers watched listlessly as Charlie and Banner parked up and began their garage inspection. One, the self-styled gang leader, took it upon himself to shout insults as they worked, egged on by his mates. After a minute or so Banner lost his patience and silenced the boy with a look and his ID card.

The first two garages drew a blank: one empty, the next occupied by a green Vauxhall Zafira. The next in line was padlocked.

Charlie turned to Banner. "Would you oblige me with a show of strength, Sergeant?"

Banner flashed Charlie a cynical smile and went to the boot of the car, returning with a heavy socket wrench. The padlock disintegrated at the first blow. He heaved the aluminium door up on its pivot.

Charlie's heart thumped with elation. "Bingo," she said to the Audi. "You are one beautiful sight."

Chapter Twenty

"Surprise surprise," Charlie muttered. "No one home."

Moran shaded his eyes and peered through the front room window. "Uh huh, but it does give us the chance to have a little look-see."

"Without a warrant, guv?"

"If you don't tell on me, I won't tell on you." Moran beckoned and made for the side gate. An untended garden lay at the rear of the house, which had been extended by the addition of a small conservatory. "Good," Moran said, taking out his handkerchief.

"Guv..." Charlie watched uncomfortably as Moran muffled a conservatory window pane and broke it with a sharp tap of his stick.

"Splendid." Moran reached in, turned the key and pulled the door open. "Shall we, DI Pepper?"

"But guv–"

"They know we're calling, so they won't be coming back for a while, am I right?"

"I suppose."

Charlie followed Moran, her nostrils twitching at the smell of stale cannabis and spice. The house was ordered and tidy, as if the brothers had had a housework blitz following their earlier visit. Which they probably had.

Charlie went into the lounge. There was nothing out of place. She caught a movement at the front of the house. Someone was in the drive, taking photographs.

"Hey!" She went to the window and struggled with the catch. By the time she had got it open the photographer had stepped into a car, which pulled away with a screech of tyres.

Moran joined her. "What was all that about?"

"I have no idea, guv. Press?"

Moran shook his head. "Unlikely. They've been fed enough scraps to keep out of our way for the time being. They have no reason to connect anything to the Ranandans." Moran's mobile went off. "Excuse me."

Charlie watched Moran's face cloud over. "Thanks. I'll be right there." He pocketed the phone and made for the conservatory. "Come on. This'll have to wait."

"Problem, guv?" Charlie followed, perplexed.

"Looks that way." Moran cursed as he opened the back gate and stumbled over a loose pile of bricks. He straightened up. "That was my neighbour. Apparently my house is crawling with policemen. She thought I'd like to know."

Moran's heart sank as he recognised not only Sheldrake but also Mike Airey standing at a respectable distance from the comings and goings in and out of his front door. A gaggle of squad cars were parked outside, blue lights flashing. What had happened? Sheldrake saw him coming and called over two uniformed officers.

"This is DCI Moran." Sheldrake nodded to the uniforms, and shoving Charlie Pepper to one side in bewildered obedience, they took up position on either side of Moran, a hand on each shoulder.

Moran tried to shrug them off but felt their grip tighten. He appealed to Mike Airey.

"Sir, what on earth–"

"You won't be surprised at how disappointed I am, Brendan. But I suppose that temptation is always there, even for someone of your vintage." Airey shook his head and exchanged a complicit look with Sheldrake.

"This is nonsense." Moran tried not to raise his voice. Charlie Pepper, he noticed with satisfaction, wore a loyal frown of indignation. "Whatever you think has happened, this is absolute nonsense, sir."

But Airey's attention had been diverted by the rapid approach of Sheldrake's DI, Sharron Flynn. "Another bag in the spare room, sir," she announced, beaming with pleasure.

"Is there. Is there really." Airey turned to Sheldrake for confirmation and received a hard nod in return.

"I knew you were up to no good, Moran," Sheldrake said. "No wonder you've been dragging your feet."

"Will someone please explain what the hell's going on?" Moran was angry now, really angry. He had a sinking feeling that he knew exactly what was going on: he'd been stitched up. Big time. The evening was warm and Moran felt sweat trickle down his collar. Along the street he saw householders gathering at their front doors waiting to devour the scandalous events that were apparently taking place on their doorstep.

"Heroin is what's going on," Sheldrake stuck his face in Moran's. "The haul you got from a Mercedes. An RTA, remember? The one you neglected to tell me about. Now I know why. It all makes sense."

It was all making sense to Moran as well. The open front door. Someone had been in his house. He turned to Charlie.

"I'm being framed. This is a complete stitch-up."

Charlie was looking at DS Flynn with an expression of concentration, as though she was trying to remember something important. She gave Moran a short, distracted nod. "'Course it is, guv."

Sheldrake laughed flatly. "You won't get out of this one, Moran, whether your lot believe you're innocent or not."

"You'll be taken into custody, DCI Moran, pending a thorough investigation." Mike Airey nodded stiffly to Sheldrake and walked briskly away towards a waiting car. Moran was bundled into a squad car, watched helplessly by Charlie Pepper.

As they drove off Moran sat quietly and tried to gather his thoughts. The heroin had been taken from the evidence room. Which had been under lock and key. The keys were held by DS Banner. He trusted Banner; He was inclined to be a little impulsive, maybe, but sound enough when the chips were down. Moran felt his head throbbing and a heaviness creeping over him. Somehow this was Sheldrake's doing. And somehow he had to prove it.

"He's been *what?*" Banner's face was comical as he tried to take in the implications of Charlie's announcement.

"You heard, Banner," Helen replied tersely.

"Why?"

"Because someone planted two bags of heroin in his house and tapped up Sheldrake, that's how."

"You are *kidding*." Banner got to his feet, knowing what the next question was liable to be.

"You have the evidence room key?" Charlie asked.

"You know I do," the DS snapped. "And I haven't let anyone else have access either, before you ask."

"All right, Banner, calm down. No one's accusing you of anything. Let's go and check it out."

Five minutes later Charlie reconvened the team. "OK, listen carefully. The guv has been stitched up. Someone took the H from this station and planted it in Moran's spare room. Obviously he can't help right now, so we sort it out. I take it no one thinks he's guilty?"

There was a general shaking of heads. Someone at the back of the room said 'No way' to accompanying murmurs of agreement.

"We're all on the same page, then," Charlie said. "So, come on – let's have some suggestions. How did whoever get in and out of the evidence room carrying two bags of class A drugs and manage to avoid detection."

Banner had a secretive, rather pleased look about him. Charlie cocked her head. "Well, DS Banner? Share your thoughts, do."

Banner waited until he had everyone's full attention. "The heroin was security marked with UV security paste. Anyone who touched it will show up like a night out in Chernobyl."

"Well, good. That's a start." Charlie lowered her voice. "But I'd still like to know how someone got in there without authorisation." She paused, making sure she had their attention. "Now, listen. What I'm about to say goes no further than this room, OK?"

A ripple of curiosity circulated, dissipating with Charlie's raised hand. "You'll all be aware that I trailed the Ranandans to a farm on the Emerson estate. They were met by a woman. I didn't get a look at her face, but

I know her voice. It was DS Sharron Flynn, and I don't think she was on duty."

There was a swell of protest and muttered refutes. Charlie raised her hand again and eventually the room fell silent. "Now I also know DS Flynn is working undercover on the Kestrel team, but what I heard at the farm makes me deeply suspicious of her motives. She was talking about a 'bust', as she called it. Obviously she was referring to what's just happened to the guv. She knew what was going down."

"How do we approach her?" Helen McKellar asked. "We can't just pull her in for questioning."

"And she'll have covered her tracks," DC Harding observed. "She'll have worn gloves, taken every precaution. If it *was* her."

"Well, we'll have to be thorough then, won't we, DC Harding?" Charlie was thinking hard. Harding was right; If Flynn was the culprit she had all the odds stacked in her favour. Charlie racked her brains trying to remember all that had been said in the farm granary. Was there any weakness she could exploit, any knowledge she had gained by eavesdropping on the conversation with the Ranandan brothers?

As if reading her mind, Banner asked: "Still want us to check out the farm?" The DS raised an eyebrow.

"Yes. Take Helen and keep me in touch. And for goodness sake keep out of sight." Charlie ran a hand through her thick hair. "No, wait. I'll get uniform to stake it out. I can't afford to have you two out of the picture right now. We need to get something on Flynn, or eliminate her from the list; either way, asap." Charlie pursed her lips. "DS Phelps is able to receive visitors, isn't he? The guv mentioned that Phelps found out a bit about Flynn from a mate in OCG. DC Harding, can you and Helen pop into the RBH and have a quick word, see if he has any suggestions?"

Harding nodded. "Will do."

Helen McKellar spoke up. "Oh, I almost forgot," she said. "As if the guv hasn't enough problems already ... his mother's been taken ill. She's too frail to move, apparently. The matron called an hour ago."

Charlie sighed. "OK. I'll get word to him. Thanks."

She surveyed the room. "Right. That's it for now. DS Banner? A word please. My office."

Banner, who had been about to disappear for a smoke, twisted his face into a quizzical smile. "That's the *guv's* office."

"Not for the time being, Sergeant. I'll be looking after it until DCI Moran is back."

Banner complied, muttering under his breath. One of his mates gave him a dig on his way past.

Charlie closed the door. "Have a seat."

Banner hovered at the door. "I'm all right."

"I said, have a seat."

Banner sat.

"Bit of a ladies' man, are you?" Charlie asked, resting her elbows lightly on the arms of Moran's chair.

"Look, I'm only mucking about. Sorry if I offended–"

"I'm not talking about me." Charlie laced her voice with a steely edge. She'd dealt with blokes like Banner before. There was only one possible approach: the direct one.

"Oh? Then why–"

"Have you been seeing DS Flynn?" Charlie watched Banner carefully, studying his body language.

Banner tried an exasperated laugh which didn't quite come off. "Seeing? What do you mean, *seeing*?"

"You know exactly what I mean."

Banner fell silent. Charlie could see the cogs turning. *How can I get out of this one?* was written all over his conniving face.

"I'm waiting."

"Look, this has nothing to do–"

"Nothing to do with the investigation? Nothing to do with DCI Moran's arrest? Get real, Banner. Or are you even more stupid than I thought?"

"I took her out for a drink, OK? That's it."

Charlie raised her eyes to heaven. "That's *it*?"

"Yeah. She's all right. Bit on the cool side."

"I'll bet she wasn't too cool to lift your keys while you were ogling her charms though, Sergeant. Where did you go for that drink?"

Banner shifted uncomfortably in his seat. "Across the road to the Falcon. As usual."

"Let me guess. She went to powder her nose and took a bit longer than usual?"

Banner was looking at the floor now. He didn't reply.

"Well?"

"Yeah, actually. Now you mention it."

Charlie rapped her knuckles on the desk in frustration. "You're supposed to be a detective. You're supposed to be *alert*." Charlie was really angry now. Not that it would do any good. With an effort she calmed herself down. Somehow they had to work together to turn this around. No point in making an enemy of Banner – but judging by the look of hate on his face she'd probably passed that milestone already.

"What was she wearing?"

Banner scratched his head. "I'm not sure."

"You asked her out and didn't bother to look at her clothes?"

"It's not the clothes I'm interested in," Banner said, with a sly grin.

"Your brain is not in your trousers, Banner. Or maybe it is, I don't know. *Think*, Sergeant. Blouse? Jacket? Colour? Style?"

"No jacket. Too hot." Banner shrugged. "Might have been orange. Or yellow. Yeah. A yellow top. *Blouse*."

Charlie leaned back in Moran's chair and exhaled. "OK. Thank you, DS Banner. In future, use your noddle. That's what you're trained for."

"But she's one of ours," Banner protested. "How was I supposed to know?"

"Intuition? Due care and attention? An enquiring, professionally suspicious mind? Shall I go on?"

Banner was studying the carpet tiles again.

Charlie stood up. "At least you had the foresight to security mark the packages. Consider that a partial redemption. And turn off the pricked balloon impersonation, sergeant. We haven't got much time and there's a lot to do."

Moran received Charlie's message with resignation and without surprise. His mother was on the way out. *A bit like you, Brendan...* What could he do? Would they let him visit? Surely, on compassionate grounds? He buzzed for the duty officer.

Ten minutes later he was led out to the car park. He was surprised to see Charlie Pepper sitting in her car. When she pulled in behind them Moran was pretty sure she wanted to make contact. Maybe the new DI had something useful up her sleeve. *Someone better had, Brendan, because you've got nothing...*

It was getting dark by the time the car pulled into the nursing home. Out of the corner of his eye Moran saw Charlie park a discreet distance away. Moran was escorted to reception and led along the corridor by the matron, a large lady in a blue uniform who seemed not to think it unusual that Moran had turned up with two uniformed police officers. Perhaps she thought it was all part of his job.

"She's not good, I'm afraid. Doctor's been in twice today. He's not ... optimistic." The matron nudged the door to room fourteen and poked her head in. "Mrs Moran? Your son is here." She gave him a sympathetic smile. "I'll leave you to it."

Moran could hear his mother's laboured breathing. His nostrils wrinkled at the smell of sickness. There was a chair beside the bed, a vase of flowers on the edge of the television table. The walls were bare. It wasn't much of a place to end your life.

As he looked down at his mother's emaciated form he forgot his own problems. This was the woman who had raised him, had suffered the loss of a much-loved child and yet had struggled on, bearing the pain and loss like the trooper she had been. Moran's father had disappeared into the Western Isles and a bottle of whisky when Moran was six years old. It was his mother who had paid his way and managed him through his teens, through college, police training, and who had eventually helped him buy his first flat. It was his mother who had been there for him when Janice was killed. And here she was now; a shadow in a dark room.

Moran took her hand and she stirred, her chest wheezing as her eyes tried to focus. "Is that you, James?"

"No, Mum. It's Brendan."

"Ah, Brendan. Are you well?"

"Yes. Very well," Moran lied. What was the point in telling the truth? "And how are you?"

"Oh. You know. I could be better." She coughed and grimaced in pain. "Are you well yourself, James?"

Moran squeezed her hand. "It's Brendan, Mother."

"Yes. Yes, I know. Brendan?"

"I'm here."

"Are you married yet?"

The question took him aback. He swallowed. "No, Mum. Not yet."

"Well, you need to be. You're getting too old to be on your own."

Moran smiled. "You're probably right."

"Am I not always right when it comes to you?" She smiled weakly. "I've always tried to do the best I can for you, Brendan."

He nodded, unable to speak. He thought of the Dass family, bonded together, united in crisis, the elderly matriarch at the centre of home life and activity, respected and cared for. Could he not have done the same for his own mother? *Should* he not have done?

"I'm very tired, Brendan."

"I know. I just wanted to make sure you were comfortable."

Liar. You wanted to assuage your conscience...

Her eyes had closed. She was asleep. Moran sat for a long time, watching his mother's chest rise and fall, listening to her infected lungs fighting for air. *Thank you,* he said quietly. *For all you did. For all the sacrifices.* He stood up but found he couldn't bring himself to walk away. *Maybe we'll meet again, one day. If there is a heaven.*

"Guv?"

Moran's heart jumped.

Tap Tap Tap. "Guv? Are you in there?"

Moran went to the window. "Charlie?"

"Guv. I'm sorry to intrude. The farm; the woman – it was DS Flynn, I'm sure of it."

"Was it, now?" Moran felt a familiar excitement ignite in his stomach.

"And Banner security marked the heroin. We just have to find traces on Flynn and we've got her."

"And how do you propose we do that?"

"She's on duty tonight, guv, so she won't be at home."

Moran glanced over his shoulder to make sure no one had entered the room quietly while his back was turned. "You're not suggesting a break-in, are you DI Pepper?"

"Only if strictly necessary, guv" Charlie said, straight-faced. "Just following your example," she added. "Would you care to join me, sir?"

Moran suppressed a smile and shook his head. "I'm in enough trouble already without slipping custody. If you're wrong, they'll hang me out to dry."

"Fair point." Charlie stuck her chin out. "But I can prove it, I know."

"And what if DS Flynn has been her usual thorough self? She'll have covered up well, if all I've heard about her is to be believed." Moran felt a wild impulsiveness competing against his better judgment. If Charlie was right they needed to nail Flynn before she got up to any further mischief. If the DS had taken the drastic step of a drug frame-up it meant she had a lot to hide. Like the murder of a colleague, for instance.

"It's worth the risk, guv. If we get Flynn she'll open up the whole case for us," Charlie pressed. "With the added bonus of your charges being dropped, of course."

"I can't pretend that's not an attractive result from where I'm standing right now." Moran smiled wearily. "Do what you can Charlie, but remember that anything you find will be inadmissible in court without a search warrant."

"Been there, guv," Charlie said.

I'll bet you have, too, Moran thought as he watched her trot back to her car.

Chapter Twenty-One

On his way out Banner dropped by to see how the police mechanics were getting on with stripping the Audi. Pepper had also asked him to catch up with Dr Bagri at the path lab; by now Father Jeffries' autopsy, which the guv had obviously been unable to attend, had already taken place. Banner looked at his watch. After half past nine; Bagri would be finished for the day. He could probably make do with a phone update.

What Banner needed right now was exoneration. He knew he'd screwed up badly with DS Flynn, added to which his humiliation at the Zodiac had made him the butt of a seemingly endless stream of wit and repartee from his colleagues. Banner wasn't used to that. *He* was the one who made the jokes. Worse still, he had to deal with a sassy new DI who seemed impervious to his charms. *We'll see about that, Ms Pepper...*

His train of thought was interrupted by the approach of one of the forensics team. "Couple of hairs in the boot. Lipstick in the glove box. Missing brake light. Nothing hidden in the panelling. That's it so far." The white-suited investigator turned back to his work.

Banner thanked him curtly and headed for the car park. Sod the autopsy result. It could wait until the morning. It wasn't top of his list anyway, and besides, he was spoiling for some action. True, the Ranandan brothers had done a predictable disappearing act, but he was pretty sure he knew where they'd show up. Banner loosened his collar. He was going to kick some ass down at the Zodiac, and this time he'd be the one who came out on top.

Nice place, Charlie muttered to herself as she parked beneath a street lamp. Sharron Flynn's address had led her to a new block of executive flats overlooking the river, complete with underground car park and security entrance system.

You seem to be doing all right for yourself, Miss Flynn ... or is someone else footing the bill?

She entered the reception area. A security guard looked up from his magazine with a lazy enquiry. "Help you?"

"Just calling for number eleven," Charlie said. "Mind if I go up?"

"Go right ahead. Second floor." The man's eyes were already back on his magazine.

Charlie called the lift and pushed the button for the second floor. She emerged into a plush corridor which evoked the feel of a five-star hotel. The carpet was silent beneath her feet; number eleven was the last flat on the right.

She knocked once. The door opened almost immediately. A woman in her late fifties stood on the threshold. She looked puzzled, as if unused to opening the door to visitors.

"Can I help?"

"Hi. I'm Charlie, one of Sharron's colleagues," Charlie said. "She asked me to pop in and pick up something she forgot. You're Mrs Flynn?"

"Yes, that's right." Mrs Flynn gave her the once-over. "I'm just on my way out. It's not like Sharron to forget anything. She's very organised."

"Yes, I know." Charlie laughed. "Puts us all to shame."

Mrs Flynn laughed. "It's just her nature. I expect she drives you all mad."

"She sure does," Charlie grinned. "We cope, though."

"Drives me mad on occasion as well," Mrs Flynn confided. "Do come in, please." She stepped aside and held the door open.

"Now, what's she's forgotten?" Mrs Flynn asked Charlie over her shoulder as they walked through into the lounge. "I expect I'll know where it is. I usually pop in to do the housework once or twice a week, so it's all familiar territory to me."

"It was her bag," Charlie replied. "The one she uses for work. It's got all her stuff in it – you know, rubber gloves, pens, notebook and so on."

Mrs Flynn frowned. "Well, she had a bag with her when she left the flat earlier on. I wonder which one she meant. I'll have a look in her bedroom. Do make yourself comfortable. I won't be a moment."

Charlie waited until Mrs Flynn had left the room. The designer kitchen was immediately opposite the lounge. She nipped across the hallway and opened the first of a seemingly endless row of drawers. It slid noiselessly open on its rail.

Mrs Flynn called from the bedroom. "I can't *see* another bag."

Charlie tried the second and third drawers. Inside the third was a key ring containing a comprehensive assortment of keys she doubted were for domestic use.

She pocketed it and returned to the lounge. Mrs Flynn bustled in seconds later. "Well, there *were* a few things on her bed. I'll put them in a plastic bag for you."

"Thanks," Charlie said with a smile. "May I use the bathroom?"

"Of course, dear. Second on the right."

Charlie went straight for the laundry basket by the basin. It was full. She whispered a prayer of thanks and started to dig. Right at the bottom was a yellow blouse. *Hey presto...*

But what if Mrs Flynn decided to do a load of washing? Charlie frowned, and then carefully removed the yellow blouse and placed it in the airing cupboard under a pile of sheets. Hopefully it wouldn't be discovered until she got hold of a warrant. She flushed the toilet and went back into the lounge. Mrs Flynn handed her a bag.

"Oh, by the way, Sharron says to say thanks."

"Send her my love," Mrs Flynn said as she led Charlie to the door and saw her out.

Charlie cocked her head, a noise attracting her attention. "What was that?"

"One of the cats, I expect." Mrs Flynn smiled sweetly. "Noisy things."

"Well, bye for now," Charlie said.

"Bye."

Back in the car Charlie called Moran.

"Any luck?" The guv's voice sounded tired and strained.

"Yes, guv. A set of skeleton keys and a yellow blouse in the laundry basket. Banner said she was wearing a yellow blouse when he bought her a drink the other night."

"Top marks, DI Pepper. No time to lose, then; when DS Flynn goes off shift and speaks to Mummy she'll know she's been rumbled. Get a search warrant authorised, pronto."

"I'll get Banner and Helen McKellar to join me for the fun, guv."

"The real fun starts in the interview room," Moran said coldly. "And I've got a lot of fun to catch up on."

His head was splitting, a pounding, relentless pulse which had tormented him all day. The tablets he had taken hadn't got close to reducing the pain.

The Kafir lay full length on the floor and writhed like a snake, as if by doing so he could somehow push the agony out of his body, and then trap it and kill it. Should he visit the doctor? No. What good would that do? More tablets, more empty advice.

Perhaps the heat was to blame. He had tried cold showers, sipped mugful after mugful of herbal tea, but it was no good. His head was on fire, his brain in torment. If he closed his eyes and tried to sleep he was disturbed by images that made no sense. A dark wood, snowfall, the distant echo of church bells, tree roots tripping him, hindering his progress through the blackness. A cowled figure waiting, watching.

The Kafir snapped his eyes open. Better to be awake with the pain than to allow sleep to take him to *that place...*

Through the mist of his discomfort the Kafir tried to focus on his enemy, something he knew would sustain him through the hours of trial. He would not be beaten, and revenge would be all the sweeter with the knowledge that his anger had been refined in the fires of suffering.

The Kafir went to the window and breathed in deeply. The air seemed cooler outside. Perhaps he would find relief in the ebb and flow of the river. Perhaps he would find peace sharing his pain with another.

Suddenly, in an instant, as though someone had flicked a switch, the hammering in his head ceased. He felt instantly refreshed. and alert. The Kafir laughed aloud. Now he *knew* where he was going; his friend had told him just what to do. He'd been wrong. He wasn't being followed; he was being *helped*.

"Thank you," he said aloud. "*Thank* you for telling me where she is."

He began to make preparations. Everything must be done with diligence, his helper had told him, and so it would be. The Kafir was happy; it was time to kill again.

Chapter Twenty-Two

"**A**sk her," Phelps said. "She didn't have anything good to say about this Jag bloke."

Helen McKellar chewed thoughtfully on an orange segment. "No. Nobody does. And Zoë gave you the Chalvey link?" she asked, helping herself to a grape.

"She did." Phelps shifted on his pile of pillows and winced. "She's all right. I reckon she'd do it."

DC Harding shrugged. "So where do we find her?"

"Oxford Road. Or the Zodiac. Or the Two Princes in Duke Street."

"OK," Helen said. "I'll call Charlie."

"We'll have to make sure Flynn's out of the way," Harding observed. "Otherwise she'll spill the whole thing."

"I have a feeling Flynn will be well out of the way by the time we get Zoë on board," Helen said. "We'll leave you in peace, Sarge. Hope you feel better. Sorry to disturb you so late."

"Disturb? From what exactly?" Phelps grimaced. "Do me a favour, Helen – see if you can't get hold of a Shakespeare commentary. Macbeth is what I'm after. The missus has banned my books."

"I'm not sure if I'd want to risk the wrath of Mrs Phelps, Sergeant."

"No," Phelps said thoughtfully, "can't say as I blame you. Just a thought."

"Keep thinking, Sarge." Harding shot Helen a wide grin. "That's what you're good at."

Banner searched the sea of faces. He'd have no trouble recognising the scumbags who doped him. This time, things would be different. He ordered a tonic water and looked down the length of the bar. Sharron Flynn was at the end, talking to a girl wearing a ludicrously short skirt and a low-cut top. Banner looked past them, towards the exit.

There. That was one of them, deffo – the tall guy with the shaved head. He had a distinctive mole on his cheek and a short goatee. Banner ducked his head, cradled his drink and risked a further glance. He cursed and scanned the crowd; the man had vanished. Banner looked at his watch. What the hell. He was officially off duty, wasn't he? He signalled the barmaid with the Aries T-shirt and ordered a proper drink.

Ten minutes later he ordered a chaser, downed it in one and ordered another beer. Still no sign of his abductor. Maybe he could get an intro to Flynn's friend. He excused his way out of his hard-won square metre and pushed his way to the end of the bar.

"Hi girls," he shouted over the music. "How's it going?" He winked at Flynn. "What's your name, babe?" he asked the girl with the long hair and short everything else.

Flynn shot Banner a look that conveyed both puzzlement and irritation. Banner returned a challenging smile.

"It's Zoë, if you must know, love." Zoë exchanged a fleeting look with Flynn. "I'm just having a chat with my friend, if that's OK."

"Don't mind me," Banner said, finishing his beer with a long swig. "Just keep an eye on your handbag. You never know what might go missing." He glared at Flynn, daring her to object. But Flynn was in character and doing a good job. She let the comment wash over her without batting an eyelid.

"What are you saying, mate?" Zoë's mouth twisted in annoyance. "On your bike. Like I said, I'm talking to my friend."

Banner was angry now, at Flynn's impregnable undercover status and at Zoë's attitude. Moreover, he was still smarting from the dressing-down he'd received from DI Pepper. Most women were only too pleased to be chatted up by Stephen Banner. They didn't tell him off *or* brush him off – no way.

He glared at Flynn, feeling the build-up of rage inside him. If she *was* mixed up in this, then his Ketamine humiliation was *her* doing. Banner's hands clasped and unclasped at his side. He opened his mouth to give her some verbal, but before he got anything coherent out a suave young Asian in a dark jacket sidled up to the group.

"You girls OK?" the man asked, looking Banner up and down with mild curiosity. Banner clocked the unmistakeable promise of violence in the dark eyes,

"Yeah. Just fine." Zoë rolled her eyes and looked away.

"We haven't met." The Asian extended his hand. "I'm Jag."

"Stephen." Banner took the proffered hand and shook it firmly. "I'm a friend of Zoë's."

"Really?" Jag replied with a half smile. "I thought I knew all Zoë's friends."

"A new friend." Banner twisted his lips into a smile. Zoë's face was still turned away. It was clear there was no love lost between them. Banner watched for Flynn's reaction to Jag's appearance, but her face gave nothing away.

"I see. Well, nice to meet you, Stephen. Have a good evening, and take care." Jag excused himself and moved off towards a table where a noisy group of students was clearly celebrating a birthday or exam success. Banner, feeling a little foolish, slid back to the bar. So that was Jag – the potential king pin, the guy who had ordered his Ketamine episode.

For the first time Banner began to feel uncomfortable. What had he been thinking, coming down here on his own? Jag obviously knew who he was – which meant trouble. But maybe he could still do something useful, claw back a brownie point or two – if he was careful. Banner knew he couldn't afford any more cock-ups.

As he ordered another beer something made him glance to one side where the barmaid was serving a new customer. Banner recognised him immediately. It was Moran's old DS, Greg Neads. Hadn't Moran wanted a word with him? Something Phelps had said? Banner frowned. Then he remembered; Neads had told Phelps he knew where that poor sod DC Hill had been taken. And then Neads had vanished. Nice one.

Banner weighed up the best course of action. If he tackled Neads directly there'd be a scene. Best just keep tabs until he had a chance to get Neads on his own.

For the next half hour Banner kept an eye on Neads, all the time checking on Jag's movements around the club and keeping an eye open for any sign of the goatee guy. Neads was behaving oddly. He had a vacant, weird look in his eyes. At one point Banner thought Neads had recognised him, but the other man seemed to look right through him as if he wasn't there.

At just after eleven, Jag made for the door with Zoë in tow. Neads came alive, downed his drink in one and headed towards the exit. *Interesting*, Banner thought, following close behind. He stepped onto the pavement in time to see Jag and Zoë getting into a BMW. Neads waited until the tail lights had gone out of sight before beginning to walk slowly in the direction the BMW had taken. Banner followed him all the way to the river until Neads let himself into a new block of flats and disappeared inside.

Moran awoke suddenly, disoriented. It took a full five seconds before the room assumed a depressing familiarity. His mother lay still beneath the bedclothes. The noise of her laboured breathing had stopped, the resulting silence plainly the cause of his awakening.

Dry-mouthed, he leaned forward, took his mother's wrist and gently explored for a pulse. As he felt the coolness of her flesh he knew he wouldn't find one. It was over. Had they spoken during the night? He couldn't clearly recall – perhaps a reassuring whisper, some small shared memory? Or had he just dreamed these fragmentary conversations?

Moran remained in his chair until the sun had fully risen and its rays reached along the worn carpet to touch his feet. His mother's face was peaceful, a faint smile creasing her lips. After a while he rose, rested the back of his hand lightly on her forehead, and quietly left the room.

"We didn't want to disturb you, Mr Moran." The duty manageress smiled sympathetically as he turned the corner to reception. The two uniforms were propped on a bench seat sipping mugs of tea. They both looked knackered and fed up.

"I've given your friends some tea," the manageress said brightly.

"She's gone," Moran told her. "There's nothing more I can do."

"We'll take care of the immediate arrangements, Mr Moran. Perhaps you could let me know which undertaker you'll be contacting in due course?"

"I can do that now." As Moran jotted down the details his mobile rang.

"Guv? It's Charlie. The keys I found in Flynn's kitchen fit the evidence room lock. The warrant should be approved within the hour."

"Good. Get that blouse checked out as soon as you can. If you get a positive result, bring Flynn in. And only let Airey know what's happening *if* we have the evidence."

"Will do." Charlie paused. "How are things, guv? Is there any–?"

"She died a short time ago," Moran said. "Thanks for asking."

"I'm sorry, guv."

"Yes. Yes, thanks."

Moran signed off. It was uncomfortably warm already, and he felt grubby, tired and numb. Death, he thought, followed him wherever he turned, one way or another. But it wouldn't do to dwell on it; that was a sure fire route to melancholia. Which was why he was more than glad to have other things to occupy his mind.

"Would you like a cup of tea as well, Mr Moran?" The manageress wore an expression of professional condolence, and to be fair she wasn't all that bad at it.

Moran passed a hand wearily across his forehead. "In the absence of anything stronger, I suppose it'll have to do. Thanks." Besides, he thought bleakly, it would allow him an extra ten minutes away from the dubious comforts of a police cell. As he sucked the hot liquid over his teeth he comforted himself with the thought that if all went to plan and allowing for a little luck, he'd be swapping places with DS Sharron Flynn before the day was done.

Chapter Twenty-Three

"**D**id you get to Dr Bagri?" Charlie pitched the question to Banner like a Graeme Swann offspinner. She was pretty sure the DS hadn't bothered to carry out her instruction. It was deliberate, of course. Banner would test her authority, and so would the rest of the team – in different ways, perhaps, but test they would, nevertheless. She was expecting it, but she knew that whatever they threw her way, she had to pass muster or else lose both face and respect, a potentially fatal result for any new DI on the block. And that, Charlie determined, wasn't going to happen to her, oh no.

Banner looked up from his screen and feigned surprise. "Not yet. I was going to call in on him this morning."

"I asked you to go last night, DS Banner, remember?" Charlie said pointedly. "We need that autopsy update. Airey's already bending my ear. What happened?"

"Nothing happened. I caught up on some paperwork, checked on the Audi and knocked off. It was late."

"It was late?" Charlie simmered. "You didn't think it was important, or what?"

By now the exchange had the attention of the other detectives in the squad room. The tapping of keyboards tailed off.

"I'll get on it." Banner got up in a leisurely fashion and slipped his jacket on.

"You'd better," Charlie told him. "If I wasn't so busy I'd make a performance monitoring note for your PDR review."

Banner froze. "Now wait a–"

"Just do it, DS Banner, all right?"

Banner stormed off without another word and Charlie withdrew into Moran's office.

She had just sat down and picked up the phone when Helen stuck her head around the door.

"Come in, Helen." Charlie indicated the chair. "Have a seat."

"Can't stop," Helen said. "Banner wants me to go with him. Just to let you know the warrant's signed and sealed. Oh, and the chiro secretary – Nalini – has sent in a list of all the past employees at the practice. On my desk if you want a butcher's."

"Great. Thanks, Helen. I'll handle the search of Flynn's flat with Harding. Don't let Banner push you around, OK? Call me if you have any probs."

"Will do," Helen said perkily and disappeared.

Right, Charlie said to herself, *time to pay you another visit, Mrs Flynn. Hope you've got the kettle on and changed the baby's nappy...*

"I see." Mike Airey stroked the bridge of his nose with his forefinger. "I see. And where is DS Flynn now?"

"We don't know, sir," Charlie said. "Something might have spooked her. But I can't think what – we've been careful."

"I'm sure," Mike Airey said. "I'm sure you have. And Superintendent Sheldrake? Have you made contact?"

"No, sir, I–"

Before Charlie could finish Airey's office door swung back on its hinges with a crash.

"Ah, Alan," Airey began, "we were just–"

"Where's Moran?" Sheldrake wasn't exactly spitting fire, Charlie thought, but he was doing a good impression of it.

"Chief Inspector Moran is on his way to the Emerson Estate, Superintendent," Charlie said sweetly. "We have reason to believe that a suspect linked to the Broad Street murder may be holed up in one of the rented farm buildings."

"What's this nonsense?" Sheldrake demanded. "Who the hell applied for a warrant to arrest my sergeant?"

"Take a pew, Alan, if you please." Airey kept his voice even and low. "I'm afraid we do have some rather compelling evidence that DS Flynn has been up to no good."

"Up to–? She's a damn good officer, what are you talking about?" Sheldrake grabbed the back of a chair and leaned over it aggressively.

"We're talking about a set of skeleton keys found at her flat, sir," Charlie advised. "And security stains on her blouse. The blouse she was wearing when she broke into the evidence room and took the heroin. Sir."

"Now look–" Sheldrake stammered.

"And, apparently, a vial of gamma-hydroxybutyrate in her bathroom cabinet," Airey concluded, poker-faced. "Now, why do you imagine DS Flynn would have such a substance in her possession, Alan?"

"There are probably all sorts of reasons," Sheldrake blustered. "She works undercover, on the Kestrel team. You know that, Mike."

"I also know that traces of gamma-hydroxybutyrate were found in DS Reed-Purvis' blood."

"Yes, but–"

"Alan," Airey said patiently, "we intend to question DS Flynn when we find her. Can I suggest that you also prepare a statement?"

"Of all the damn cheek!" Sheldrake exploded. "You'll regret this, Airey, by God you will!"

And Sheldrake was gone, leaving papers flying in his wake.

"Sorry about that, DI Pepper." Airey cleared his throat. "Now, tell me about this Jag fellow, and what was discussed with Sergeant Phelps."

Moran knocked on the farmhouse door. He had a pretty good idea of the layout of the farm from Harding's Google Earth printout. There were many interesting features in and around the property, the granary where Charlie had eavesdropped on the Ranandans being one, but what interested Moran most was the field beyond the granary, which was long and smooth and featured a windsock at the end nearest the farm buildings. A private airstrip, no less, with two corrugated hangers next to the grain silo. Very handy, Moran had little doubt, for the import and export of illegal substances. The fact that the Ranandans and DS Flynn had recently been on the premises gave Moran a pleasant warm feeling in the pit of his stomach, more pleasurable even than his release from custody and Mike Airey's back-pedalling speech of remorse, even though it hadn't come across as entirely sincere:

'Never doubted you, Brendan. Had to go through the procedure. Sure you understand...'

Was Flynn here? Probably. If not, it was only a matter of time before they ran her to ground. What concerned Moran more was Jag Ranandan and his sibling. Or sibling*s*, if you included the missing sister. Nevertheless, he was confident that Ms Flynn would be able to point him in the right direction.

"Can I help?" A smartly dressed man in his sixties was framed in the open door. He was wearing tweeds, a checked shirt, an olive green tie with stitched club logo, and a pair of worn but expensive-looking brogues.

"DCI Brendan Moran. Thames Valley Police.

"That so? Won't shake hands, if you don't mind," the man said. "Doing a spot of DIY. Damn taps playing up again. Probably the heat. " He pocketed an oily cloth and stuck his chin out inquisitively. "So, what can I do for you?"

"I'm looking for Sharron Flynn. Can you help?"

"Goodness, what's the girl been up to?" the man said, tucking his chin into his collar.

"You know her?"

"'Course I know her," he replied, blowing out his cheeks. "My daughter."

"Ah. Mr Flynn."

"Colonel, actually." He stood aside. "You'd better come in."

"Thanks," Moran said. "If you don't mind. It won't take long."

The interior of the farmhouse spoke of a comfortable retirement. It was cosy, but with the suggestion of one-time affluence here and there: a signed first edition print by a nationally famous artist, an original Giles cartoon, expensive-looking antique furniture, a well-stocked bookcase and, most notably, a magnificent grandfather clock with a hand-painted face depicting pastoral scenes of times gone by.

"Like it?" Colonel Flynn said, noticing Moran's admiring expression. "Eighteenth century. Scottish, you know."

"Very nice," Moran said. "Clocks used to be a bit of a hobby of mine. No time these days, if you'll excuse the pun. But let's talk about Sharron, shall we?"

"Yes. Yes, of course." Colonel Flynn bobbed his head. He had a Brylcreemed fringe of white hair and an almost cartoonishly gleaming bald pate. A pair of pince-nez completed the elderly country gent look. "Busy girl. Always working, y'see. Can't get enough of it."

"She enjoys her work?"

"Good grief, yes. All she ever wanted to do after … well, after her disappointment."

"And what was that?"

Colonel Flynn raised his eyebrows as if he thought it odd that Moran didn't know. "Flying, of course. Applied for three of those charity jobs, you know. In Africa. Flying supplies and so on. Turned her down, all of 'em."

"That's a shame," Moran prompted. "Why?"

"No idea, really. Well, tell you the truth, she's a little hot-headed. Doesn't get on with people too well. Don't know where she gets it from, I'm sure. Her mother's very affable, and as for me, well, I'll talk to any Tom, Dick or Harry. Saving your presence, no offence."

"None taken. And how do you get on with her? Sharron, I mean."

Colonel Flynn's face clouded. "Not too good, I suppose, if I'm honest. We don't see eye to eye. The mother does all the social stuff. We do see each other occasionally – Christmas and so on … and when she's flying I might catch the odd glimpse, but she never calls in. Sad, I suppose." He trailed off.

"And where is she now, Colonel Flynn?"

"Where? Oh, I thought you knew." He cupped his ear. "Listen, can you hear it? Sounds like she's on her way back."

A faint buzzing could be heard, like the drone of a large mosquito. A single-engined plane – a Cessna, maybe, or one of those kit planes Moran had heard people built to keep the costs within an attainable budget.

"She turned up an hour ago. Often flies to relax when she's come off shift. If we're quick you can meet her when she's down," Colonel Flynn said. "She doesn't normally hang about after she's landed. More's the pity," he added wistfully.

They went outside and walked through the garden at the rear of the property. A large area had been wired off for a chicken run, and beyond this lay the fence which ran behind the two hangers at the airfield's edge.

"Who else uses the airstrip?" Moran asked as he scanned the sky for visual contact.

"Not sure, to be perfectly honest. Don't get involved. Some private club, I believe. Couple of foreign-looking fellas."

"So the land doesn't belong to you?"

Colonel Flynn guffawed. "I wish. No, we own the farmhouse and one or two of the outbuildings. The rest is owned by Lord Emerson and the estate. Rents a lot of it out privately. Time are tough, you know, even for the landed gentry. Austerity and all that."

"I'm sure." Moran could see the plane now. It was turning in towards the end of the runway at a few hundred feet. No, wait, – it was climbing again. Or–

"What the deuce is she up to?" Colonel Flynn shielded his eyes from the sun's glare. "Damned aerobatics again, I shouldn't wonder. She's good at it, you know. Likes to show off a bit."

Moran felt a coldness in the pit of his stomach, a premonition of catastrophe. "Is she in radio contact? Can we talk to her?"

"Talk? Well, she'll be in touch with ATC, but I don't have the equipment – oh, I say..."

The aeroplane had reached the zenith of its climb, where it hung for a moment, suspended like a high explosive shell at the very tip of its trajectory. Then its nose dipped and it began to plummet earthward.

"Seen this before," Flynn said. "Scares the life out of me. You watch."

Moran was rooted to the spot, unable to take his eyes off the plunging machine. *Pull up,* he muttered. *Pull up...* But something told him that Sharron Flynn had no intention of pulling up. Or no *way* to pull up. The machine continued to fall, propeller whirring at full revs, urging it on to terminal velocity.

A few seconds later it was clear to both men that, whatever the pilot's intentions, there was no chance of the plane pulling out of the dive. Colonel Flynn raised his other hand, as if by some miraculous power he could somehow reach out and pluck his daughter's tumbling aircraft to safety. Moran took a half step forward, paralysed by his powerlessness to intervene.

The aircraft hit the ground roughly halfway down the airstrip and crumpled like a paper toy. For a split second it seemed as if there would be no fire, but then the wreckage heaved and exploded with a sheet of orange flame and a thump which shook the crows from the trees

213

at the field's perimeter. Bits of metal were flung into the still air and a pall of black smoke puffed up in the wake of the detonation.

Moran gripped Colonel Flynn's arm and tried to restrain him, but the old man tore free with surprising strength and set out on a shambling trot to the airfield gate.

"Wait! *Colonel Flynn...* There's nothing you can do! It's not safe!" Moran yelled himself hoarse at the running figure. He took out his phone and gripped it hard to stop his hands trembling. Emergency services answered and Moran directed them to the farm. He then set off in pursuit of Flynn, who had got to within fifty metres of the fireball before the heat had brought him to a standstill. As Moran entered the field and broke into a run he saw the old man sink slowly to his knees and bury his head in his hands.

Chapter Twenty-Four

"We had no idea," Mrs Flynn said quietly. "That she was, was–"

Colonel Flynn put an arm around his wife's shoulder. "Now then, let's be calm and try to help DC McKellar, shall we? This business isn't over yet."

"But drugs! I mean, *why*?" Mrs Flynn wasn't exactly wringing her hands, but she was as close to it as Helen had seen in a long while. "Oh, there he goes again." She got up at the sound of a baby's cry. "The poor little thing, without his mummy..." She put her hand to her mouth to stifle a sob and rushed out of the room.

Helen waited tactfully for a few moments before speaking. "Colonel Flynn. I understand how hard this must be, but I do need to ask you a few questions."

"Course you do. Understood." Colonel Flynn gazed reflectively into a half-tumbler of malt. "Got a few questions myself, as it happens."

"You didn't know about the baby?"

"Not a thing. Can you credit it? Me, a grandfather, and I had no idea. Suppose she thought I'd disapprove. Probably do, come to that. Unmarried and so on."

"I understand," Helen nodded.

Colonel Flynn looked up. "Do you? Not many would these days. Try to do the decent thing, bring up your children the way you think best. Teach them a good moral code and so on. For what? So they can just go off and do whatever they like, eh?"

"Your wife thinks Helen was too ashamed to tell you about the baby. She was struggling, needed money. It turned her head."

Colonel Flynn shook his head. "Silly girl. Should have come to me. Prodigal son and all that. Daughter, anyway. Same thing. I would've been angry, of course I would, but I'd never have turned away my own flesh and blood. Never."

"She must have been a proud woman."

"Proud? I suppose so, yes. Stubborn, too. Like me." He shook his head self-deprecatingly and sipped his whisky.

Helen wondered how long it would be before the Flynns discovered that their daughter had, in all probability, been involved in the death of her fellow officer DS Reed-Purvis, intentionally or not. That wasn't somewhere she wanted to go today, but once the press got hold of it...

"I'm afraid your daughter *was* mixed up in a drugs operation, Colonel Flynn. She was working undercover, but at some point she made the decision to switch allegiance. There have been repercussions, and we need to find out who she was in contact with. I have a couple of names."

"Fire away." Colonel Flynn waved his hand. "What does it matter now? She's gone."

Helen took a breath and carried on. "Jagdip and Atul Ranandan. Do those names ring any bells?"

Colonel Flynn shrugged. "Not to me they don't, I'm afraid. I told your Inspector that a couple of foreign-looking fellows have come and gone – using the airfield, you know."

"Yes, I know. It may well be them. Can you remember the last time they were here?"

Colonel Flynn scratched his head. "A couple of weeks or so, give or take a few days. Never paid much attention. Told your Inspector that as well."

Helen gave him a tight smile. "Yes. Thank you." Helen closed her notebook. "I'll leave you my number. It's very important that you contact me if you see them on or around the farm again."

"Understood. Anything to help." Colonel Flynn knocked back his drink and looked wistfully at the half-full bottle on the dining table.

"I'll leave you in peace now," Helen said, getting up from the sofa. "Thank you for your help. I'm very sorry for what's happened here today."

Colonel Flynn made a broken noise in his throat and lowered his head. Helen made her way out of the lounge and left the Flynns to their grief.

Moran flicked through the pile of papers on his blotter. At the bottom of the pile he found a note from Helen McKellar pinned to Nalini's list of the chiropractic clinic's ex-employees. There she was, highlighted in green. Jaseena Ranandan.

What happened to you, Jaseena? Had her brothers dealt with their awkward family situation in some permanent way? It had happened before. Moran remembered a recent story concerning a young girl whose own parents had murdered her to prevent her marrying – or absconding with – a Western boy. He hoped Jaseena would not prove to be another of these horrendous statistics.

Moran was about to put the list to one side, but then a name further down caught his eye. He did a double-take. *Surely not...* He checked again in case he'd completely misread it. But he hadn't; Shona Kempster's name was three down from Jaseena's.

Moran scrunched the paper into a ball and flung it at the corner of the office. Shona had lied to him. He got up and paced the room. *Why?* This called into question her entire motivation for contacting him. Had she manufactured the whole situation? If so, what on earth for?

A short rap on his door and DS Banner appeared. Seeing Moran on the prowl he hesitated briefly before withdrawing into the safer environment of the squad room.

"Come in, Banner," Moran called through the gap. "And bring some good news while you're about it."

Banner reappeared. "Nice to see you back, guv," the sergeant remarked, to Moran's ears rather disingenuously. "Dr Bagri has some observations regarding Father Jeffries' murder."

"Sit." Moran indicated the empty chair.

Banner cleared his throat. "No witnesses, as we've already established, guv. Throat slashed in much the same way as Bling Boy's – and Slough Boy's."

"Mr Dass," Moran said. "Slough Boy has a name."

"Yes, guv. Same as Mr Dass' wound, then."

"There's more, I trust?"

"No prints. No weapon. A mint on the floor of the box."

"A what?"

218

"A mint, guv. A Tic-Tac; you know, the little mints in clear plastic boxes? There was one on the floor of the box where we found Father Jeffries."

"A *confessional*, Banner. It's called a confessional."

"Right. Anyway, it wasn't fresh from the packet; *partly consumed*, I think was the way Dr Bagri put it."

"So we have a DNA sample. Excellent. How do we know it didn't come from Father Jeffries' mouth?"

"Checked with his understudy, guv. Father Kearney. Young bloke, bit of an old woman if you ask me, but he said Father Jeffries would never consider eating or drinking on the job." Banner grinned stupidly. "If you get my meaning, sir."

"Yes, Banner, I get it." Moran exhaled with a heavy sigh. The rush hour traffic rumbled in the background, horns blaring impatiently. Moran felt the headache that had been threatening all day rise another notch on the pain scale. He sat down and rubbed his cheek, a twenty-four-hour growth of stubble rasping against his fingertips. "Come on then; what else did Father Kearney have to say?"

"Plenty," Banner said. "Not much that was useful, though. No grudges against the victim. Jeffries was well liked by his parishioners. Kept himself to himself. Bit of a shining star, I suppose."

"So," Moran nodded. "Apart from the fact that he was a practitioner of religion, we have no apparent motive."

"None that we've been able to establish so far, guv."

"What's DC McKellar up to at the moment?"

"Finishing off some paperwork, guv."

Finishing off your paperwork, I shouldn't wonder. Moran allowed the thought to pass without vocalising it.

"You've heard about Flynn?"

"Yes, guv. Unbelievable."

"Isn't it?" Moran said. "Especially since we'd gone to some trouble not to alert her to our suspicions, wouldn't you say?"

"Yes, guv."

"I wonder what spooked her, then?"

Banner licked his lips and shrugged. "The mother probably told her McKellar had called."

"Nope. We had mum under obs. She hadn't made contact with her daughter before the airfield incident. I heard you took her out for a drink. That right?"

"Yes, guv. Nothing wrong with that."

"Apart from the fact she borrowed your keys, of course."

"I'm sorry about that, guv," Banner replied. He was beginning to perspire in the sticky heat of Moran's office. "It won't happen again."

"No?" Moran shook his head. "I'm pleased to hear that, DS Banner." Moran paused and rested his elbows on the desk. "You didn't by any chance meet up with DS Flynn at a later time? Last night, maybe?"

Banner visibly flinched. "I inspected the Audi last night, guv. Knocked off and went for a drink."

"At the Zodiac?"

Banner hesitated for a second too long.

"Correct, yes?"

"Yes, guv. I was–"

"You weren't thinking, were you?" Moran held the sergeant's eyes. "For the second time in recent history."

"I didn't say anything to spook her, guv. I was just, you know–"

"Letting off a bit of steam? Fancied a bit of revenge?"

Banner sniffed and looked away.

Moran drummed his fingers on the desktop, a long, rhythmic pattern of military precision. "Good job Flynn's still alive then, isn't it? Otherwise you might develop a life-long guilt complex."

"Alive?" Banner looked up in surprise. "But–"

"But she went down in the aircraft? The one I witnessed crash and burn on the Emerson Estate?"

Banner looked bemused. "Yes. Exactly."

"Well, my internal radar says she didn't. And you and Helen are going to prove it," Moran said. "And no cock ups this time, if you think you can manage that?"

Moran turned into the road, a normal, suburban pocket of late twentieth century houses. The address had been on Nalini's list and Moran had no reason to suppose that Shona had moved, recently or otherwise.

He parked with some difficulty, trying to find a section of road that would not obstruct a driveway, but the houses were packed together in usual new estate fashion, like sardines in a tin. He turned the engine off and tried to gather his thoughts. What would he say? Eventually, realising he'd just have to wing it as usual, he got out and approached the house.

The front room curtains were drawn, the drive empty. He knocked. No response. He pushed the letterbox open a fraction and caught a flicker of movement. He called through the gap.

"Shona?" He hammered with his fist. "Open the door. *Police.*" He squinted through the letterbox a second time. Someone was coming. It wasn't Shona. He stepped back as locks scraped and the door hesitantly opened inwards.

A pretty Asian girl in her mid-twenties stood on the threshold. It didn't require a PhD in ophthalmics to see the fear in her deep brown eyes.

"Jaseena Ranandan, I presume?" Moran showed his ID. "May I come in?"

"So let me get this straight," Moran said. "I've been told that your brothers didn't approve of your relationship with your boyfriend? That true?"

Jaseena nodded. "My family are strict Muslims. Simon is an Englishman."

"And Shona offered to put you up so that you could hide from your brothers?"

"They want to send me home in disgrace. I've done nothing wrong."

"OK. I see." Moran felt some compensatory relief that Shona seemed to have been acting in good faith rather than for some hidden nefarious purpose. "But what does your boyfriend think of all this? I understand there was a fracas at the clinic?"

"Yes, there was. He is a little volatile. But I haven't seen him for a long time. He was beaten up, you see, by my brothers. He was in hospital." Jaseena bit her lip. "They hurt him badly."

"Did he report the assault?"

"I doubt it."

Moran cocked his head at the sound of a car engine and wondered fleetingly what Shona's reaction would be when she found him in her sitting room. "Jaseena, are you aware that your brothers are involved in drug trafficking?"

Her hand went to her mouth. "No. What are you saying? They wouldn't. Jagdip is in business. He's not–"

"I'm afraid the evidence is mounting."

They both turned their heads as a key snecked in the lock and Shona came in. When she saw Moran she stopped and put down the shopping bags she was carrying.

"Ah. Brendan. You're here. I *was* going to tell you..."

"I wish you had. Might have saved me quite a bit of time and hassle."

"I'm sorry. I'm doing it for Jas."

"I know. To protect her from her brothers."

"Her brothers? Her boyfriend's the scary one. The brothers might want to send her home, but God only knows what Simon's capable of."

Moran raised an eyebrow. "You make him sound like a psychopath."

The two women exchanged knowing glances.

Moran gave Shona a hard look. "Come on. Tell me more."

"Didn't Jas tell you? Her brothers beat him up. I saw it happen." Shona took a deep, resigned breath. "I'd popped into work to collect a cheque; the clinic owed me some money. He was hanging around outside, asking for Jas. I said she wasn't in and he stormed off. He was ranting and shouting. I thought he might do something to himself, you know . . . then, by the canal ... well, they nearly killed him, that's all."

Shona paused, worrying the strap of her handbag. Moran gave her time to collect herself.

"I called the ambulance," Shona continued. "Waited for the paramedics to arrive – I mean I didn't want the poor guy to die or anything." She looked over at Jaseena appealingly but the girl's head was bowed, as if embroiled in some exigent inner turmoil.

Shona moistened her lips. "Since then he's changed. Something happened to his head; he was a bit odd before, but now–"

"I'm scared he might be, might have–" Jaseena began, but Shona cut her off with a look.

"Might have what?" Moran asked.

Jaseena took a breath. "Might have killed those poor boys. The stabbings in the newspapers," she blurted. "He hates Asian people now."

Moran sat down heavily in an armchair. He looked at Shona with shocked reproach. "You knew about this guy and you didn't tell me?"

"It's probably nothing to do with him." Shona fumbled in her handbag and produced a packet of cigarettes. "I'm only saying he's a bit of a nutter. Sorry, Jas." She lit up and winced at Jaseena, who shook her head and looked miserably into her lap.

"I'll be the judge of whether or not it's anything to do with whomever, or whatever." Moran said, aware that his anger was making him less than coherent. His thoughts and words tumbled over each other. "You should have told me."

"I'm sorry, Brendan."

"What's this man's name?"

"Simon Peters," Jaseena said. "He's a nice guy, mostly, really he is–"

"Spare me," Moran said shortly. "Where can I find him?"

"That's just it. I don't know where he is anymore." Jaseena shrugged. "He's disappeared."

"Where did you meet him?"

"He came to the clinic a few months ago. He had problems with his back. An accident, he said. We talked, and then after his last session he asked me out."

"Distinguishing marks? Habits?"

"He wears gloves a lot of the time. He burned his hands badly in a fire."

"Anything else? What does he do? Job-wise, I mean?"

The women looked at each other. "He's retired," Jaseena said. "On health grounds, with a good payoff. He writes poetry. He's very good at it, too."

"Really." Moran jotted the facts down.

"I have a photo." Jaseena brightened. "Wait a moment." She got up and Moran heard her footsteps on the stairs and then the creak of a bedroom floorboard.

There was an awkward pause.

"Brendan, I feel very foolish. I know I should have told you."

"Yes. You should have. You lied to me, Shona; I asked you if you knew the practice."

"I didn't work for Suri," Shona protested. "It wasn't really a lie. I worked at the chiropractic clinic, not the physio."

"Oh, come on," Moran said under his breath. He was seething with anger, struggling to rein it in before he said something he might later regret.

"We can still see each other, can't we? I mean, it needn't spoil things, need it?"

"I'll think about it, Shona. Right now I've got too much on my plate."

"I understand."

An aeroplane hummed somewhere high in the stratosphere. As it faded the sound merged into the staccato rattle of someone's lawnmower.

Jaseena's footsteps pattered down the stairs. "Here. I couldn't remember where I'd put it." She handed a small, passport-sized photograph to Moran. "Can I have it back?"

Moran took it. "Of course you can. I just–" He broke off, staring at the picture in his hand.

"What? What is it?" Shona demanded. "What's wrong?"

"*Simon Peters*? This isn't Simon Peters, or Simon anyone. This is Gregory Neads. My ex-sergeant."

Chapter Twenty-Five

Banner edged his way past the granary towards the hangers. He could hear an aero engine firing and missing, as though a mechanic was working on some fault of timing or ignition.

They had called at the farmhouse first and found only Mrs Flynn at home. She had been unable to confirm her husband's whereabouts, but she had looked shifty to Banner. He'd left Helen in the farmhouse to make sure that the faithful wife didn't alert Colonel Flynn to their presence.

Banner reached the hanger door and peered cautiously into the open space. A single-seater plane took up most of the space, one of those kit jobs that Banner would never have entrusted his life to. Two people were busily attentive to the open engine compartment; the first was Colonel Flynn, the man who claimed no aeronautical interest or involvement. The second was Sharron Flynn.

Banner retreated a few paces and called in the uniform support he had positioned on standby a few hundred metres down the lane. As he waited for his backup's customary tyre-screeching arrival Banner reflected on Moran's finely tuned intuition. Colonel Flynn had all but convinced Helen of his role as grieving and ignorant father, but Moran had spotted something else: Colonel Flynn had been cleaning his hands with an oily rag when Moran had called. Nothing odd about that, except the old man had told Moran he'd been fixing some plumbing problem – not the sort of repair work you'd usually associate with oil. That, and the fact that the Flynn's bookcase had contained a number of aircraft-related books and a well-thumbed wedge of aeronautical magazines, had aroused Moran's suspicions.

Banner felt a pang of jealousy. Would he have spotted the tell-tale signs? Maybe, maybe not. Still, at least he was on site to make the arrest. That always made him feel better. Once he was done here he'd decide what to do about Neads. He hadn't told Moran yet that he'd followed the ex-detective sergeant, that he knew where Neads could be found. Knowledge was power, Banner reminded himself. You had to be careful who you shared it with.

"He's calling himself Simon Peters," Moran announced. "I want a check made of all recently rented flats or houses in the area under that name."

Helen raised a hand.

"Yes, Helen?"

"Do we have any evidence actually linking Greg Neads to the murders, guv?"

Moran hesitated. Apart from the fact that Neads had every reason to be both anti-Muslim and anti-Catholic, there *was* no hard evidence. But that might change once he'd interviewed Sharron Flynn.

"Honestly, no," he told Helen and Harding. "But it fits. Neads appeared to know what was going down in Jag Ranandan's operation, even to the extent of claiming to know where DC Hill was being held. Banner tells me that he spotted Neads at the Zodiac stalking – or at least keeping tabs on – Jag Ranandan himself."

Helen bit her lip and looked away at the mention of Hill's name.

"Which means he's been playing detective." Harding chewed his pencil.

"Yes. And he's pretty damn good at it, too," Moran said. "The question is, what will he do next? What are his motives?"

"Revenge." Helen shrugged. "Against the Ranandans. And their family," she added.

"And you too, guv," Harding said. "He sounds crazy enough. And he did threaten you."

"Uh huh." Moran paced the floor. "I can look after myself, DC Harding. But thanks for your concern."

A few corridors away Charlie Pepper and Banner were in the process of softening up Sharron Flynn for the main event: Moran's interview. He was itching to get on with it, but Neads had to be found as a matter of urgency. *Blind, Moran, that's what you are – blind...* He now admitted that he hadn't *allowed* himself to include Neads as a potential suspect. Why? *Guilt, that's why, Moran. Plain, idiotic, blind guilt...*

He shook the thought away and went on. "According to the hospital, a Simon Peters was discharged a week ago from the RBH. The doctor I spoke to confirmed the description, and also surmised that Neads could be suffering from what he called 'cognitive disruption'."

"No wonder, after what he's been through," Harding muttered. "Why the name change, though?"

"A fresh start? Rejection of his past life?" Helen offered.

"Quite possibly. But whatever the reason," Moran continued, "he's not in his right mind. Whatever thoughts of revenge he was harbouring as fantasies might now be translated into real action. That means he could well be our killer. And it also means he's extremely dangerous."

229

Moran sat down heavily at a spare desk and rubbed his eyes. "I'd like to take the lead on this, Helen but I've got Flynn to sort out first. Take Harding with you, make sure you have backup, and bring in Gregory Neads. Do whatever it takes, but do it *fast*."

Sharron Flynn looked up briefly as Moran entered the interview room and then let her gaze drop back to the tabletop. Banner took his cue and made a swift exit. Charlie spoke to the recorder.

"DCI Brendan Moran has just entered the room. DS Banner has left the room."

Moran sat at the table and fixed his eyes on Sharron Flynn. She looked terrible. Her eyes were dark and sunken, her skin pale and unhealthy-looking. Too much stress? Too much time spent tinkering with aero engines? Too much sampling the contraband?

"So. Back from the dead," Moran stated. "How does it feel?"

Flynn compressed her thin lips and said nothing. Her fingers described vague patterns on the tabletop.

"We're interviewing your father next door," Moran told her. "So you might as well tell us everything."

Flynn toyed with a lock of her hair. "About?"

"Let's begin at the beginning, shall we?" Moran was making a huge effort to keep his cool. If he was right, then this woman was partly responsible for the deaths of two police officers. He noticed Charlie shooting him an anxious glance.

Flynn shrugged.

"It all began well, didn't it?" Moran folded his arms. "High profile operation. Working with an experienced and respected SIO."

Flynn worked her facial muscles and carried on with her patterns.

"And then the laws of attraction came into play. You got too close to said SIO. You fell pregnant. Not good."

Flynn gave Charlie a look, as if she were seeking some kind of female empathy for her actions.

"And then what? Money too tight? A wicked idea came to mind?" Moran leaned forward. "*Maybe I could threaten to spill the beans,* you thought. *Unless, Mr SIO, you give me a nice little paycheck every month.* Is that what you were thinking, Sharron?" Moran leaned back and watched Flynn's expression, noting a small droplet of sweat appear just beneath her hairline before it was wiped away with the back of her hand.

He went on. "But – oh dear, what then? Mr SIO doesn't have enough dosh to shell out without Mrs SIO getting suspicious. So he tells you he doesn't know what to do. His career and marriage are at stake. *No problem,* you say, *I'll do a little deal with Mr Ranandan. We'll turn a blind eye to his operation and he'll give us a cut. In fact, we'll even help him out. We'll let him use the airstrip and I can fly for him. We'll double the profits and take an even bigger cut. Problem solved – Ranandan and Co. get the old bill on their side, Mrs SIO is kept in the dark and we both get rich.*"

Flynn shifted uncomfortably in her seat. "Can I have a drink?"

Moran nodded to Charlie, who went to the door and asked for three mugs of tea.

"And a jolly nice flat you have too, by all accounts, DS Flynn. I bet you couldn't pay for that on a sergeant's take-home pay, eh?" Moran raised his eyebrows.

Charlie sat down again and Moran got up. He went to the window and folded his arms behind his back. "But then you had a little problem, didn't you? In the shape of DS Reed-Purvis. She was a *good* cop. And she sussed you out, didn't she?" He came and stood behind Flynn, placed his hands on the back of her chair. "*Didn't she?*"

Flynn's hands were shaking. She clasped her right wrist with her left hand.

Moran leaned down until his mouth was by Flynn's right ear. "So you drugged her. With GHB. That's gamma-hydroxybutyrate, Sharron. But you know that, don't you?"

"I didn't mean to kill her. I just wanted her out of the way that evening. She was alive the last time I saw her. Honest to God. She left the club, but I felt bad. I wanted to make sure she was OK. I was going to call her a cab."

"Is that so?" Moran straightened up. "But you didn't. Perhaps you'd like to tell DI Pepper and myself what happened next." Moran went to the radiator and leaned on it. The evening sun spilled into the room and fell across the table. It made Flynn's face appear even paler.

"I went to the exit, but Val was already walking down the street. Then she stopped. I saw someone run across the road. I heard her call out. She'd seen something. I followed. There was a guy in a doorway – he was dead, I could tell. And then I saw Val chasing this guy who was running away. Then he turned round and caught her. I didn't know what to do. I had no backup."

"No *backup*?" Charlie's mouth fell open. "You poisoned your own colleague and then thought about getting *backup*?"

232

"I didn't mean to hurt her," Flynn shouted. "It wasn't me. The guy she chased, he did it. There was a struggle. She fell over and he put her in the boot of his car."

"Oh my God." Charlie's hand was at her mouth. "She couldn't fight back. The GHB had kicked in."

Flynn nodded.

"And then?" Moran prompted.

"He drove off. I went back to the Zodiac."

"You walked away. All sorted, right?" Charlie's voice caught and she cleared her throat huskily.

The door opened with a peremptory knock and a uniformed sergeant brought in a tray of tea.

"Thank you, Sergeant. I think we all need that." Moran smiled thinly.

Moran returned to his seat and sipped the hot tea. Flynn stared at her drink but her hands remained clasped as if manacled together. Moran placed his mug carefully on the table.

"Who was in the plane?"

Flynn ran her tongue around her lips and looked at the window, as if it might suddenly open and allow her to escape.

"Come on, Sharron. We'll find out anyway, once forensics has pieced it all together."

"Was it one of the Ranandans?" Charlie asked.

"No."

"Then who?"

"A friend. A mechanic. He tests the planes for us, services them."

"I see. An expendable friend," Moran offered, his tone steady and reasonable.

"It was my father's idea. He–" Flynn began, but broke off, coughing.

"Have a drink," Moran suggested.

Flynn took a deep breath before continuing. When she looked at Moran her eyes were defiant. "He fixed an aileron so it wouldn't function at a certain height. I didn't want to go that far, but–"

"No. It's always someone else, isn't it, Sharron? Not your fault." Charlie's voice was almost a whisper.

"He loves me," Flynn protested "Any father would protect his daughter. Do you know that the farm has been in my family for generations? And they're taking it away from him, piece by piece? Do you know how much that hurts him? How much it *costs* him?"

"Daddy's another beneficiary of your scheme, is he, Sharron?" Moran took a mouthful of tea to mask the bitter taste in his mouth. "Anyone else currently enjoying your largesse that we should know about?"

Flynn shook her head.

"What was the next move, then, Sharron?" Moran pressed on. "A new life in Australia? A forged ID? A short hop over the Channel and then a long haul to the Outback?"

"Close. Thailand, actually." Flynn sniffed and tapped the edge of her mug.

"Plenty of opportunity to offer your trafficking expertise there, I expect," Moran observed caustically.

"Can you describe the man you saw attack DS Reed-Purvis?" Charlie had brought herself under control. Her face was composed, her mouth set in a determined line.

"Six foot. Fair to blond hair. Limped."

Moran nodded. It had to be Neads. Unluckily for him, a police officer had spotted him just seconds after his first murder. *Unlucky, Gregory. Unlucky again...*

"What will happen to me? And Alan?" Flynn's eyes were flat, resigned.

"That's not up to me, DS Flynn," Moran said icily. "Luckily for you. Now, if you'll excuse me, DI Pepper is going to ask some more questions regarding the Ranandans. I strongly suggest you co-operate." Moran nodded to Charlie. "Carry on, DI Pepper."

Moran left Charlie to conclude the interview and dialled Helen's number for an update on Neads.

Chapter Twenty-Six

"Got it, guv." Helen's matter-of-fact tone belied the excitement Moran knew she must be feeling.

Almost immediately Banner was at Helen's desk. Moran wasn't much slower. They all focused on the photograph and description on Helen's laptop screen.

"I know it, guv." Helen looked up, her face slightly flushed. "It's a new development near Caversham Bridge, overlooking the river. Quite posh."

"I know it as well," Banner said. "Must have had a nice payoff. To afford a place like that, I mean."

"He would have done," Moran said tersely. "The annuity lump sum would have covered most of it." He straightened up. "Nice work, Helen. Let's pay Mr *Peters* a visit, shall we?"

"Ascetic," Moran said, taking in the bare apartment with its Spartan rectangular strip of carpet, unused kitchen and pristine pine dining table.

Helen crossed the room and opened the fridge. It was empty, sterile. She stuck her head into the small bedroom and frowned. "No bed either. Are we sure he's actually been living here?"

"Oh yes," Moran said. "I can smell him. He's been here all right."

Banner loosened his collar and stuck his head out of the Velux. "Nice view. Wonder why he chose the penthouse?"

Moran took a last look around the empty flat. "He used to climb. Big hobby of his. Maybe high places make him feel superior to the rest of us. I'll bet he feels like a god up here."

"Some god." Helen shuddered, thinking of the photographs of Father Jeffries' mutilated body.

"Well, god or loony," Banner said, closing the window with a bang that made Helen jump, "the million dollar question is, where the hell is he now?"

The Kafir knocked on the door. If he'd timed it right they'd both be here. He'd taken a great deal of care deciding on the order of events, and his final decision pleased him. He had also spent a long time marvelling at the wonderful serendipity of it all. Jag Ranandan and DCI Moran at the same time. Surely it had all been predetermined by his helper? It was all meant to be. And now, here he was; this was the *coup de grace*, the end game to avenge all the wrongs done to him. He felt a little dizzy at the prospect.

The security chain jingled and Jaseena's face appeared. The door began to close almost at once, but he'd been ready for her reaction. His foot was in the gap, his shoulder against the wood. The chain split and the door flew open. He heard another voice call out.

"*Jas*? Are you OK?"

He closed the door behind him, bent and severed the BT line. Jaseena was backed against the wall, her mouth open in horror. "What's the matter, Jas? Aren't you pleased to see me?"

Another woman appeared in the lounge doorway –
Shona Kempster. Moran's love interest. Excellent; both
eggs safely in the basket. The Kafir grinned a greeting
and held up the kitchen knife so that both women could
see it.

"I wasn't sure which one to bring," he told the
cowering women. "This one is brand new. Nice and
sharp." His voice roughened. "Pack a bag," he told them.
"I can't wait to show you where we're spending the
weekend."

"Brendan? Someone to see you." Denis Robinson, the
Duty Sergeant, shrugged an apology.

Moran groaned. It was late. He had Flynn and
Sheldrake in custody, all units were on alert for Gregory
Neads, aka Simon Peters, and he had hoped for a
nightcap with Shona followed by a decent night's sleep.
Not that he'd sleep much anyway. Now that the others
had knocked off and he was alone with his thoughts they
kept returning his mother lying motionless beside him as
he dozed. Drifting into eternity on her own...

"She seems upset, Brendan," the sergeant prompted.
"I'd best go back down and make sure she's all right.
Can't leave the front desk unattended."

"Who is it, Denis?" Moran asked wearily.

"Young girl. Indian. Says her name's Nalini – or
something like that."

"I'll be right down."

"Right you are, Brendan. By the way–"

"What?"

"You look knackered. You should go home and get
some kip."

"Thanks, Denis. I'd never have thought of that."

Moran logged off his PC and made his way down the stairs to reception. Nalini was on her feet as soon as he appeared.

"Mr Moran. I had to tell you. He made me. I'm sorry. I am very frightened."

She seemed it. She was shaking like a sapling in a storm. Moran took her arm.

"All right. Take it easy; you're safe now – Denis?"

"Yep?" The sergeant's head popped up at the reinforced glass counter.

"Can you rustle up a cup of tea for this young lady? We'll be in number one."

"Right you are."

Moran ushered Nalini through and sat her down. "Now, slowly does it. Tell me what's happened."

"It's Simon. He came to the practice again. I was alone. He frightened me. He was *different*." Nalini covered her face with her hands. "Now, I think he is even more crazy. He called himself this strange name, *Kafir*... 'I am not Simon,' he said. His voice was different. He wanted to know if Jag had been back to the practice. If I'd told him anything. He said he knew where Jaseena was now. I was very frightened."

Moran felt a chill run down his spine. "What else did he say?"

"He said she was with her friend, Shona Kempster. Shona used to work in the practice, last year. She's very nice. Very kind. I am frightened for her, I–"

"It's all right, Nalini. When did this happen?"

"This evening. He let me go eventually. He said a lot more crazy stuff, and then he said his helper had just told him where Shona lived. I wouldn't have told him, Mr

Moran, I came straight here. On the bus. It took a long time. I'm sorry."

"Tea?" Sergeant Robinson came in and plonked a tray on the table. There were two sachets of sugar and two teaspoons lined up neatly by the mugs.

"Go on," Moran encouraged. "It'll do you good."

"Thank you."

As Nalini sipped her tea Moran slipped out and told Robinson to get Banner and Helen McKellar over to Shona Kempster's house sharpish. He gave them strict instructions to take no action, just observe. Then he rejoined Nalini, who was looking a little calmer – considerably calmer than Moran himself felt. Why had he not anticipated this? How could he have been so short-sighted? *You stupid Irish tosser, Moran...*

He tried to keep his voice steady and reassuring. "What else did he say, Nalini? Anything at all, even if it sounds silly or irrelevant."

"He was smiling and laughing a lot. Talking nonsense. I thought he would hurt me. He talked about going away, going to a clean town?" She shrugged. "I'm not sure. He didn't make much sense to me at all. I was so happy when he went."

Moran nodded. "Thank you. You did the right thing coming to see me. I'll get one of the female duty officers to give you a lift home." He caught the anxious look in Nalini's eyes. "Don't worry. We'll keep an eye on you. I promise."

Just after Nalini left Moran received a call from Banner. They'd checked out Shona's house: no one home. Moran's heart did a slow roll. What was in Neads' head?

What would he do? He recalled the consultant's dry pronouncement: *cognitive disruption...*

"Clues?" Moran barked down the phone, his voice sounding harsh and flat.

"Funnily enough, guv, yes. There's a note pinned to the front door, a cartoon of a knife. And a message."

"Go on." Moran clenched the receiver hard.

"It says: 'Leaving the smoke for an elevated view of a cleaner town. See you there, Brendan.'"

"That's it?"

There was a brief silence at the other end. "There's a PS," Banner said, reluctance clear in his voice.

"Spit it out, Banner."

"It says: 'You have until dawn. Then one dies. If you're still a no show, Brendan, the second dies at midday tomorrow. I haven't decided who's first yet. Oh, and come alone. No funny stuff or they both get the chop. Don't be late.'"

Chapter Twenty-Seven

"What does he want?" Helen McKellar's brows knitted into a frown which made her look vulnerable and attractive at the same time. She pushed the hair away from her eyes and folded her arms.

"He wants me," Moran said. "I'm to blame for this whole ludicrous mess."

"Come on, guv, that's not true," Helen protested. "The guy's got a screw loose."

"Yes, and I'm the one who undid it."

"With respect, guv, that's bullshit," Helen spread her hands in a gesture of appeal. "You did everything you could at Charnford. It wasn't your fault."

Moran sighed. "I wish I could believe that, Helen."

"What are you going to do?"

Moran paced his office. The sound of a motorcycle engine filtered in through the open window. The room was humid and airless. All Moran wanted was a shower, a change of clothes and Shona Kempster. He didn't want to dwell on what she might be going through right now; given his emotional involvement, that would be counterproductive. It was down to him to get her out of the mess she'd inadvertently got herself into. *That you've got her into, Moran...* He stood at his desk and rattled his fingers on the desktop.

"I'm going to have a quick word with Sergeant Phelps, Helen. Then I'm going to make an end of this. In the meantime, I want you and DI Pepper to talk to our friend Zoë. Use whatever powers of persuasion you can bring to bear. I want Jag Ranandan off the streets, and Zoë is our best bet."

Charlie Pepper sucked an extra strong mint and tried to push Sharron Flynn out of her head. In all her experience she had never met anyone as cold and callous as Flynn. How anyone could betray a colleague the way Reed-Purvis had been betrayed was beyond Charlie's imagination. Her success in trapping Flynn, feather in her cap though it might be, wasn't nearly enough to cleanse the bad taste in her mouth. She suspected that even Jag Ranandan's entrapment would fail to restore her spirits.

But she'd been here before; this wasn't the first time a fellow police officer had come to a bad end on Charlie's patch, and, she reflected, it probably wouldn't be the last. She knocked on the door of the dark blue Vauxhall Movano van and waited to be admitted. When the door opened she clambered in and slid it shut behind her.

"All right, boss?" DC Harding settled back into his swivel seat in front of the surveillance desk. Charlie could hear the low-volume monitored sounds of the Zodiac emanating from the stereo speakers built into the desk's panelling. The aircon was bliss after the stifling heat of the town centre. Charlie undid her blouse a notch to allow the cool air to circulate around her skin.

Her mobile bleeped. A text from Helen – Zoë was in situ. Good. Now all they had to do was hope that Mr Ranandan turned up. Charlie wondered how patient Zoë would be in her role as *agent provocateur*, how long it would take before she lost interest. It hadn't taken a great deal of persuasion to get her to agree to the job; she hated

Jag with a vengeance, and this was her chance to get him off her back for good.

"All working?"

"So far," Harding grinned. "Let's hope he doesn't suss her out."

"She's cool," Charlie said. "There's no flies on Zoë, so I've heard. The original streetwise kid, apparently."

"Hmmm. Oh, by the way, I was wondering..." Harding said casually.

"What?"

"If you might be free for a drink tomorrow night?" Harding beamed his best, most winning smile.

"Let's keep our minds on the job, DC Harding, shall we? I'll give you an answer later." Charlie turned her head to avoid showing Harding the grin she was struggling to suppress. *Men. Talk about one track...*

"Sure thing, boss. No problem. Is Helen joining us?" Harding transitioned smoothly back to work mode.

"Soonish. I told her to hang around for a bit, just in case Zoë needs any help. And Harding?"

"Yep?"

"Please don't call me 'boss'. It makes me feel like an extra from *The Godfather*."

"Fair enough." Harding adjusted a slider and put a set of headphones to one ear. "Zoë? Can you hear me OK?"

"Loud and clear." Zoë's voice, laconic and long-suffering, came back through the speakers.

Charlie dipped her head closer to the microphone. "Hi Zoë. Charlie. Any sign?"

"Atul's here somewhere. No Jag yet."

"OK. Keep us posted."

"This had better be worth it, doll."

244

"It's always worth getting scumbags like Jag Ranandan off the street, Zoë," Charlie said with feeling.

"Hang on," Zoë said. "He's here."

"Good luck. Take it nice and easy." Charlie bit her lip. So, Moran had been right. Even though Jag must have known what had gone down at the farm earlier that day, he was still arrogant enough to maintain his local profile. *Well, Mr Ranandan,* Charlie muttered to herself, *your profile is about to be significantly lowered...*

"Wondered when you'd be back, guv." Sergeant Robert Phelps was sitting in a chair next to his hospital bed.

"Am I being rebuked, Robert?"

"Not at all, guv. Busy man, I understand."

"You can say that again." Moran slumped into the visitor's chair. There was a pile of magazines and an unopened carton of cereal bars on the bedside table. "How are you?"

"Fine," Phelps said. "No, actually, that's a lie. I'm bored out of my bloody mind."

"Physically?"

"Consultant reckons I'll live a bit longer. Provided I make a few sacrifices."

Moran smiled. "That's great."

Phelps shook his head vehemently. "No, it's not. How am I going to survive without a fag? Or a glass of Glenfiddich?"

"Take it easy. Don't get yourself excited."

Phelps guffawed. "A bit of excitement wouldn't go amiss. So, come on, let's cut to the chase. It's way past visiting time. Something's up, right?"

Moran was enjoying the hunger in Phelps' eyes. He was still a copper, coronary survivor or not. Moran would have given a lot to have Phelps with him for the next twelve hours.

"It's Neads."

"Why am I not surprised?" Phelps scratched his cheek and raised his chin interrogatively. There was something incongruous about a big man like Phelps dressed in pyjamas and a dressing gown. The sergeant was like a fish out of water in his hospital garb and surroundings.

Moran ran a hand through his hair. God, he was tired. He took a deep breath and went on. "Looks like Neads flipped. Some heavies beat him up and chucked him into the canal a week or so back. They didn't want him to date their sister. And get this – we now have a witness who saw Neads attack DS Reed-Purvis the night Bling Boy was killed."

"OK. Sounds promising so far."

"It gets worse. Neads has just abducted the sister and Shona Kempster."

"Whaat? That's the girl who you–"

"Yes."

"I'm sorry, guv." Phelps shook his head. "That's just unbelievable."

"Isn't it. Problem is, I don't know where he's taken them."

"Ah. That's where I come in?"

"What do you remember about Greg Neads? What made him tick?" Moran leaned forward. "He left a note."

Phelps watched as Moran fished a piece of paper from his trouser pocket. *Leaving the smoke for an elevated view of a cleaner town.* "I mean, what the hell is all that about?"

"He's being his usual self," Phelps grunted. "An arrogant little shit."

246

"I have to find him, Robert. He's given me until dawn. Then he's going to kill them both."

"Will he do it?"

Moran got up and drummed his fingers on the bedstead. "I think so, yes. He's not in his right mind. *Cognitive disruption*, the consultant reckoned."

Phelps was silent for a few moments, pondering. "He fancied himself as a poet. Used to read stuff to me. It wasn't bad."

"What else? *A cleaner town*?" Moran forced his tired brain to think. "Are there any clean towns? Unpolluted? Is that what he means? There's pollution everywhere. It can't be that."

Phelps was grinning. "I know what he means. He's having a laugh."

"I'm glad someone is."

"Bath."

"Bath?"

"Can't get any cleaner than that, guv."

Moran batted the side of his head. "Right! You're a ruddy marvel, Robert!" Then he frowned. "But what's the elevated bit?"

"A high place. He was into mountains, wasn't he? Climbing?"

"He was." Moran thought of the penthouse, the lofty view.

"OK, so maybe you're after the top floor of a hotel in Bath?"

Moran shook his head. "He wouldn't choose somewhere so public."

"All right, then. A hill? Bath is in a valley."

Moran retrieved his iPhone and googled Bath. "Solsbury Hill? Just outside the city?"

"He'd want somewhere secure, guv."

Moran clicked on the next link. "Beckford's Tower?" He scanned the page and read the blurb with a growing sense of excitement.

"Heard of that," Phelps said. "It's a Landmark Trust building. You can rent it. Me and the Missus have stayed in a few Landmark properties in our time. BK, that is – before kids."

"It's perfect," Moran said. "But is it right?" He tapped a key on his mobile. "Banner? Can you check if Beckford's Tower in Bath has been booked for the weekend? If so, by whom? Straight away please. Thanks."

Two minutes later Moran's phone rang. "Guv? Banner. Yes, it has. To a Mr Simon Peters."

Phelps raised his arm in poker-faced farewell as Moran made for the door. His sergeant's parting words followed Moran into the car park, resonating in his head like a tuning fork.

"Watch him like a hawk, guv," Phelps had warned. "Right now he's got all the aces, and I'd hate you to finish up holding the joker."

Chapter Twenty-Eight

Charlie felt sweat run down her back as she listened. They'd killed the engine and the aircon had gone with it. Zoë's voice was beginning to fade into the escalating background racket as the pubs emptied and more punters arrived for their after-hours entertainment, which made it difficult to hear what was going on, even despite the supposed sophistication of Harding's surveillance equipment. Charlie puckered her lips and tried to concentrate.

"You heard about the arrests?" they heard Zoë prompt, casually.

"Yeah. So what?" Jag's voice was calm and unruffled.

"So, she might grass you up."

"Not a chance," Jag replied with a snort. "She's got nothing on me, anyhow. Nobody has."

"That copper, Moran. He knows you're involved."

"Why are you suddenly so interested in my welfare?" Jag's voice probed silkily.

"'Cause I don't want to get done, neither. I've got a living to make an' all."

"You do a good job for me, Zoë. Have I ever let you down?"

"What about the other copper? Flynn's boss?"

"Sheldrake? He won't make any trouble. He'll go down, anyhow. Flynn will stitch him up. Why shouldn't she? As for the others, the ones that matter are in my pocket, sure thing." There was a rustle as Jag tapped his chinos to illustrate his point. "Even the new ones," he added smugly.

"Cool."

"How much are you taking tonight?" Jag asked matter-of-factly.

"Usual."

"Good. I'll see to it."

Come on, girl, keep going. Charlie ransacked her mind for another angle she could feed through to keep the conversation going, but Zoë had it all under control.

"I might need more than usual next weekend," she said.

"Oh? That's good." Jag sounded both puzzled and pleased. "Why?"

"Because I've made a couple of new contacts. Thing is, they want a mixed bag."

"What exactly?" Jag's voice was edged with curiosity – and something else. Greed.

Zoë lowered her voice so that Charlie had to strain to make out the words. "Couple of bricks. Some smack."

"No problem."

"And some GHB. You know, the stuff you got for Flynn."

"Why?"

"Comes in handy when I need to make a quick exit. Know what I mean?"

"You're evil, Zoë," Jag laughed. "That's why I like you. Listen, not so easy to get the GHB. It took a little time before."

"Did the job though, didn't it?"

"Yes. Bloody good thing, too – that copper was going to blow the trumpet, that's for sure. Anyways, Atul will deal with it. No worries."

"Can he get it OK?"

"Yah, yah. Just a bit tricky, that's all. Give me a few days."

"Thanks."

"I'll be back."

"I'll be waiting, big man," Zoë trilled.

Harding swivelled in his chair and made elated thumbs-up signs to Charlie. She sat back, relieved. They'd got all the evidence they needed. She high-fived Harding.

"No excuse to turn that drink down now, right?" he beamed.

"Drink later. Food now," Charlie said firmly. Having missed out on supper yet again, her stomach was rumbling. "There's a late chippie around the corner. Interested?"

"Am I ever?" Harding enthused, "And you'd better get something for Helen, too. She eats like a horse."

"I'm sure she'll be delighted with that observation, DC Harding," Charlie chuckled. "Fish supper coming up."

Charlie slipped out of her seat and slid open the door catch. As she walked briskly along the street she reflected on her first few days in TVP. *All in all, not a bad start, Charlie.* DCI Rawlings, her old guv'nor, would have been proud of her. She made a mental note to give him a call in the morning.

She thought of Harding's invitation and smiled to herself. He wasn't bad looking, but her rule was to keep the job well separate from her private life. She'd seen too many relationships founder under the spotlight of the incident room.

Charlie followed her nose into the chip shop and noted with satisfaction that the owner was in the process of laying out a fresh batch of newly-fried cod. Her mouth began to water at the delicious smells, but then she guiltily remembered Moran. She might have got a result tonight, but Moran had the tougher task. As she waited to be served she wondered how her new DCI was getting on.

Moran gripped the steering wheel and tried to stick to the speed limit. It wasn't easy. His satnav display read: *Bath: 51 miles*. What would he do when he got there? What appeal could he make to Neads' malfunctioning mind? The call he'd made to Bagri half an hour before he left had raised more questions than it had provided answers.

"I am no expert in psychiatric conditions, Detective Inspector Moran," Bagri had admitted. "But it sounds to me, from what your young chiropractic receptionist has told you, as though your fellow could be suffering from what is known as dissociative identity disorder."

"Go on," Moran had prompted.

"I am having to remember carefully; it is a long time since I studied these things. Now, yes, dissociative identity disorder is characterised by the presence of two or more distinct or split identities or personality states that continually have power over the person's behaviour. Your Mr Neads may have difficulty recalling key personal information. He may have memory variations which fluctuate with his split personalities. All the different identities will have their own age, sex or race, each with his or her own postures, gestures and very distinctive way of talking. Each personality controls the poor man's behaviour and thoughts. I am thinking it is

252

called 'switching'. Now, this switching can take seconds, or minutes, or days. He may have headaches, amnesia, time loss, all sorts of bad mental disruptions. Maybe even he will begin to self-persecute. Maybe he will be violent. Detective Chief Inspector," Bagri had warned solemnly, "I am thinking you must be most careful."

Despite Bagri's analysis of Neads' possible condition, Moran didn't believe he would hurt Jaseena – by the girl's own testimony he had professed to love her only weeks before. No, he wanted Jaseena on board to get back at Jag. On the other hand, Moran fretted, Shona was a different matter; the ex-sergeant was plainly aware of Moran's close attachment to the pretty physiotherapist, a fact that Moran was sure Neads would have no hesitation in exploiting.

His thoughts returned to Charnford, where it had all started. If only he had kept Neads with him that night instead of sending him to interview a suspect, none of this would be happening. *If only... No good, Moran, no good thinking that...*

He checked the mileage again. *Sod it*, he thought, and put his foot to the floor.

Harding turned at the sound of the rap on the van door. It wasn't quite the signal they'd prearranged, but he imagined Charlie juggling packets of hot chips and reached for the lock with a grin of anticipation.

As the door slid open the first thing he saw was Helen's blank expression. Before he had time to register alarm she had been pushed, sprawling, into the body of the van beside him, followed by Zoë, yelling and cursing at the top of her voice. Her cries were abruptly cut off as an arm reached in and struck her on the head. Zoë collapsed like a sack of potatoes.

All this happened in seconds. Before Harding was able to react the door had closed and he heard a heavy bang as something smashed into the lock. Harding swore and heaved at the handle, but the mechanism had been effectively disabled. He turned to Helen who was nursing a bruised forehead.

"Are you OK? What's going down?" He tried to keep panic out of his voice. *Calm, Ken, calm... Charlie'll be back any time, it's cool...* He shook Helen by the shoulders. "Helen?"

But Helen was groggy and clearly unwell; she sank to the floor, retching and moaning. Zoë was out cold. Harding squeezed past her prone body into the driving cab. What he saw next froze the blood in his veins.

Two guys outside were sloshing liquid all over the van from plastic canisters. *Petrol.* Harding banged on the windscreen, pulled at the door handle. A face looked in at him, a man in his thirties with a goatee and a mole on his cheek. His face was expressionless. *God, they can't, they wouldn't...*

Harding threw his weight on the passenger door, but it was solid, reinforced and customised for police work. He banged on the windows, frantically scanning the pavement for passers by but the streets were quiet. Either everyone had gone home for the night or they were continuing their evening in the clubs. Where was Charlie?

The goatee man stood back and his accomplice, hooded and half-masked across his mouth, flicked a Zippo. The bluish yellow flame flickered as he brought the lighter towards the Vauxhall Movano's bonnet. *Oh God, oh God...*

Harding felt a hot gush between his legs as a sheet of flame leaped skywards and enveloped the cab. The flames quickly spread to the roof and found their way into the engine compartment. Harding screamed and covered his face with his hands.

As Charlie turned the corner she heard the crump of the explosion before she saw the fire. A gust of petrol-laden wind ruffled her hair and she staggered back, dropping the bundles of hot fish. She clung to the wall of the corner shop in horror, unable to believe what her eyes and ears were telling her. *Harding... Oh my God, Harding...*

She broke into a wobbling run, calling for help as she stumbled towards the conflagration. She couldn't get within five metres; the van was burning like a funeral pyre, shooting flames and acrid black smoke high into the atmosphere. Charlie shrieked and tried to move closer, shielding her face, feeling her skin starting to sting in the intense heat. She became aware of hands trying to restrain her; people had appeared from nowhere, drawn by the noise of the exploding petrol tank. She shrugged the hands off.

"Someone's *in* there. My *friend* is in there." Charlie dropped her hands to her side and fell to her knees as she realised it was all futile. If Harding was still in the van he had no chance. Sirens ululated, the sound drawing closer. Soon two police cars swerved into view.

Charlie allowed herself to be led towards the first uniformed officer to emerge from his patrol car. She couldn't understand why everybody seemed to be moving in slow motion. When the uniform asked her who she was and what had happened, she could barely speak her name.

Chapter Twenty-Nine

Charlie cradled the hot mug of tea in her hands. The shaking had stopped, at least for the time being, and all she felt now was a numbing paralysis. The shock had been bad enough at the time, but then she had been told that *three* bodies had been recovered from the Movano's charred wreckage. Two had already been identified as DCs Helen McKellar and Kenneth Harding. The third, in all probability, was Zoë Turner. Charlie sipped her tea without tasting it and tried again to understand what had happened.

A tactful cough reminded her that she was still sitting at Superintendent Mike Airey's desk, and that the DCS was waiting for a response.

"Sorry, sir. What did you ask me?" Her voice sounded slurred and distant. Charlie supposed that the mild sedative the paramedics had administered a few hours ago was still doing the rounds in her bloodstream.

"That's quite all right, DI Pepper. You've had a ghastly shock. Ghastly." Airey shook his head. "As have we all."

"Sir."

"Tell me again what you saw. Was anyone walking away from the van, or maybe watching from the other side of the street?"

Charlie tried to think. She lifted the mug to her lips but the shaking had started again. She slid it onto the corner of Airey's desk where it deposited a watery half-circle of tea.

"Take your time."

"I got to the corner. That's when I heard the bang. I looked up. I couldn't believe what I was seeing. For a moment I thought it was some other vehicle, that Ken had moved the van. It couldn't be our van, not with Ken inside and..." Charlie broke off as her voice began to quaver. She didn't want to break down completely in front of the Chief. She was supposed to be an experienced DI, for God's sake...

Airey, hands folded in his lap, was staring at his blotter, but he nodded supportively. "No one running from the scene?"

She shook her head. "No. This is Jagdip Ranandan's doing, sir," she blurted. "He must have sussed Zoë. He knew where we were."

"He didn't know you'd left the vehicle."

"I was lucky." Charlie wiped a hand across her forehead and absently wiped soot and grime onto her jeans. "God, listen to me. *Lucky*." She looked at Airey. "I should have died with Ken and Helen. And Zoë. That poor girl. I *persuaded* her to help us. She *trusted* me."

"We'll get him, don't worry, DI Pepper – Charlie," he added, a touch awkwardly.

"Will we?" Charlie felt her eyes sting with unshed tears. "How? The evidence has gone."

"Nevertheless," Airey stood up and folded his arms behind his back, "justice will be done. I trust Brendan Moran. He'll find a way forward." Airey sat on the edge of his desk and looked at Charlie with a paternal smile. "And you must support him in every way. Keep busy. That's my advice."

258

"Yes, sir."

"Good. By the way, where *is* DCI Moran?"

Charlie frowned. She had no idea where Moran was.

There was a sharp rap on the door and Banner appeared. He looked flushed and excited. "Sir? Can I have a word? It's urgent."

"Come in, DS Banner." Airey waved his arm informally.

"It's DCI Moran, sir. He's gone off on his own, to Bath."

"Explain."

Banner outlined Moran's discoveries regarding Neads and Jaseena. "I've just spoken to Sergeant Phelps, sir. The guv'nor – I mean DCI Moran – went to see him tonight. They worked out between them that Neads is holed up in this gaff called Beckford's Tower. And get this." Banner lowered his voice to a gruff whisper. "He has two hostages. And I'm afraid he also has a gun. We checked the Firearms Training log. Neads never signed his weapon back in."

"What the hell does Moran think he's doing?" Airey flushed with anger. "Get the ARU on the phone. We'll need at least two Rifle Officers."

"Shall I call Avon and Somerset?" Banner's eyes were gleaming.

"I'll handle the liaison, Banner. And save me a car, would you?"

"Yes, *sir*."

"Unmarked cars, Banner, not the Smaxes. We approach with stealth and caution. One of our own will be in there with Neads. Remember that."

Banner looked like a child who'd just been given the keys to a chocolate factory. Charlie tried to summon the energy to get up, but her muscles were limp and rebellious.

"You sit this one out, DI Pepper," Airey said, pulling his jacket on. "You've been through enough for one day. Go home. Get some rest." He strode out leaving Charlie alone with her thoughts.

She knew why Moran had gone out on a limb; it was because he felt responsible. To him, Neads was still his protégé, someone Moran felt he had let down badly. He wanted to reason with Neads, help him. But it seemed as if Neads was beyond help, certainly the sort of help Moran – or any other police officer for that matter – could provide.

Charlie got up and went to her desk. What should she do? Moran was walking into a death trap. She had lost two colleagues already. Banner had invoked an armed response unit; this could only end badly. She picked up her mobile. The least she could do was warn the guv what was heading his way. She looked at her watch. It was a quarter to three in the morning.

Charlie drove slowly out of the station car park. Home and sleep seemed an irresponsible destination, at least while Jag Ranandan still walked the streets. Charlie felt a surge of hatred.

She stopped at a set of lights, right indicator clicking. The lights held her there a long time, and as she waited she wrestled with her conscience. *Yes*, she muttered under her breath. *Yes*. She cancelled the indicator and drove straight on instead. She was pretty sure she could remember the way to the Ranandans' house. *Follow signs for the M4 and Earley...*

"Why have you brought us here, Simon?" Jaseena's voice was calm and soothing. The Kafir wasn't fooled. He'd anticipated that the women would try to soft-soap him.

They were sitting in the plush living room of Beckford's Tower. It felt opulent, fit for purpose. A portrait of the eccentric William Beckford looked down from the wall, his impassive features faithfully preserved on the canvas. The Kafir admired Beckford; shunned by society, the maverick had built this grand folly to store his priceless collection of *objets d'art*. The Kafir understood. He got it. The tower itself was something he strongly identified with. It was an eyrie above the masses, aloft and isolated. Superior.

The Kafir regarded the two females huddled together on the antique settee. "Why? Because I want you both to understand."

"Understand what, Simon?" Shona Kempster wasn't quite as adept at hiding her fear. Her voice caught as she spoke, a slight tremor giving her away.

"Firstly, what I have become. Secondly, what I must do to continue my work."

"Your work?" Shona's mouth twisted. "You murdered a policewoman and two young men. How is that *work*?"

"Religion is the opium of the people," the Kafir replied. "Do you know who said that?"

"Marx," Shona muttered under her breath.

"Yes. He spoke of dulled minds, oblivious to the corrupting power of fundamentalism," the Kafir spat. He toyed with the knife, twirling it between his fingers. "Marx was right. He knew. He was a visionary."

"Religious freedom is part of the fabric of a free democracy," Shona said firmly. "You're free to practice atheism if you wish, or any world religion of your choice."

The Kafir crouched beside her and placed the knife against her cheek. "But a day is coming when it will be imposed on you, can't you see that? Islam is gaining in strength, slowly but surely, creeping into the *fabric* of your democracy. How long before Sharia law is practised legally in the UK? Very soon, you'll see."

"So what will you do? Kill all the Muslims?" Jaseena's voice was trembling now.

"Someone has to take the lead, before it's too late." The Kafir removed the knife from Shona's cheek, leaving a white indentation on her skin. "And your brothers? You *know* what they're like." He sat on the arm of the settee next to Jaseena and put his mouth by her ear. "You know what they did to me," he whispered.

"I am Muslim. Will you kill me too, Simon?" Jaseena said softly, and moved to touch his hand.

The Kafir felt a stab of some old emotion as Jaseena's fingers brushed against his flesh. *No.* He snatched his hand away. "I am not Simon any more. I have a new name now, one you cannot utter. You may not address me by it, or by any other name."

"You need help," Jaseena said. "You are ill."

"Not so," the Kafir smiled. "I need nothing."

He stood back and looked at each woman in turn, enjoying the feeling of power. Moran would arrive soon, and then the circle would be complete.

Chapter Thirty

Charlie parked in a dark spot a few metres from the lamp post outside the Ranandans' house. She looked at the clock and doused her lights. Six minutes past three. The Ranandans were mostly nocturnal, she reckoned, so her vigil might take a while.

She settled back and shut her eyes. *Bad idea.* She opened them again fast, blinking to dispel the vivid images of the night's earlier events. She turned the radio on, listened to the DJ's chatter. It was company of a sort. Anything to distract her from what had happened.

But she couldn't escape it. Zoë's cynical expression haunted her thoughts, the need for reassurance that the girl had tried to hide. *It's OK, Zoë,* Charlie had told her, *we're right outside. Any problems, I'll be there for you.* And Zoë's sarky response: *You'd better be, babe...*

Charlie swallowed hard. She dared not think of Helen McKellar and Harding. She hadn't known them long; just long enough to recognise two dedicated people, kind, friendly, maybe in Helen's case a little insecure. Good coppers. Team players. They would have become firm friends, given time. And Jagdip Ranandan had had them burned alive. What sort of man would do that? How desensitised to the suffering of fellow human beings did you have to be to stoop *that* low?

Ken Harding had fancied her. He'd asked her out. Now he was dead, his charred remains spread out on some cold pathology lab bench. It wasn't right that they should be dead. Charlie began to sob, great gulping sobs that would not be suppressed. She rocked back and forth in the seat, her forehead banging on the steering wheel. *Why, why, why, why...*

After a while she regained control, the sobs becoming more and more infrequent until all she could feel and hear was her erratic breathing and gradually slowing heartbeat. Maybe Airey was right. She should go home. Have a drink, rest – forget.

The car slid into the drive, headlights doused, almost before she was aware of its stealthy approach. Charlie stopped breathing. Jagdip Ranandan got out. He was alone. She watched him walk up the path and enter the house. The front door closed. After a moment the lounge light went on.

Charlie switched off the radio and argued with herself. What could she do? What did she hope to achieve? *I want him to know that I know*, she realised. *I want him to know he's not going to get away with this...*

She stepped out onto the pavement, locked the car and stood silently outside the Ranandans' house, composing herself. Then she walked briskly to the front door and rang the bell.

The headlights picked out the brown heritage sign that read *Beckford's Tower*; confirmation that Moran had reached his destination. He pulled over in front of the gateposts and turned off the engine.

He was still trying to grasp what Charlie had told him; the news that Harding and Helen McKellar were dead had shaken him badly, but he couldn't afford to dwell on this unexpected disaster. Banner's cavalry would be here within the hour, and he had only a small window of opportunity to handle things his way before Mike Airey took over. Experience told him that once the ARU were on the scene, casualties were highly likely. And that, Moran vowed, was something he intended to prevent at all costs.

OK, Neads had lost it, was suffering from some kind of trauma-induced schizophrenia. That being the case, a court of law might well decide that the ex-sergeant could not be held responsible for his actions. He needed medical help, a chance to recover not only from his Charnford experiences but also from his brutal beating at the hands of the Ranandans. How *could* Neads be held responsible after what had happened to him? Yes, he had taken lives, but not rationally, not premeditatively...

No, the responsibility lies with you, Moran. You know it does. This is all happening because you made a bad call, took the wrong decision...

Moran silenced his negative thoughts by getting out of the car and making his way cautiously towards one of the small arches which formed part of the grand entranceway to the Tower gardens. The arch had a wooden door which was ajar, and a sign riveted to the stonework beside it:

Lansdown Burial Ground
Beckford's Tower and Museum

Emerging from the shadows on the other side of the arch he found himself in a graveyard. Straight ahead, beyond the cemetery's perimeter wall, he could see the lights of Bath twinkling in the distance. To his right loomed the squat shape of William Beckford's grand folly with its belvedere-topped tower stretching high above it like a single candle on a tiered birthday cake.

The building stood in total darkness, an apparently deserted mausoleum. Moran began to fret. Maybe he'd got it wrong. Maybe they weren't here after all. But if not here, then where? *Worry about that when you've proved there's no one home...*

He continued along the graveyard path, senses humming like a radar dish, alert for the first sign of trouble. The moon was almost full, lighting his way between the headstones. If Neads was watching from the tower he couldn't fail to spot him, but that was OK with Moran. He wanted Neads to let him in, to give him a chance to talk to him.

He exited the graveyard and found himself directly in front of the building. A wide stone stairway led up to the main entrance porch which featured a large central door and two smaller portals to the left and right.

Should he knock? He hesitated for a moment, unsure. But then his next move was decided for him; the door on the left creaked open and Jaseena's frightened face appeared, silhouetted in the narrow crack of light emanating from the building's interior.

"Come in, DCI Moran." Neads' voice came from behind Jaseena, and Moran saw the glint of a knife at her throat. "It's been too long."

Jag answered the door immediately. When he saw Charlie his lips parted in a wide smile.

"Ah. An attractive young woman knocks at my door in the middle of the night. Why is this, I wonder? I can't recall placing an order."

Charlie showed her ID. "DI Pepper, Thames Valley Police. Mr Ranandan, I'm investigating an incident near the Zodiac nightclub in the town centre. I have reason to believe you may be able to help us with our enquiries."

"Do you?" Jag's expression was one of mild amusement. "And why is that?"

"You know what I'm talking about. Two police officers were killed in a van fire just before midnight. On your orders."

Jag narrowed his eyes. "That's a serious accusation, Ms Pepper. I hope you have supporting evidence."

Charlie's self-discipline buckled. "You bastard, Ranandan. You murdered my friends in cold blood. *And* an innocent girl. I know what you are and what you've done." She took a step forward until her face was close to his. "And I'm going to nail you, trust me. You are going down for a very, very long time."

"Listen, bitch," Jag spat. "You have *nothing* on me. On the contrary..."

He disappeared inside the house and came back brandishing an envelope. "Here. Take a look. You're the sad cow with the explaining to do."

Charlie snatched the envelope and shook out the contents. A photograph. Moran and herself, in the Ranandans' front room...

"Breaking and entering, no warrant. I'll be pressing charges, naturally. Now piss off, before I have you thrown off my property."

The door slammed in her face, leaving Charlie fuming and tearful on the threshold. *Bastard. Bastard. Bastard.*

She wept as she drove away, hardly aware what she was doing or where she was going. She found a late-night kebab van parked by a parade of shops and stopped for a coffee. It was bitter but hot, and after she'd drunk half of it she was able to quell her emotions a little. *Time to go home, Charlie...*

She restarted the engine and drove towards her flat in Woodley, trying to work rationally through the events of the last twelve hours. Jag Ranandan had known what was going on at the club. He had been prepared. But how? Nothing had been shared outside the team – all the briefings had been held behind closed doors. Who had been present? Banner, herself, Helen, Harding, Moran. And the DCS, naturally.

Charlie felt her eyes drooping as she turned into her road. Maybe she would sleep, for a while at least.

She grabbed her handbag from the back seat and locked the car. A cat brushed her leg as she fumbled for her door key, making her jump. The cat, alarmed by her reaction, sped off across the neighbour's garden.

A thought popped into Charlie's head. The conversation between Jag Ranandan and Zoë. He had told Zoë that certain police officers were 'in his pocket'. And he had said something else, a throwaway comment which had struck her as odd at the time. She turned the key in the lock and bent to pick up the pile of letters scattered on her doormat. Then it came back to her. *Even the new ones*, Jag had said, proudly. *Even the new ones...*

She froze. *How long had Mike Airey been in post? He was new, wasn't he...?*

The blow had been aimed at her head, but the action of bending for the post probably saved her life. Something struck her hard across the shoulders with enough force to send her sprawling. She tried to scream but the pain was so intense she could only gasp. The door was kicked shut and she saw the intruder for the first time – a tall man in his thirties with a goatee and a dark birthmark on his cheek. The face was handsome, East European perhaps, but the expression was cold and compassionless.

His arm went up to strike again, and as it came down Charlie saw the businesslike cosh nestled in his gloved grip. She raised her arm to ward off the attack but instinctively recognised that the cosh was heavy enough to break bone and instead rolled to one side an instant before the cosh descended. Off balance, her attacker stumbled, his arm shooting out to save himself from tumbling forward. Charlie lunged at his legs, using the man's energy to propel him towards the front door.

The cosh hit the door's glass panel and the intruder's arm smashed through, followed by his upper body. On her knees, Charlie grabbed him around the waist and used her weight to drag his torso down onto the stalagmite-like shards of glass poking from the wooden frame. He screamed as the glass penetrated his stomach and tried to pull back, but Charlie hung on, knowing that he would kill her for sure if she let go. Sobbing and shouting she held him until his struggles became weaker and finally stopped.

Charlie scrabbled backwards, her outstretched hands sliding in a pool of blood. There were raised voices now, people crowding her porch, neighbours in dressing gowns and hastily pulled-on pairs of jeans and non-matching tops. She heard someone gasp and swear, and another voice called for someone to call an ambulance.

The door was pushed open and hands gently lifted her. Her knees wobbled and a sudden surge of nausea made her retch until she was violently sick on the floor. She tried to stand unaided but her balance had gone. With a soft moan she felt the blood leaving her brain, and she pitched forward into the supporting arms of her neighbours.

Chapter Thirty-one

Charlie regained consciousness slowly, her eyes smarting in the light thrown from the standard lamp she had bought at a local emporium a few weekends back. She blinked. Two uniforms were sitting in her armchairs and her neighbour, Mrs Tredray, whom she had met only briefly on the day she moved in, was sitting beside her on the arm of the sofa with a jug of water and a glass at the ready.

"Drink this, my love, you'll feel better."

Charlie held out her hand to receive the water, but it was shaking so badly that Mrs Tredray bent forward and held the glass to her lips.

"Thanks."

"DI Pepper," one of the uniforms spoke, "when you're up to it I'd like to ask you a few questions."

Mrs Tredray frowned and gave the policeman an old-fashioned look, which under normal circumstances would have made Charlie chuckle.

"It's OK, Mrs Tredray," Charlie wrapped her fingers around the glass and found that she was able to drink unaided. "I'm all right, really." Then, with a jolt of realisation Charlie remembered everything that had happened. The van, Jag Ranandan, Moran, Airey... *Airey...*

She tried to get up, but Mrs Tredray pushed her firmly back into the sofa. "No, no, dear, you've had a terrible shock. You need to rest."

"I know," Charlie said. "But I need the bathroom."

"I'll help you," Mrs Tredray offered.

"It's all right. I can walk. Look." Charlie levered herself into an upright position. "See? I won't be a minute."

There was no time for explanation or to share her suspicions with the uniforms. She had to get the proof she needed *now*. As Charlie made a play of shuffling unsteadily to the downstairs loo she checked for her keys. She prayed she hadn't left them in the door, hoping that she'd slipped them into her pocket instead. She felt the key ring cold against her groping fingers. *Yes...*

Locking the bathroom door behind her, she slid back the window bolt and opened the pane. The neighbours had dispersed, the lone police car's presence the only indication of the earlier drama. Charlie scrambled over the window ledge and hit the ground running. The uniforms could wait for their statement; if she was right, her new guv was in even greater danger than he realised.

"Back again?" Sergeant Denis Robinson's thick eyebrows arched in surprise as Charlie appeared in reception. "Don't you lot ever sleep?"

"I could ask the same of you, Sergeant," Charlie called over her shoulder without waiting for a reply.

The team's office was in semidarkness. No one around. Good. Charlie fretted that Airey would have locked his private office door, but her fears were unfounded. She hit the light switch, made a beeline for the computer and wheeled Airey's plush office chair from under the desk as the machine booted up.

Come on...

If anyone challenged her she'd have a lot of explaining to do. She wondered how long it would take the uniforms to figure out where she was.

The monitor flashed at her. *Enter password:*

Damn.

She tapped her nails on the desk. It would have to be six characters and include at least one number and one upper-case letter. She tried to remember what she'd been told about Airey. Married? No, she thought not. Not kids' names, then. Sporty? No, not by all accounts.

Workaholic? That was nearer the mark. So, what's he been involved in? Kestrel, obviously. Charlie puckered her lips in concentration. The upper-case letter was usually the first character. So, *K* for Kestrel, followed by *e s t r e l*. The number, almost inevitably, would be the suffix. *Hopefully...* She typed *1*.

Password Incorrect. Number of retries left: 4.

She bit her finger. OK, another obvious one.

Kestrel0.

Password Incorrect. Number of retries left: 3.

In the empty open-plan office a phone rang. Charlie frowned. The IR was closed between eleven at night and eight in the morning. It must be Denis. Frowning, she went quickly to answer it.

"Hello?"

"DI Pepper? Denis here. Chief Superintendent Sheldrake wants a word. I've sent him up, OK? Just to let you know."

"Thanks." Charlie crashed the phone down and sprinted back into Airey's office. *What was Sheldrake doing out of custody?* Someone was pulling strings, big time.

Kestrel10, enter. *Please please please...*

Password accepted. Please wait.

Charlie heard the whine of the lift as it began its slow ascent. Her fingers fumbled the keys as Windows finished loading. *MS Outlook... Sent Items...*

She scrolled through the sent mails with no idea what she was looking for. *You'd better be right about this, Charlie...*

She came to a mail with an attachment. She opened it. Outside, the lift motor continued to whirr. She had only a few seconds, and she still needed to cross the open plan to the back stairs before Sheldrake emerged from the lift. Charlie double-clicked the attachment and simultaneously scanned the contents of the email.

It was brief and to the point. It gave the surveillance van's registration number and description, and a time. She felt her heart begin to pound.

*It **is** him...*

Charlie made a note of the email recipient string and waited until the .jpg had loaded before hitting Ctrl P. She selected the HR printer two floors below, clicked the monitor power off and pelted out of Airey's office towards the swing door leading to the back stairs. As her hand reached for the door handle the lift pinged, announcing its arrival on her floor. She flung the door open and took the back stairs three at a time.

As she came out into the HR area she could hear the printer delivering its incriminating evidence. Two minutes later she was back in reception, and she breathed a sigh of relief that Denis' familiar profile was absent from the reception window; now there was a good chance that Sheldrake would waste time looking for her.

Back in her car she took a few minutes to calm herself. OK, she had the required evidence. But that wouldn't help Moran in the short-term. She daren't call the guv in case she compromised his current situation – whatever that might be. The bottom line was that Moran was out on a limb with no back-up. Small wonder Airey had wanted to head up the ARU; Jag Ranandan had sent an assassin for her, and Mike Airey clearly intended to take care of Moran.

She wrestled with her options. Someone else had to know what she had discovered. Who should she tell? Banner was with Airey. Harding and Helen ... she bit her lip savagely.

There was only one official way to go with this, she knew: she should inform the Chief Constable. But would the formidable Sara Stevenson believe her? Would she take immediate action? Was *she* trustworthy? Charlie grabbed her iPhone and quickly composed an email. She reread it. The whole thing looked utterly fantastic in printed form. She couldn't risk it. Whether the end result was commendation or crash and burn, she had to go it alone.

No choice, Charlie... None at all...

She saved the email in the drafts folder, ground the car into gear and headed for the M4.

Chapter Thirty-two

The interior of Beckford's folly was lavish, sumptuous even. Moran examined his surroundings as Neads led him through the modern kitchen area into an elegant drawing room.

The first thing he saw was Shona, sitting rigidly in a chair, her mouth covered with gaffer tape, hands tied behind – and to – the back of the chair. Her eyes followed Neads' every move, mutely expressing her terror as Neads settled Jaseena onto the settee and sat beside her, the knife gently brushing her leg.

"Please. Have a seat, Brendan." Neads indicated a high backed antique rocker. "What do you think?" He made an all-encompassing gesture. "The scarlet drawing room. Appropriate, don't you think?"

Moran nodded and settled himself against the worn contours of the rocker. The atmosphere was humid and stuffy. Moran took in his surroundings. The windows were securely fastened, no external doors led directly from the drawing room, and the only way out was via the kitchen. He didn't recall Neads locking the front door behind them, although he had made a play of placing a bunch of keys on the mantelpiece beneath a gilt-framed portrait that Moran assumed to be a representation of the great eccentric himself, William Beckford.

Neads fell silent, distracted by some thought or notion he chose not to share with the company. Moran watched his ex-sergeant carefully; he knew he had to somehow get inside Neads' mind, find a way of probing beyond the torn curtain of mental illness.

He glanced at Shona and found a tight smile of encouragement as he waited for Neads to speak.

"So," Neads began, and paused again, apparently struck by another thought. Then he shook his head and chuckled quietly to himself as if listening to some private conversation. "No, no," he muttered under his breath. "That won't do at all." After a moment he looked up and went on.

"Have you noticed how often people begin their conversation with the word 'so' these days, Brendan? Especially the youngsters. I imagine your new DI speaks like that. Anyway–" he rapped the settee's armrest with the butt of the knife, making Jaseena flinch. "Here we are, and here you are. With these charming young ladies," he added, smiling at Shona and Jaseena in turn.

"What are you looking for, Gregory?" Moran asked gently. "I'd like to help, if I can."

"Looking for?" Neads toyed with the knife, twirling the point on the armrest. "Ah, no. my *looking* days are over, Brendan. I've found what I was looking for, you see."

"Which is?"

Neads leaned forward suddenly, his mouth twisting in a dismissive sneer. "A reason. A purpose. *The answer.* Call it what you like."

"And the answer is murder?" Moran kept his body language as unthreatening as he could, relaxing into the rocking chair, fingers entwined casually in his lap, as though chatting with an elderly aunt over afternoon tea.

"*Cleansing*, Brendan, not murder. There's a difference."

Moran nodded. "Who are you?"

The question appeared to confuse Neads. A flicker of panic clouded his eyes for a moment and then his face broke into a wide grin. "Ah ah, Brendan, I know what you're up to." He waved the knife mock-threateningly. "You're psyching me out, right?"

Moran shrugged. "It's a simple question."

"Well, it might be a simple question, Brendan, but the answer may not be as simple as you think." Neads' voice had risen in volume, crackling with emotion. He sprang to his feet and covered the distance between them in three long strides. The knife was at Moran's throat.

Moran didn't move. With an effort he kept his expression neutral.

"Don't play with me, Brendan." Neads' breath wafted in Moran's face, minty and warm. "I'm finished with games. This is real now, Detective *Chief* Inspector. More real than you can understand." He let the knife drop and backtracked to the sofa, keeping Moran in view. Jaseena's eyes met Moran's in an unspoken question. *Shall I jump him?* Moran warned her off with a slight shake of his head.

"We should begin, shouldn't we?" Neads announced. "You'll see what I'm about once we begin, Brendan." He stood behind Shona's chair, tossing the knife from hand to hand. Shona's eyes bulged, tears of terror tracking down her cheeks. She wriggled and tried to turn her head to second-guess Neads' intentions, but she was securely tied and could only sob in frustration. Moran's heart banged against his chest. What could he say to stall Neads?

"So, a knife, then. Or this perhaps?" Neads reached into his inside jacket pocket and produced a sleek looking handgun. Jaseena gasped and pressed herself against further into the sofa.

"Nice, isn't it?" Neads held the revolver up for inspection. "Oh, don't worry, Brendan, I know what you're thinking; but my fingers are still strong enough to pull a trigger. Your generous employers gave me this little beauty a while back. Firearms Training issue, but they never missed it. Sloppy, don't you think?"

"Very. I didn't know you'd trained, Gregory. When was this? Before you transferred to TVP, or afterwards?" Moran wanted to capitalise on Neads' current state of mind – while he was able to recall his past life as a police officer Neads' murderous alter ego had to take a back seat, which was exactly where Moran wanted to keep him.

"Before. In the Met," Neads replied. He aligned the barrel with Shona's right ear.

Moran held out his hand, palm up. "Greg, how about you sign it back in now? We can talk this through."

Once again Neads seemed wrong-footed. He dropped his hand and held the revolver loosely at his side. Shona was shaking, a low note of terror humming in her throat.

Neads touched her shoulder. "Shut up."

Shona flinched.

"I said shut *up*." Neads gripped her neck and jammed the revolver into her shoulder.

"Gregory–" Moran began.

"*Not* Gregory." The voice had changed subtly. "Gregory was a failure. *I* am the success."

"You weren't a failure, Gregory. You were a victim. There's a difference."

"Is there?" Neads shrugged. "I choose the victims now. The past is of no consequence."

"This is *all* about the past, Gregory. About Charnford, about your suffering. Is that why you killed Father Jeffries?"

"Yes, Gregory killed him," Neads said. He had moved slightly away from Shona, although the revolver was still held purposefully in his right hand.

"Gregory? Not you? Who *are* you?"

"The other – the other..." Neads stammered, squared his shoulders and gathered himself. "I am the *Kafir*."

"The *Kafir*?"

"Yes. They hate me. Tried to kill me. So I hate them."

"I don't hate you, Simon," Jaseena said, quietly. "The man I know was kind. He was in trouble, yes; he was hurting, yes – but in his heart he is a good man. You told me you *loved* me. Don't you remember? Why did you lie to me? Why did you pretend to be someone else?"

"Simon?" Neads turned towards Jaseena, puzzled. "Yes. I remember him, too. Gregory's policewoman friend introduced him to you, didn't she? Told him you would help his pain?"

Jaseena nodded in a mixture of sorrow and despair. "That's right, you remember. Sharron Flynn was her name, the detective sergeant. Look, Gregory, Simon, whoever you are. I still love you. Do you understand? I can't help what my brothers did. I can't help what happened to you before. But I will try to understand, I promise you. Please, give the gun and the knife to DCI Moran. You don't have to harm anyone any more. We want to help you, can't you see that?"

Neads appeared to consider the entreaty carefully. The room seemed to hold its breath as the competing personalities inside his head struggled for supremacy.

Moran was still processing the information that Sharron Flynn had brought Neads and Jaseena together. Is that how Neads had been able to keep tabs on everything so easily, how he had known where DC Hill had been imprisoned? Not cyber networking then, as Moran had surmised, just good old fashioned social networking. He wondered if Flynn had also thought to inform Neads that the woman who had interrupted his first killing had been a policewoman? Moran's suppositions were curtailed as he noticed with alarm that Shona had worked an arm loose from the strip of tape securing her to the chair. Moran watched helplessly as, taking advantage of Neads' preoccupation, she gradually eased it free. He wanted to tell her to stop, to warn her that any attempt at escape would probably end in bloodshed, but he could see the desperation and panic in her eyes.

Jaseena baulked as Neads went to her side and stroked her hair. "You were very important to Simon," he told her. "You helped to heal his body. But things have changed."

While Neads' back was turned Shona wrenched at the bindings holding her left arm. Her eyes darted this way and that, always returning to the half-open door of the drawing room. Moran shook his head frantically as he watched her weighing her options.

Don't...

Neads bent and gently kissed Jaseena's forehead. "Simon doesn't want to hurt you, Jaseena. But your brother must be taught a lesson."

At that moment Shona ripped the tape from her mouth, propelled herself from the chair and half-hobbled, half-staggered towards the kitchen. Moran could see what was going to happen, and a second later it did: inevitably, her circulation-starved legs let her down and she collapsed, sprawling onto the kitchen floor.

Neads moved fast, but Jaseena grabbed his shirt and hung on. He brought his arm down in a vicious swipe and she fell back, stunned. Taking a step forward Neads gripped the revolver awkwardly in his clawed fingers, levelled it at Shona and squeezed the trigger.

The noise of the report was deafening in the enclosed space. The bullet buried itself in the skirting board by Shona's feet, throwing up splinters; Shona yelled – whether in pain or fear Moran couldn't tell – and rolled to the left, away from Neads' line of fire. She scrambled to her feet and disappeared through the kitchen, Neads following hard on her heels.

Ears ringing, Moran cast about for some weapon, realising belatedly that he'd left his stick in the car. *Good planning, Brendan...*

He reached the front door to find that Shona had somehow managed to wrench it open. He watched her lurch into the gap as Neads drew a bead and fired again. Shona tumbled to the right and rolled down the entrance steps into the car park.

Moran hit Neads at knee level, the impetus propelling them both out of the building into the porch. Moran landed on top of Neads, the breath driven from his body as the butt of the gun caught him in the solar plexus. Neads grunted and dropped the revolver which clattered away, spinning on its axis, into the shadows.

Moran writhed in pain, fighting for air. A second later the porch was illuminated by an intense white light and the metallic harshness of a loudhailer split the silence.

This is the police. Lie still with your hands on your head.

Moran wasn't in a position to comply – he was fully occupied trying to fill his lungs, far less being able to move his arms in any given direction. The next few moments passed in a kind of sluggish slow motion as he fought for air.

After what seemed an eternity Moran's chest began to rise and fall sporadically. He breathed again. The loudhailer repeated its warning. Moran's intuition told him that Neads would ignore the instruction. He was right: Cursing and groaning Neads levered himself to his haunches and prepared to dive for the cover of the balustrade on the far side of the porch. Moran opened his mouth but could only croak an inarticulate warning.

*No! They'll kill you ... stay **still**...*

As Neads sprang forward Moran summoned his remaining strength and went for another tackle. He heard the flat crack of a rifle, something punched him hard on the shoulder and Neads gave a pained cry of surprise. Then they were behind the balustrade, Moran on his back, Neads crumpled against the tower door. The light remained on, and all was still.

Moran moved his arm experimentally and a bolt of pain fizzed through his upper body. He tried again, and although he felt something warm and sticky trickling down his back, this time the pain was bearable.

*Do **not** move again or we will shoot to kill.*

"Still there, Brendan?" Neads' voice was a whisper of pain.

"I'm here."

"I wanted to show you the belvedere," Neads rasped. "You would have understood then."

"The belvedere?"

"The top of the tower. You can see the world for what it is up there."

"Gregory, let me call them in. You need a doctor." Moran raised his head cautiously, making sure he was still in the shadow of the balustrade. Neads had propped himself up, his back against the woodwork. He still had the knife, which he held pressed to his own flesh.

"Call them in and I'll cut my throat. You know I'll do it."

"I'll make sure you get help," Moran insisted. "You have to trust me."

Neads laughed, a throaty gurgle. "Trust you, Brendan? I trusted you before, against my better judgement. And what happened?"

Moran could see a spreading stain on Neads' chest. The bullet had torn through his own shoulder and into Neads' torso. If he didn't get help soon Neads would bleed to death. And, for that matter, so would he.

"I understand why you killed those boys, Gregory. They were members of Jag Ranandan's family. The first – he was an illegal, wasn't he? That's why we couldn't ID him."

"Yes. Anoop. He hated me. They all did."

"And you thought they'd taken Jaseena away, sent her back to India?"

"Yes."

Neads' unbalanced alter ego – the Kafir, had he called himself? – had gone, at least for the moment. This was just plain Gregory Neads. Moran changed position and grimaced. His shoulder was throbbing but he didn't think the bullet had hit anything vital. Then with a start he remembered Shona. He twisted, but he could only make out a vague crumpled shape at the foot of the steps.

Keep talking to him, Brendan…

"Gregory, why didn't you tell us where DC Hill was?"

For a while Moran didn't think Neads had heard. Then the ex-sergeant spoke in a rasping, strained whisper:

"I didn't think they'd kill him, Brendan. Sharron was a mate. She had a nice little thing going. Who was I to spoil it for her?"

"Four serving officers are dead, Gregory. It didn't have to be that way."

"I didn't know she was a copper. She ran after me. Had to kill her," Neads' voice was weakening.

"Let me help you, Gregory. Please." Moran dragged himself forward a few inches.

"One more move like that, Brendan, and I'll do it," Neads warned. The knife glinted in the harsh glare of the police lights as he brandished it in front of his face.

Moran's mobile bleeped. "Can I answer it?" he asked Neads.

Neads weakly waved an affirmative.

"Moran."

"This is Mike Airey, Brendan. What's the situation?"

"I have a wounded man here, sir, but he won't let me near. I recommend extreme caution."

"Am I on loudspeaker?"

"Yes, sir."

"I intend to bring a paramedic to tend to the woman," Airey's voice said. "And I will come to you, unarmed. Is that clear?"

Neads hissed through his teeth.

"I wouldn't recommend it, sir, at present. Just the medic might be OK. Gregory?"

Neads nodded. "All right. Just the medic."

"I only want to talk to you, Neads," Airey said. "There's no harm in that, surely?"

"So talk."

"Better face to face," Airey said. "Don't you think?"

"Sir–" Moran began.

"Just me. On my own. I'll show you my hands."

Moran was rigid with tension. *Don't push it, Airey...*

"I'm walking to you now." Airey rang off.

"It's all right, Gregory. He's trustworthy." Moran said. "No one's going to hurt you." But Neads was drifting into unconsciousness. Any longer and it might be too late. Maybe Airey was right; they had to pre-empt matters, move things on somehow...

Moran heard a scuffle of feet, the mutter of a low voice. The medic had reached Shona.

A shadow fell over the porch. Mike Airey appeared, empty hands raised. He saw Neads' unconscious body and dropped his hands to his side. "Are you hurt, Brendan?"

"Not badly. Be careful, sir – if he sees you–"

Airey stepped over Moran and stood over Neads' inert body. He reached in his pocket, pulled on a pair of rubber gloves and retrieved the knife. Moran admired his coolness.

"I'm sorry, Brendan," Airey said, stooping down. "I really didn't want it to come to this. But, you see, I haven't much choice."

"Sorry?" Moran head was fuzzy. He couldn't make sense of what Airey was saying.

Airey crouched low and hefted the knife. Then Moran understood. He tried to shift away from the deadly point but his brain was fuzzy and his body wasn't responding.

Blood loss...

He raised his arm and the pain in his shoulder made him gag. Airey's face was a blur, the knife a slice of descending silver. Moran closed his eyes.

Chapter Thirty-three

*P*ick up Banner, pick up... Charlie stabbed her finger at the red 'End' bar displayed on her iPhone and refocused her attention on the motorway. A pair of HGVs loomed in the distance, playing a racing game in the slow and middle lanes. Charlie pulled into the fast lane and sped past them. She clicked Banner's number again with the same result: straight to voicemail.

She screamed in frustration. According to the satnav Beckford's Tower was still thirty-two minutes away; thirty-two minutes she didn't have. The speedo reached a ton. She willed the car on.

By the time she got within visual distance of the tower Charlie could pick out the police incident lighting silhouetting the entrance archway and the trees beyond. She screeched to a halt beside two parked police vehicles, flung herself out of the car and hurried along the verge towards the light where she found a knot of officers gathered in the driveway. Banner saw her coming and raised a warning hand. She wondered briefly at the absence of the Avon and Somerset constabulary before it dawned on her that Airey had probably never made that call. He was winging it, and Charlie knew why.

"Where's Moran?" She grabbed Banner by the shoulder.

"Hey, what do you–"

"Where *is* he, Banner? Tell me." Charlie pushed her way past Banner to where two ARU officers were positioned, weapons trained on the building.

"Behind the balustrade. With Neads. He's down – the Chief ordered a shot."

Charlie's heart was hammering against her ribs. "Airey?"

Banner pointed. Now she could see the medic crouched beside a prone body at the foot of the steps and a tall figure framed in the centre arch. "Who's injured?"

"We think it's Shona Kempster. Moran's significant," Banner added with a wink. "Neads has taken a bullet. Moran's hurt, but he's just spoken to the chief on his mobile." Banner looked pleased.

"This isn't a bloody paintballing excursion, Banner. What's Airey doing?" Charlie could hear the note of panic in her voice and Banner picked up on it. He peered closely at her face.

"God, what happened to you?"

"I'll explain later. Give me those." She snatched the field glasses from Banner's grip and zoomed in on the balustrade. "Oh God..."

"What?" Banner grabbed at the field glasses but Charlie's grip was firm.

Charlie spun and pointed at the first ARU rifleman. "What's your name?"

"Schouten – Mike Schouten. And you are–?"

"DI Charlie Pepper. I'm working with DCI Moran. Line up a shot."

"No way. Neads is down..."

"Do it. *Look at Airey*. Look *through* the balustrade – he's on his hands and knees..."

Schouten squinted through his telescopic sight. "Shit. Am I seeing things?"

"No, you're not. On my mark." Charlie put the binoculars to her eyes and watched Airey continue his stealthy movement towards Moran's motionless body.

"Wait. You can't make that call." Banner took her arm.

"I'm the senior office here, Banner. I'll take the rap."

"Not until you tell me what the hell's going on."

"No time." Charlie waved him away.

Airey had reached Moran's side. There was a long, thin blade in his hand. His arm went up. Charlie froze.

*No way ...I **can't** make this call ... what if...*

But even as she hesitated she saw that Neads, somehow conscious again, had levered himself into a squatting position and was trying to stand up. What the hell was he up to? Charlie held her breath as the ex-sergeant took a stumbling step towards Airey.

A loud report shattered the silence, the sound of a discharged bullet. For a second Charlie couldn't work out what had happened. Then she saw the slight Asian girl emerge from the left, a revolver held in her outstretched hand.

Charlie swivelled the field glasses. Airey was on his back, blood seeping from a ragged hole in the side of his head. The Superintendent's eyes were open but unseeing. Neads was slumped unmoving against the balustrade. The girl staggered, leaned on the pillar for support. The revolver fell from her grasp and bounced down the steps.

There was a long, frozen silence. Somewhere in the distance the sound of sirens began, rising and falling like a discordant glissando.

"Schouten, Banner, *you*." Charlie gesticulated wildly at the second Rifle Officer. "Go. Go. *Go!*"

"She was aiming at Neads," Charlie told Banner.. "Never fired a gun before, so her aim was off. Fortunately for DCI Moran."

Banner grunted and waved to the ambulance man as he shut the rear doors and turned on his siren. Two one-time lovers within. One in shock, the other fighting for his life.

Moran had already been whisked away to Bath A&E in the first ambulance. He had been *compos mentis* enough to give her a weak smile and a wave as they loaded him in. The tough old sod.

Charlie watched as the DCS from Avon and Somerset trudged wearily down the steps of Beckford's Tower. He hadn't been impressed with what he'd found when he'd arrived on the scene. There'd be an inquiry, for sure, and she'd be in the middle of it. Thank God the evidence she'd found on Airey's PC seemed irrefutable. The message she'd printed off had been sent to an email address belonging to the Ranandan brothers. No defence barrister would be able to explain that one away easily.

"So," the Avon DCS said dourly. "You and your commandos can push off back to Berkshire now, DI Pepper. I'll handle the SOCO activity from here. Of course, you will be expected to provide a full written report to your senior officer within twenty-four hours. And I'd like a copy asap. Understood?"

"Yes, sir. I'll see to it," Charlie told him. "And sorry about the lack of communication."

"Yes. So am I," the DCS replied with a humourless smile. "Your CC will be hearing from ours in due course."

"Sir."

Charlie turned away and made a face at Banner, who was deep in conversation with the two firearms officers. They'd fired only one shot; it had been effective, and she hadn't had to order a second. So that was a result, wasn't it?

Charlie turned her back on Beckford's Tower and retraced her steps to the gate. It was only when she reached the car that the tears finally came.

"Hello, guv." The female voice broke into Moran's semi-conscious state.

He opened his eyes a crack. So far, so good. Then he tried to move, but that turned out to be a very bad idea indeed. His shoulder and upper arm felt as though someone had stuck a hot branding iron on his flesh and left it there.

"Such language from a senior officer," a second, male voice observed. "And in front of a lady as well."

There was something familiar about the voice. Moran couldn't quite place it; his brain felt foggy and stupid, as if it was filled with cotton wool.

"How do you feel?" the female voice asked.

Then it came back to him in a rush. *Airey...* He jerked his upper body in an effort to sit up, but the pain defeated him and he sank back onto the heaped pillows. A hand rested lightly on his good shoulder.

"It's all right, guv. It's DI Pepper. It's over."

Moran groaned a question. "Neads?"

The hesitation told him all he needed to know. He screwed up his face in frustration. "Damn, damn, damn."

"Sorry, guv," Charlie confirmed. "He died on his way here. But Miss Kempster is going to be all right," she added quickly. "Still in ICU, but doing well. She's in good hands."

"The Royal Berkshire?" Moran asked, knowing the answer.

"A fine establishment," the male voice said. "Gets on your nerves after a while, though. Especially the food."

Phelps... Moran opened his eyes fully. Sergeant Phelps was sitting in a visitors' chair in his dressing gown, a folded newspaper in his lap and a biro wedged behind his ear. Charlie Pepper was standing over him, her face lined with fatigue and concern.

Moran forced the corners of his mouth into a smile. "The RBH and I are old friends, Robert. With my frequency of attendance they'll soon be naming a ward after me." He glanced at Charlie. "You'd better tell me what happened, DI Pepper. I have the feeling I'm missing something."

Chapter Thirty-four

Mrs Flynn poured a third glass of sherry and walked unsteadily into the empty lounge. Three glasses – one for each week. It had been three weeks since everything had spiralled out of control. Three weeks of tears, three weeks of visiting Ernest in custody, three weeks of recriminations, three weeks of talking to pessimistic lawyers, three weeks of wondering how her life had so rapidly fallen apart.

Outside the sun blazed relentlessly, slanting through the picture window and showing up the threadbare patches on the worn carpet. They'd needed a new carpet for years, but Ernest had forbidden it. Too expensive. Ironic that now, just as her husband had sanctioned the purchase of a gorgeous oatmeal deep-pile replacement, he wouldn't be here to enjoy it. For a long, long time. Never, in fact, because he would be in prison, until he died.

She took another gulp of sherry and gazed out onto the airstrip, where a blackened area of grass was all the evidence that remained of the wreck of the light aircraft her daughter had regularly flown. At least Sharron hadn't been inside when it had taken gentle Mark Barnes to his death. No; her husband had made sure it had been Mark. Her husband had killed the mechanic, to protect Sharron. Sharron, her once lovely daughter, now apparently a corrupt, drug-dealing, embezzling murderess.

Mrs Flynn started as a tentative cry followed by a loud gurgle announced her grandson's awakening. Time for another feed.

Mrs Flynn gripped her glass and fought back tears. There was no one left for the baby, except her. And what did she have to offer? A grieving, ruined woman in late middle-age. She was no company for a growing child; a child needed a mother, someone to cherish and look after him. Boys especially needed their mums, even when they'd grown up. But there was no one. And who was to blame?

That, at least, was an easy question to answer. The brothers, Jagdip and Atul Ranandan. She'd known from the off that they were bad news. Ernest wouldn't listen to her concerns – Sharron could do no wrong in his eyes – and by the time the Ranandans were using the airstrip regularly Sharron was probably in too deep to pull out even if she had wanted to. Silly, silly girl. Mrs Flynn set her glass down on the coffee table, and crossing her arms around her trembling body, burst into tears. *How could this have happened?*

The baby's cries grew more urgent. She couldn't just ignore the little mite, but she wasn't up to dealing with his demands day and night. She was nearly sixty-five, for goodness sake. She should be taking life easy, relaxing into old age...

Mrs Flynn sat on the edge of the sofa, and when her tears had subsided she tried to remember where her husband had kept the keys to the gun cupboard. She went to his office and rummaged in the desk drawers. The baby's escalating cries were hard to resist as her searching fingers eventually found what she was looking for. The cartridges would be in the cupboard along with the shotguns.

The shotgun cupboard was her husband's domain. She had never touched a gun before – she had never had the desire or need. But she had seen Ernest and the farmhands using them. It looked quite simple: you broke the gun and inserted two cartridges, clicked it shut, checked the safety switch was off, and that was it. All ready.

The baby's wailing reached a new level of urgency; he'd always had a good appetite, even when he'd been poorly with chicken pox. He had, Mrs Flynn thought sadly, the potential to grow into a big strapping lad. A rugby player, maybe, or a footballer.

She tucked the gun under her arm, as she'd seen Ernest do so many times, and carefully closed and locked the gun cupboard. It wouldn't do to leave anything to chance. You never knew who might be snooping around these days.

"I'm coming, darling," she called. "Granny's just coming."

"Thanks for agreeing to see me," the smartly-dressed woman said, rising to her feet. "It helps a little, to know who she worked with. Who her friends were. Thank you again. You've been very kind."

Moran, groping for suitable words, could only nod and smile a tight-lipped farewell as he watched Mrs McKellar walk out of his office, head held high. Proud and hurting, dying inside. He let his breath out in a long sigh and rubbed his shoulder where the sling was beginning to chafe his flesh raw.

Charlie Pepper's attractive features peeped in through his slatted office window. A second later she knocked and came in.

"Charlie. How are you?"

"Never mind me. How are *you*, guv? You shouldn't be here, you know. You need rest."

"I'm all right, Charlie. Weary, aching. Nothing new." Moran laughed sardonically. *Aching in my soul...*

"How was Mrs McKellar?"

"Brave. Nice woman."

"Tough job," Charlie said sympathetically. "Telling her what happened."

Moran shrugged. "Had to be done. So," he said, wanting to move on, "what's up?"

"Sheldrake's told all. He and Airey go way back apparently – all the way to cadets. Airey was a gambler, did you know? He didn't look like one, did he? Anyway, he ran up some horrendous debts, and Sheldrake bought him into the gang over a few beers. Didn't take much persuasion, so Sheldrake says."

"Desperate times, desperate measures." Moran massaged his shoulder again and grimaced. "There's no accounting for the lengths to which people will go to extricate themselves from their self-inflicted messes. What about the Ranandans? Have we got enough to bring them in?"

Charlie flushed slightly at the mention of the name. "OK. We have the hard evidence of Airey's email but the acting Super wanted them kept them under close obs for a few days before we picked them up. He was hoping we might net one or two of their European buddies as well, but no show so far." Charlie hesitated. "I was just going

297

ask, guv, if Banner and I could do the honours? If you're happy to authorise it?"

"I'll speak to DCS Higginson now," Moran replied. "I want the Ranandans in custody sharpish before they get any ideas about foreign travel. One thing though, Charlie." Moran frowned, he hoped in a kindly way.

"Guv?"

"Keep your feelings well in check. Don't let them get the better of you. We all feel the same about Helen and Harding. You can join me in the interview room. If you feel you can handle it."

"Oh, I can handle it, guv. Don't worry about me."

Moran studied Charlie's expression. She would handle it all right, he had little doubt.

"There's something else, guv. I just got a call from Denis. Someone's dumped a baby in reception."

"Uh huh." Moran frowned. "And that's significant because–?"

"There was a note pinned to the baby's carry cot. It's Sharron Flynn's baby."

"Who wrote the note?" Moran said without thinking, and then the obvious conclusion came to him. "It was her mother, wasn't it?"

"Right," Charlie confirmed. "The note says she can't cope with the responsibility. Thinks the baby deserves better, but surely she knows we'll only take him back, so I don't see–" Charlie broke off as she registered the look on Moran's face and realised what it meant. "Oh God, she's going to–"

Moran was already on his feet and moving. Pausing only briefly to retrieve his stick he grabbed Charlie by the shoulder and spun her out of the office.

Banner looked up from his desk. "What's going on?"

"Get out to the Flynn's farm, pronto. I don't think she'll be there – but then again she might be." Moran swiftly explained the situation to Banner and then propelled Charlie towards the lift.

"So; where to, guv?" Charlie guided the car quickly out of the over-populated car park and onto the IDR.

"Jag Ranandan's place. Put the siren on."

"Guv."

Charlie pedalled the accelerator and wove expertly through the traffic queue at the lights until the road opened up in front of them.

In contrast with the siren's racket, Moran sat quietly, hating himself. *Idiot. Idiot. Idiot...*

Chapter Thirty-five

As she parked near the Ranandans' house Mrs Flynn's attention was diverted by a neighbouring garden. Whoever tended the colourful borders knew what they were about; they had done a wonderful job. She particularly liked the contrast between the reds and pinks of the dahlias and the yellow snapdragons, which together formed a crowd of colour that, for a brief moment, made her forget the purpose of her visit. She paused at the garden wall, the weight of the shotgun incongruous in the crook of her arm.

It had been a beautiful summer – far too hot for Ernest – but she herself had always been a bit of a sun worshipper. Mrs Flynn tilted her head to feel the warmth on her cheeks. Somewhere in the distance she heard the noise of children playing, a bicycle bell, an ice cream van's discordant tune. It reminded her of her own childhood. Here, with her eyes closed, drinking in the scent of the flowers and the sun's rays warming her flesh, she could be a nine-year-old girl all over again. If only! If only she could go back, rewind the clock, start over.

She tarried for a few minutes, unwilling to spoil the illusion. Someone across the road closed a window with a bang and she reluctantly opened her eyes. The ice cream van's jingle had stopped and now she could hear the sound of a distant siren. Her time was up.

It took only a few strides to arrive at her final destination. She raised her fist and knocked loudly. She heard footsteps approaching. The door opened. Atul Ranandan's face twisted into a sneer.

"What do *you* want?"

Mrs Flynn could see past Atul's body to where his brother sat at a table in the front room. *The big man. The cause of it all.* She could also see the task the brothers were engaged in. Neat bundles of notes were stacked at Atul's empty place, and Jag, who hadn't bothered to look up, was busy counting. The house smelled sickly sweet, heavy with the scent of marijuana.

Mrs Flynn brought the gun up from her side and levelled it at Atul's stomach. "What do I want? I want an end. I want closure."

Atul's eyes widened and he backed away, holding his hands in front of him as a makeshift but hopeless barrier. "You crazy old–"

Mrs Flynn squeezed the trigger and the gun leapt. The noise was shocking, brutal. Atul was thrown backwards along the hallway, his chest torn open by the blast. Blood splattered, pebble-dashing the carpet and walls.

Mrs Flynn advanced, closing the front door behind her with a deft kick of her heel. She stepped over Atul's body and clicked the gun's breach lever, ejecting the spent cartridges. Then she walked slowly and purposefully into the lounge.

Jag had leapt from his chair, but instead of trying to escape or dive for cover he froze as if petrified, eyes darting between his brother's broken body and the woman in the door frame. He licked his lips and picked up a bundle of notes. "Take it. Take it all."

Mrs Flynn inserted two new cartridges and closed the action. "Why? What would I want with money?"

Jag's mouth opened and closed. He had no answer to a question that, to him, seemed nonsensical. "What then? What can I give you? Anything–"

Mrs Flynn raised the gun a second time and Jag screamed. She waited for him to run out of breath and said quietly in the resultant pause: "You can give me your life."

And then she squeezed the trigger.

Mrs Flynn looked down at Jag's twitching body. There was a great deal of blood. He hadn't died straight away, like his brother had. Maybe she hadn't hit any vital organs. No matter. He would die soon. A sudden weariness overcame her and she sank into a nearby chair. The carpet was covered with blood and torn bank notes. The siren she had heard earlier was outside now, very close, but her fingers were crochet-nimble and she had the gun reloaded very quickly.

As the front door crashed open she placed the stock of the gun on the floor in front of her and the barrel in her mouth. She allowed herself one last thought, one last recollection – her baby girl, her Sharron, taking her first steps at the farm. The toddler's innocent face looked up at her and smiled, full of simple, guileless trust. With that image firmly in her mind Mrs Flynn hooked her thumb around the trigger and pressed it down.

Moran gritted his teeth as he stepped over Atul's body. The house smelled of blood and cordite. He heard Charlie gag behind him and then a covert, rustling movement in the lounge. His heart raced. For a brief moment optimism blossomed, but before he could reach the lounge a shotgun blast ripped his hope away.

Moran entered the room cautiously. Flakes of wallpaper and plaster were dropping from the ceiling like bloodied butterflies. Mrs Flynn – at least he had to make the assumption it was Mrs Flynn – was sitting in one of the carvers, a shotgun propped against her thigh. Most of her head was missing, but he was able to recognise the dress she had worn at the farm interview. The clumps of hair adhering to the wallpaper also aided his identification; Mrs Flynn had worn her grey hair proudly and long, even in late middle age, foregoing the usual temptation to colour and perm. Traditional country stock, the Flynns. No frills – just honest, hardworking people who'd taken one wrong turn, and then another, and another after that, through life's deceitful and perplexing maze.

Charlie was at his side, pale but composed. "Shall I call the SOCOs, guv?"

Moran looked down at Jag Ranandan's ruined body. It was justice, he supposed, of a kind. Maybe the only kind Jag Ranandan and his ilk could understand. He nodded.

"Yes. Better had, DI Pepper." Then he turned and limped out of the house without another word.

The sun was still shining. The hum of rush hour traffic drifted over from the motorway junction. Life went on, as it always would. Moran smelled the fragrance of flowers on the light evening breeze and noticed that the garden two doors away was resplendent with colourful blooms. Shona liked flowers; freesias were one of her favourites, he recalled. He made a mental note to pop into the florist on his way to the RBH. Or maybe, he reflected, it would be wiser to give the visit a miss altogether.

Moran sat on the garden wall and listened to the sound of the world passing by. The clear atmosphere magnified each individual noise; cars, voices, the erratic drone of a dragonfly buzzing through the suburban flora. Moran closed his eyes and allowed the sun to bathe his upturned face. If only, he thought wistfully, if only the warmth could slip under his skin, penetrate his soul, revive his wounded spirit.

If only. If only...

The *DCI Brendan Moran* series continues with

Death Walks Behind You

Available from

www.scott-hunter.net

Did you know that *DCI Brendan Moran* also appears in

The Trespass

Read on to sample the prologue & first chapter

Prologue

Smithsonian Institution expedition, March 1920
Location: classified

He placed his hands gently upon the stone, probing and pressing. It would open, given the correct sequence. And he knew the sequence; he'd worked it out. The question was, should he use this knowledge?

"Come on, Theo. Quit stalling."

He felt a prod in his lower back. Theodore swallowed hard. He had no choice. That had always been the case. No choice. *Let posterity remember that, if nothing else.* He turned his attention to the task, fingers moving over the smooth surface. And then a rolling of tumblers, the wall folding away. He heard the American's gasp of surprise and a collective intake of breath from those following. Theodore mopped his brow and squinted into the opening. He'd been expecting wonders, but nothing could have prepared him for this.

Before them was a chamber, empty except for a raised platform upon which rested a large sarcophagus, an object of such beauty he could only stare in awe.

"I said move it, Theo. What are you waiting for?"

Theodore advanced reluctantly, his heartbeat a pounding ostinato against his ribs. Torchlight flickered as they jostled him forward. *No choice. I have no choice.* He stumbled and put a hand out to save himself, grasping the corner of the dais. It was cold to his touch and he pulled his hand away with a gasp. It made him feel – *unholy.*

"Okay, let's get it open."

He was pushed roughly aside, and stepped back in trepidation. *This is wrong. This is not for us to see...*

But the others were heaving at the heavy lid, crowbars grappling for purchase. Slowly it lifted, then fell to the floor with a crash that shook the chamber from top to bottom. Theodore covered his ears and muttered a prayer. *Forgive them. They don't know what they're doing...*

An abrupt silence descended. Heads craned, peering into the sarcophagus. Theodore found himself drawn by a terrible fascination. For a moment he saw nothing, a swirl of colour, then his eyes were brought sharply into focus and he fell back with a cry of astonishment, covering his face in anguish. *It's true. I was right...* With this thought came a renewed conviction. *I can't let them do this – they don't understand...* He felt the weight of the revolver in his pocket, then he was pointing it, the muzzle wavering in his sweat-slicked grip. He heard himself call a warning. A hand reached from behind and grabbed his wrist. The gun exploded towards the chamber roof sending a splinter of rock skittering. He lashed out with a kick but a grip of steel encircled him, pinning his arms. He felt the needle slide into his flesh and he was falling, spinning in slow motion towards the floor. There was no pain but he heard a distant groan; with a shock he realized it was his voice. *I must stop them...* He tried to crawl but bizarre shapes zipped and twirled across his peripheral vision, diving and swooping at him like gulls. He covered his eyes with one hand and groped forward like a blind man in a storm. He felt a boot crunch against his ribs and heard sibilant, chattering laughter. He ignored it all. With his remaining strength he reached out towards the sarcophagus, felt its cool surface under his fingertips and was comforted. As darkness descended he thought he saw angels surrounding the dais, enfolding it with their powerful, protective wings.

Chapter 1

Simon Dracup's head ached as he walked briskly along the hotel corridor. Surely it couldn't be true? Perhaps his grandfather had invented the whole thing. But why do that? It *had* to be genuine. He tutted with irritation. No point in speculating now – he needed to study the diary in depth before he jumped to any conclusions. The phone was ringing as he swiped the key card over the lock and pushed impatiently into his room. He threw his overcoat onto the bed and made a grab for the beeping instrument.

"Dracup."

A woman's voice said, "Where have you *been?*"

Dracup felt his hackles rising. His ex-wife's directness still rankled. "Give me a moment." He thumbed the phone onto speaker and shrugged off his jacket. The diary was still in his inside pocket. He fished it out and placed it carefully on the bedside cabinet. Unremarkable in appearance, but the contents, if factual, were no less than mind-blowing.

"Are you there?" Yvonne's voice barked through the speaker. "Are you coming on Saturday? What do I tell Natasha?"

"If you'd let me –"

"She has to have continuity. She's only eight years old and it's been difficult enough with –"

"Now listen," he heard himself shouting; Yvonne never failed to light his touchpaper. "I will be there at 9 a.m. That's nine in the morning. I will return her at 4 p.m., afternoon, GMT, okay?"

"There's no need to shout, Simon. I can hear you perfectly well." Yvonne's voice spoke evenly across the miles.

"Tell Natasha I love her. I'll be there." He felt his eyes prickle and bit his lip angrily. "How is she?"

"She's fine. She gets on so well with Malcolm. They're real buddies."

"That's great." He gritted his teeth. "I'm her buddy too. And I'm also her daddy."

"Yes, well. You should have thought of that before –"

There was a soft but clear knock on the door. Dracup swore under his breath. "Just a minute; there's someone at the door."

"Oh, yes?"

The ambiguity in her tone was not lost on him. "For heaven's sake, Yvonne –"

"I'll see you at nine on Saturday then." The line went dead.

The soft tap came again.

"Yes. All right. Just a second." Dracup strode to the door and yanked it open. A tall man in a dark suit stood on the threshold. His face was sallow, saddened by drooping eyelids and matching downturn of mouth. In the eyes, however, Dracup discerned a keen intelligence.

"Mr – *Professor* – Dracup?"

"Who wants to know?" Dracup asked, more aggressively than he'd intended.

The visitor smiled thinly. "I hope I'm not interrupting anything? I left my card with reception – James Potzner."

Dracup fished the card out of his trouser pocket. It read:

James Potzner
US Embassy,
Grosvenor Square,
London

"Well. What do you want?" Even as he phrased the question he knew the answer. It was in the buff envelope on the bedside table: the diary.

"If I may –" Potzner took a step forward.

Dracup hesitated. Hold on, he told himself, it might not be anything to do with the diary. Then why this sense of foreboding? Well, if he was right Potzner could at least answer his questions – and he had plenty of those. He stood aside to let the visitor in. "Of course. Be my guest."

Potzner entered the room and walked to the large picture window. The lights of Aberdeen winked in the failing light. "You know, you have a great view here." He admired the scene for a moment, then bent over and flicked a button on the bedside console. The electric blinds folded the view away. "Can't be too careful." Potzner offered a smile and lowered himself smoothly onto the two-seater settee.

Dracup frowned. The diary had been a strange enough addition to his day. And now this stranger settling into his room like an old school friend…

"You don't have something to –?" Potzner made the shape of a glass with his hand.

"Of course. Forgive me. What can I get you?" Dracup fumbled with the cabinet doors under the TV until he found the minibar. "There's coke, white wine, gin." He peered at a label. "Scotch–"

"That's the one."

Dracup poured himself a gin and tonic and sat on the edge of the bed. "So what can I do for you, Mr Potzner?"

"I'll give it to you straight, Mr Dracup. You have something we need." Potzner took a pull at his Scotch.

Dracup's heart skipped. "Need? That's a strong word."

"It's appropriate, Mr Dracup."

"Well, go on, I'm listening."

"You've come to Scotland to hear your aunt's will. The solicitor gave you a diary this afternoon. It belonged to your grandfather, Theodore. Your aunt kept it a secret for many years. She had it placed under lock and key. Until her death." Potzner produced a gold cigarette case and offered it to Dracup.

"No thanks."

"Do you mind?"

"Carry on."

Potzner thumbed his Zippo and inhaled deeply.

Dracup watched him suspiciously. "How do you know what I may or may not be doing in Scotland?"

Potzner sat forward. "Professor; it's my business to *know* things." The American went on. "Your name is Simon Andrew Dracup. You are forty-five years old. You were brought up in India, but relocated to Berkshire when your father was offered a consultant post at the Royal Berkshire Hospital. You wanted to follow him into medicine but your father dissuaded you. Your first girlfriend was Susan, your best friend's sister. The relationship didn't last because when you visited you didn't know if you were there to see your friend or Susan and neither did they. Boy, that was a bummer. She really loved you.

"You got straight As at A level and went to Bristol University to escape home, even though Reading offered a better course in Anthropology. You married Yvonne when you were twenty-eight, although you weren't sure and your friends even less so. Your daughter Natasha was born eight years ago after your wife – sorry, ex-wife – had undergone a prolonged course of fertility treatment. Politically you swing to the left but enjoy a lifestyle that is definitely headed over to the right. Your students respect you and you're known as a reliable guy. Professionally, you're a hot potato. Your special interest is physical anthropology and you've made many field trips to many different countries. Your marriage ended because of the strain produced by successive failures of IVF, but your subsequent and unexpected love affair with one Sara Benham, a student at the University, has kept you on an even keel. You're trying to make a go of it, but your ex and her new man are giving you a hard time. And the other side of the coin is tough too because, irrationally for a man of logic, you blame Sara for taking you away from Natasha, so you're not sure how –"

Dracup had his hand up. "All right. All right." Shaken, he took a long swig from his tumbler. Whoever Potzner was, he had all the facts straight. Detailed facts.

Potzner read his expression. "It's my job, Mr Dracup. Nothing personal."

"Nothing personal? That's my *life*."

Potzner crossed one long leg over the other and flicked ash into the wastepaper bin. "It all goes in the shredder after you give me the diary. You have my word."

Dracup had his doubts but his curiosity was aroused. What else did Potzner know? Why was this so important? He went on the offensive. "So it's genuine?"

Potzner raised an eyebrow.

"What the diary records about Noah's Ark," Dracup continued, "or at least the remains of some ancient vessel – that it was discovered in Turkey in 1920."

"Yeah," the American nodded thoughtfully, "the traditional Biblical location."

Dracup shrugged. "Mount Ararat? Look, I've seen all sorts on the web about possible sites – blurred photos that show boat-shaped anomalies, stories about expeditions that never got off the ground – but my grandfather..." The idea was still preposterous, however he approached it. He frowned. "Theodore was actually there?"

Potzner got up and walked to the window. He moved the blind aside for a few seconds, then turned and faced Dracup. "Yeah. He was there."

Dracup levelled his gaze directly at Potzner. "And how did you keep a discovery of this magnitude under lock and key?"

For a split second, Potzner looked uncomfortable. "Before my time, Professor. The Department took care of the details."

"I see." Dracup sipped his drink. A cover-up, then. A big one.

"But the fact is, Professor, your grandfather was part of another expedition – *after* the one that found the Ark. You might say it was inaugurated as a consequence of the success of the first."

Dracup nodded. "Go on."

"I'll tell you as much as I can, Mr Dracup, but in the interest of security – and your own safety –"

"Oh, please, cut the crap."

"Now you're sounding more stateside than I do." Potzner smiled briefly. "Okay. I'll keep it simple. The Ark of Noah contained a number of –" Potzner searched for the right word, "– interesting finds. One in particular created a big stir. It pointed to another location where cargo from the Ark was apparently taken after it grounded. So, the second expedition followed this up six months later and returned with…" Potzner scratched his blue chin with a long forefinger, "… something priceless; something we have kept securely since it was first brought back to the US."

"And my grandfather was part of all this?"

"Oh yeah. Up to his eyeballs. He was a key member of both expos. It was his expertise – and his colleague's – that revealed the second location. He was not only a first-rate geologist but also a gifted historian. Seems that brains run in the family, right, Professor? Anyhow, his colleague, guy by the name of Reeves-Churchill, was the archaeologist on both expeditions. We have no record of what happened to him. But as you know, although your grandfather made it back in one piece from both expos he didn't keep too well after his return to the UK."

"That's an understatement. He was committed in 1921, the year after this diary was completed." Dracup had picked up the diary from the bedside table, but quickly put it down again with a silent curse. Brilliant, Dracup. Now he *knows* you've got it.

If Potzner was excited at the sight of the diary, he didn't show it. He reclaimed his former position on the settee and nodded. "Right. It was tough. A brilliant mind wasted – but it wasn't all for nothing. Like I said, they found something extraordinary."

Something in the American's tone sent a cold wave down Dracup's neck. He cleared his throat. "The discovery of the Ark is extraordinary enough, but it might help my understanding if you told me exactly *what* they found in this… other location."

The American shook his head. "I'm not at liberty to say any more about that, Professor."

Dracup leaned back against the headboard and folded his arms. He appeared to have reached the inevitable brick wall. The one that read 'Classified'. "All right. So what do you want from me?"

Potzner hesitated and once again looked uneasy. The cigarette case appeared. "The item I'm referring to has been – mislaid."

"Mislaid?"

"Okay. Stolen."

Dracup exhaled slowly. So that was it; they needed Theodore's record. Some clue, perhaps, to help them find – what? He emptied the dregs of his tonic water into the heavy bathroom tumbler. Another thought occurred to him. "But you knew my aunt had the diary. So why didn't you ask her for it?"

"Our problem has only recently arisen, Professor, otherwise we would have done." Potzner drew on his Winston. "So your little acquisition has come at about the right time for us."

"*Little?* If this is genuine, the implications are – staggering." That's putting it mildly, Dracup thought. He swigged back his tonic and looked at the American. "So how exactly will the diary help you?"

"I really can't tell you any more, Professor."

Dracup shook his head in exasperation. He wondered how far he could press the American. Potzner hadn't threatened him – yet. He caught Potzner's gaze and held it. "Perhaps I'll keep hold of it for the time being."

Potzner laughed softly. "Mr Dracup – I can't emphasize enough – your cooperation would be a real convenience for us."

"And if I refuse?"

"I'll tell you what." Potzner consigned the second stub expertly to the recesses of the waste bin. "I'll let you sleep on it, okay? Have a read through if you like; hell, I'd do the same myself under the circumstances." Potzner was on his feet and at the door. "I'll look you up in the morning. Perhaps you'll see things in a fresh light."

Dracup got up to see him out. "I'm not parting company with the diary until I know what this is all about."

Potzner shrugged. "Your decision."

Dracup watched him walk down the corridor; a tall man in his late fifties, with a slight limp. Before he entered the lift he called back: "Professor Dracup?"

"Yes?"

"Take care, won't you?" The lift doors opened and Potzner was gone.

Dracup sat quietly for ten minutes before kicking off his shoes and lying back on the king-size bed with a fresh drink. So it was true. It had to be if the CIA were after the diary. Dracup had no doubts concerning Potzner's 'Embassy' role. But more fascinating was their stolen item. He picked up his grandfather's diary and began to read. He studied the first entry:

21st Apr '20

First night in situ. Hardly believe we're on board, after all the anticipation. RC is elated. Estimates are that we're in the mid section – 3 fragments theory seems vindicated. The size of it is what thrills me! OT seems spot on re dimensions. It's vast – the decking is clearly visible and quite well preserved

Three fragments? Presumably referring to the condition of the Ark – the way it had broken up over the years. OT? Dracup frowned. Of course – Old Testament. Dracup shook his head in disbelief. Could this vessel really be the Ark of Noah? A dark stain obscured the next two lines. Dracup raised the book to his nose and took a sniff. Impossible to say what had caused it. He picked up at the next legible point in the entry:

RC is concerned re the location of the sarcophagus. Clear indications that it was on board during voyage – the sceptre may hold the answer. I have many reservations.

Sarcophagus? The tone of his grandfather's entry sent a chill down Dracup's spine. He shook his head in puzzlement. Potzner wanted something precious that had been on board Noah's Ark and then taken to another location…

Clear indications that it was on board during voyage

Dracup began to hum quietly. Something they had found on the Ark – some clue – had pointed Theodore to that other location.

the sceptre may hold the answer.

He flipped on a few pages.

27th Apr '20

Never been so cold. Descent halted for the day – driving snow. Tevfik's death has shaken us all. A has not spoken of it, but seems consumed with fear. RC nervous that he'll disappear and leave us. Constantly mutters under his breath. 'Bekci, Bekci' – apparently means 'The Keepers, the Keepers'. Some local superstition about the Ark we think. Despite it all I feel frustration above everything else – could only bring one or two finds of interest – the larger finds have to stay of course – have taken some samples from drogues. RC has the curious iron piece – I must say the CF is extraordinary even though I'm no expert! No wonder RC so excited. I just pray we get down safely and can examine all at our leisure.

Tevfik. A Turkish name. Dracup clucked his tongue. That fitted with the Ark's location: Mount Ararat. He read on:

30th. Still in cave. Storm too severe to attempt any further descent. RC is out of his mind with fright. I must hold him together or we'll [here there was a smear across the page] ... eepers, the keepers'. It is unsettling to say the least; there must be a rational explanation. But am compelled to be honest – I saw it too. A was lifted away – not the wind; not a hidden crevasse ... [unclear lettering here] .. as taken. Hope to God we are near the track way – not that we'll ever get our bearings in this weather. Food is nearly gone. Resorted to last tin of corned beef this morning. Wait! I hear it again.

Something out on the mountainside. RC is muttering in his sleep – he probably hears it too. God preserve us and help us away from here. Tomorrow we must go and face whatever we must face. Whatever happens I shall cling to these treasures. There is much significance in them, I am convinced.

Dracup shivered. What had happened to them on the mountain? Could it be linked to the missing sarcophagus? Was that what Potzner was after? If so, who did the sarcophagus belong to? And why was it so important? Frustratingly the diary appeared to cover only the first expedition. There was no mention of the mysterious second location. He took a gulp of tonic water. At any rate, he knew what to do next. It was what he always told his students: when in doubt, examine available source material. Reluctantly Dracup fished in the bedside cabinet and found the inevitable Gideon's Bible. Clearly it had rarely, if ever, been opened. Dracup flicked the pages and found the book of Genesis. Did it mention burials or death on the Ark? What should he look for? Something valuable; a wide remit.

An hour later and none the wiser he placed the Bible next to the diary, leaned over and clicked a button on his console. The electric blinds hissed open and the lights of Aberdeen invaded the room. He was glad of their company.

Dracup snapped awake. His bedside light was off. Something was wrong. He tried to recall the geography of the room. Which way was he facing? He opened his eyes slowly. The room was filled with moonlight; he could pick out every detail. Somewhere in the bowels of the hotel, a door slammed. The moon went behind a cloud and the quality of light deteriorated. A subtle movement, a paler shadow in the darkness, drew his attention. There. By the opposite bedside table, a tall figure leaning in towards him. Dracup was a big man but he could be agile when the occasion demanded and something told him this was such an occasion. He rolled just as a soft *pop* preceded a thump on his pillow where a second before his head had rested. A pungent, burning smell filled his nostrils, but by this stage Dracup was on the floor and groping frantically for a weapon. His brain raced in panic. Come on, he told himself. Think. That's what you're good at...

His assailant was doing the obvious thing. All he had to do was walk round the foot of the bed and shoot him. Dracup had nowhere to go. They both knew it. And that made Dracup angry. Somewhere in the back of his mind he recognized this as a good thing; anger might give him an edge. He heaved the bedside cabinet in front of him before the next shot came. The round tore into the MDF of the cabinet and a splinter glanced off his forearm. He yelled out and reflexively pushed forward, rewarded by the sound of a soft curse as the cabinet connected with the man's shin. Dracup threw himself forward in a clumsy rugby tackle, desperately aware of his lack of fitness. He caught the man around the waist but the assassin was strong; he wrenched himself free and aimed a kick at Dracup's head. The blow caught Dracup on the shoulder and threw him back into the corner. The figure lifted its arm again, lining up with Dracup's head. Dracup scrabbled around the floor for something solid. There was nothing. Wait. His hands closed around the cool plastic of the control console. It might do. He clicked the button. Please God let it be the right one…

The electric blinds began their automatic sashay, summoned into life by Dracup's frantic fingers. It was enough. The assassin spun in surprise and Dracup was on him with the full force of his six-foot frame. The impact carried them both to the opposite wall, onto the twisted wrought iron wardrobe handles. The assassin lifted his arm. Dracup remembered his games master's advice: *If you're in a fight and he's bigger than you, a knee in the groin will stand you in good stead.* Dracup brought his knee up between the man's legs. The shot went wide, cracking against the glass of the picture window. The blinds were almost closed. Dracup kicked out wildly, feeling his strength ebbing away. But it was a lucky kick, catching the intruder's arm just under the wrist and knocking it upwards. The bullet passed through the fleshy part of his assailant's chin and continued on its altered trajectory up into his brain. The assassin slipped to the floor, leaving a dark trail against the light wood of the wardrobe, and flopped forward grotesquely onto the carpet.

Dracup remained standing, legs slightly apart, panting like a dog. His arms shook, the tremors quickly spreading to the rest of his body like some fast-acting virus. He sat heavily on the bed. His shoulder throbbed and he felt stickiness on the tips of his enquiring fingers.

Not my blood…

There was an anxious knock at the door. Dracup froze. Again. "Mr Dracup?"

"Yes?"

"It's the concierge. Is everything all right?"

"I'm fine. I had a dream, that's all." Dracup felt his heart beating wildly.

The footsteps receded. Dracup lay back and listened to his breathing. After a while he retrieved the console and turned on the main light. He looked at the body. A faint mist was rising from the pool forming by the head of the man he had killed. The enormity of the word hit him like a sledgehammer. He swallowed hard and bent down for a closer look.

First thing: it wasn't the American, Potzner. He hadn't expected it to be. But had Potzner sent him? This man was olive-skinned – Mediterranean? No, Middle-Eastern by the look of him. Dracup remembered Potzner's parting words: *Take care.*

Second thing: the diary. He made a quick search under the bed. He realized he was holding his breath just as he caught sight of the little book by the bed leg. He retrieved it and breathed again.

Third thing: the body. He reached for the phone, then checked himself. Would they believe him? His mind conjured an image of the police interview, his reaction as they produced false but compelling evidence fabricated by the CIA, heard his protests overruled by stony-faced Scotland Yard officers…

Dracup stumbled into the bathroom and was violently sick. He retched into the bowl until there was nothing left in his stomach. His legs would barely support him as he splashed cold water on his face and examined his forearm. An angry gash, but not too deep. Could have been a lot worse. He realized he was speaking aloud but his voice seemed distant, as if it belonged to somebody else.

He freshened his mouth with toothpaste and sat on the edge of the bed to consider his next move. Police or no police? He looked at the diary; a small thing, nestled in his shaking hands. He squatted down next to the corpse and made himself examine the pockets. He pulled something out. And froze. He was holding a photograph of Natasha in his hand. She was standing outside her school, lunchbox dangling at her side, backpack askew. Smiling.

Oh God. No.

The telephone shook in his hands. His fingers were jabbing Yvonne's number. He waited. Nothing. *Come on.* The ring tone went on and on. Then he remembered Yvonne's habit of turning down the ring volume at night. *Please. Please pick up.*

Five minutes later he slammed the phone into its cradle. He glanced at the digital clock: 02:25. Dracup took a deep breath and got hold of the corpse's shoulders. The body was heavy. It took him five minutes of heaving and sweating to get it into the bathroom. He closed the door, fished another miniature of Johnnie Walker from the minibar and downed it in one. No police; no time. A handful of tissues took care of the bloodstained furniture. He stuffed his belongings into a suitcase and looked into the corridor. There was no one about. He closed the door behind him and headed for the fire escape.

A free book of short stories is available at:

www.scott-hunter.net

Made in the USA
Coppell, TX
23 July 2023

19513853R00194